CHAPTER ONE

Jack Powers checked his shoelaces for the third time. It was a ritual he'd started after a nasty fall that resulted in a broken thumb. His laces had become tangled during a wall run. The procedure involved him racing up a wall and following it up with a tricky hop over a thin railing, and he'd fallen forwards. He would have landed on his face if he hadn't saved himself with the thumb on his left hand.

The wall he was facing now was higher, and he rehearsed the steps he was going to take in his head.
"You won't make it."
Sharon Billing was a seasoned traceuse. She'd been practicing the fine art of parkour for five years now, and she could perform moves that not many people could. Sharon knew she was good, but she didn't make a big deal out of it.
"Your head's not in the right place," she said.
"I'll make it," Jack insisted. "Just give me a minute to focus."
"Approach the wall from the side," Sharon advised. "Run in a wide arc and forget about your arms until you're sure that your legs have enough momentum in them to propel you upwards."
"That's what I was planning on doing."
Sharon pointed at the graffiti on the wall. "See the top of the *N*. That's what you need to focus on. Your right foot has to be dead on it. Push up from there and you'll have enough lift to grip the railing at the top. Do you want me to show you?"
"Please," Jack said.

He watched her go through the motions of her warm-up. Sharon took five deep breaths and closed her eyes for a few seconds. Jack knew that she did this to plan the route up the wall in her head. No sooner had she opened them, she was on the move. With the agility of a ballet dancer, she approached the wall and then she was airborne. Her right foot hit the tip of the N on the *North Side* graffiti, and she pushed herself upwards. Her hand gripped the railing, and she flung herself over. When she looked down at Jack she was barely out of breath. She gave him an encouraging smile, and he prepared himself for his own wall run.

Five seconds later, he was at the top, standing next to Sharon. She gave him a high five and told him she thought his run-up could have been better. He needed to find the sweet spot between full pelt and maximum lift potential. Too fast, and he risked hitting the wall, face on but he had to be quick enough to channel the forward energy into upward energy.

"Looks like we have a challenger," Sharon said.
She nodded to the figure approaching from the direction of the river. The man was wearing a hooded top and a pair of large sunglasses. A black bandana was covering his nose and mouth. Jack and Sharon watched as he stopped a few metres away from the wall.

"You're going to need a longer run up if you're planning on doing the wall run, mate," Sharon told him.
The man looked up but remained quiet. He stayed where he was.
"Let's go back down," Jack said. "If he's going to face-plant, I want to see it from down there."
They made their way down the steps. The stranger ignored them. He stretched out his arms, revealing the edge of a tattoo on his lower back as his top rose up. Jack thought it looked like a spider's web.

Without warning, the man raced towards the wall and before Jack and Sharon knew it, he was at the top. He didn't stop there. He performed a vertical leap and landed on the railing. He sped along the thin metal rail and jumped across the gap to the bridge five metres away. He was over and gone in a flash.

Jack stared at Sharon with his mouth open wide.

"What the fuck just happened?"

"Who was that alien?" Sharon said.

They didn't know that they'd witnessed the capabilities of the man who called himself *The Spider*. They were also unaware that they'd just had a glimpse of the most prolific serial killer the city of York was ever going to see.

CHAPTER TWO

Detective Sergeant Jason Smith was panting loudly. He was out of breath, and he'd only run the short distance from his house to the park at the bottom of the road. He was definitely out of shape. Now his fortieth birthday had come and gone he'd made up his mind to get more exercise. It had been a long time since he'd taken a run, and he was determined to do something to improve his fitness. He'd cut down on his smoking, and he was planning on doing something about his beer intake too. But not yet – he wasn't quite ready for that yet.

He stopped to catch his breath close to the entrance of the park. It was early March and there was a chill in the air. Spring still felt like it was a long way off. Smith could smell rain too. He set off again in the direction of the small lake at the bottom of the park and he soon settled into a comfortable rhythm. He was nowhere near as fast as he once was, but he'd taken the first step. He reckoned he would probably be stiff all over tomorrow.

He took another breather by the lake and gazed across the surface of the water. Two ducks were swimming away from him. Smith watched as they reached the bank on the opposite side and hopped onto dry land. Soon they would have a troop of ducklings to take care of, and the thought made Smith smile. The worst of winter was over and there was the promise of warmer weather on the cards.

Smith debated whether to continue with his run but decided to walk instead.

"Baby steps," he said to nobody in particular.

He reached inside his pocket for his cigarettes and remembered that he'd left them at home. It probably wasn't a great idea to have a smoke during a run anyway. He followed the path around the lake and stopped when he reached the tree that always made him shiver. It was an old oak and Smith and the tree shared a history. This was the exact spot where a sniper had taken out one of his victims during the *Deadeye* investigation and Smith would never see it as anything else.

He left the tree behind and caught up with the ducks on the bank of the lake. He was glad he hadn't brought the dogs with him. Theakston and Fred always liked to tease the ducks and even though the porky Bull Terrier and the grotesque Pug were getting on a bit, they still managed to find the energy to chase them.

Smith's wife, Detective Sergeant Erica Whitton had taken the girls to visit her mother. Whitton's father Harold had passed away only a month ago and Jane was still getting to grips with the changes that his death brought with it. Smith missed him too – they hadn't always seen eye to eye, but they'd become close in the end and life wasn't going to be the same without Harold.

It was uphill all the way back to his house, but Smith decided to jog there anyway. By the time he stopped outside number 16 Greenway Avenue, he was exhausted and the muscles in his legs were burning. He was definitely going to be sore in the morning. The door to number 18 opened and Darren Lewis came outside. Smith owned this property too. He'd bought it when it had become a bit crowded next door. Smith and Whitton had three daughters - Laura and their two adopted daughters, Lucy and Fran. Lucy had a baby too and Andrew was coming up to two years old. There simply wasn't enough room for all of them in the three-bedroomed house so Smith had bought the place next door. It was where Lucy, Darren and Andrew lived. They paid Smith a token rent, and everyone was happy.

"What happened to you?" Darren said.

"Nothing happened to me," Smith said. "I went out for a run."

"You look like you're about to have a heart attack."

"Rubbish," Smith said. "I'm a bit out of practice, that's all. What are you up to?"

"Enjoying the peace and quiet. Lucy is at Erica's mum's house, and my parents have Andrew for the weekend. You really do look unwell."

"Shut up," Smith told him. "I reckon a beer is in order."

He went inside his house and made a beeline for the fridge in the kitchen. He cracked open a beer and took a long drink. His phone beeped on the table. He picked it up and saw that it was a message from Whitton. It consisted of a single photograph, and it made Smith smile. It was clear that a lot of baking had gone on at Jane's house. Laura and Fran were proudly displaying trays of biscuits.

Smith put down his phone and debated whether to smoke a cigarette. He decided that one smoke wouldn't kill him. He grabbed the packet and the lighter and went outside to the back garden. He lit the cigarette and took a long drag. He was interrupted halfway through by the sound of the doorbell. He cursed and stubbed out the cigarette in the ashtray.

It was a man who looked to be around the same age as Smith.

"Can I help you?" he said.

"You must be the Australian pig."

Smith wasn't expecting that.

"What do you want?"

"The name's Rob," the man said. "And I want what's mine."

"I have no idea what you're talking about."

"Let me make myself a bit clearer then. Robert Rogers. Does that make things easier to understand?"

"Rogers?" Smith said. "You were Sheila's husband."

"You're not as dumb as you look," Robert said. "Where is she?"

"Shelia's dead."

"Not Sheila, you prat. Where's my daughter? Where's Fran?"

"Let me make something clear to *you*," Smith said. "You gave up the right to call Fran your daughter when you walked away from her all those years ago."
"She's mine."
"Fran is not an object, Mr Roberts," Smith said. "She is a little girl who lost her mother. You were contacted before we began the process of adopting her and you didn't want anything to do with her. This conversation is over."
"It's far from over."
"Fuck off." Smith couldn't help himself. "Fuck off and don't come back here."
"You haven't heard the last of this."
Smith replied by slamming the door in his face. He locked the door to be on the safe side. The letterbox opened.
"She's my flesh and blood," Robert screamed. "And I'm taking her back."

Smith walked back to the kitchen. This wasn't how he'd expected his day to turn out. He finished his beer, and he was about to get another one when his phone started to ring. It was a familiar ringtone, and it was one that told him his day was probably about to get worse.

He wasn't mistaken. After Elvis Costello's *Oliver's Army* was cut short, the four words that DI Smyth spoke left little room for interpretation.
"We've got a body."

CHAPTER THREE

The address DI Smyth had given him was in Bootham and Smith got there in fifteen minutes. It was a terraced house in a row of identical houses. Smith parked behind DI Smyth's car and got out. Grant Webber's vehicle was parked directly outside the property as Smith expected it to be. The Head of Forensics was always one of the first people at the scene of a crime.

DI Smyth was speaking to DS Bridge outside. Smith walked over to them.
"What do we know?"
"Not much right now," DI Smyth said. "The woman's name is Christine Snow. Her husband came home from playing football and found her upstairs in the main bedroom. It looks like she's been stabbed repeatedly."
"What's with the gym gear?" Bridge asked.
Smith hadn't bothered to change out of the tracksuit he'd been wearing when he went out for a run.
"Long story," Smith said.
"You're not wearing your glasses."
"I forgot to pick them up in the rush to get here."

He looked at the house. It was a typical terraced property, the likes of which were common in this part of town.
"Where is the husband now?"
"He's with a neighbour," DI Smyth said. "He seems to be taking it rather well."
"He's probably in shock. I presume Webber is inside."
DI Smyth nodded. "He and Billie are busy going through the motions. If you want to take a look, you know the drill."
Smith did, and for once he decided to let Webber work in peace for a while. He would speak to the man who found the body first. Bridge came with him.

Peter Snow was a slim man with thinning hair. He was dressed in a similar manner to Smith in a blue tracksuit and trainers. Smith remembered that he'd discovered his dead wife upon returning from playing football. An elderly woman was sitting in an armchair opposite him. She introduced herself as Barbara Walsh and asked if they wanted something to drink.

"No thanks," Smith replied for himself and Bridge.

"I imagine you'd like some privacy," Barbara said.

"If you could just give us a moment," Smith said. "Thank you."

He looked across at Peter Snow. His facial expression was difficult to read, and Smith couldn't quite gauge what he was thinking. He was no stranger to people left behind in the wake of a murder, and there was not one size fits all where relatives of murder victims were concerned, but Peter's reaction to his wife's death was a strange one.

"We need to ask you some questions," Smith said.

"I know," Peter said. "Why else would you be here?"

"Is there someone we can call for you?" Bridge asked. "A family member or a friend perhaps?"

"What good will that do?"

"We can arrange for a family liaison officer to come and see you," Smith said.

"No thanks."

"Can you tell us a bit about Christine?"

"What is there to tell?" Peter said. "She was my wife, and now she's dead."

"How long have you been married?" Bridge said.

"Seven years. It's actually our wedding anniversary today."

And you chose to spend it playing football, Smith thought.

He didn't share this with Peter.

"When did you last see your wife?" he asked instead.

"This morning," Peter said. "Christine was still in bed when I left."

"What time was that?" Bridge said.

"Eight. I play in a Saturday League team, and we had a match against Clifton."

"What position do you play in?" Bridge said.

"What's that got to do with anything?"

"You left the house at eight," Smith said. "To play football. Is this a regular thing?"

"I play every Saturday," Peter said. "I also play five-a-side four nights a week. In different teams."

"You lead a busy life," Smith said.

"What did Christine do for work?" Bridge said.

"She didn't work," Peter said. "She didn't need to."

"What is it that you do?" Smith said.

"I'm an accountant. I'm a partner in a firm. Why are you asking me about what I do for a living?"

"It's just routine," Smith said. "How was Christine when you left her this morning?"

"She was in bed. What else do you want me to tell you?"

Something was terribly wrong with Peter Snow's attitude, and it was bothering Smith.

"Can anyone corroborate your claim that you played football this morning?" he asked.

"What?"

"Could you just answer the question please," Bridge said.

"I played football in Clifton. Twenty-one other blokes can confirm it, as can a few dozen spectators. Am I being accused of something?"

"It's a question we need to ask," Smith said.

"Oh, you mean that thing about it always being the husband. Well, I didn't kill Christine. Why would I?"

"OK," Smith said. "Talk us through what you did when you got home. Was the front door locked?"

"I always lock it behind me when I leave the house," Peter said.

"What about the door at the back?" Bridge said.

"That was locked too."

"Are you sure?" Smith said.

"I made sure of it."

"Do you know if Christine had made any plans for today?" Smith said.

"Not that I'm aware of."

"She wasn't planning on meeting anyone?" Bridge said. "Perhaps a friend was popping round."

"She didn't mention anything to me," Peter said. "When can I go back inside my house?"

"The forensic team could be some time," Smith said. "That'll be all for now. If you do think of something that might be relevant, please give me a call." He took out one of his cards and left it on the coffee table.

"And we're going to need the details of the people who you played football with this morning," he added.

"I'll give them to you with pleasure," Peter said. "Would you have any objections to me taking a walk? To clear my head a bit."

"Of course not," Smith said. "You're free to do whatever you want."

"Why doesn't it feel like it?"

CHAPTER FOUR

"What did you make of him?" Bridge asked outside in the street.

"It seems like they had a strange relationship," Smith said. "Who plays football five times a week?"

"And I imagine his job as an accountant takes up a lot of his time too. When does he find the time for Christine? What's the point in getting married if you never see your spouse?"

"People are strange," Smith said.

"Do you think he was involved?"

"I don't doubt that he was telling the truth about where he was this morning," Smith said. "He probably knows it's one of the first things we look at, but I haven't ruled out Peter Snow just yet. I'm going to have a look inside the house."

He walked over to Webber's car and opened the boot. The Head of Forensics never locked his car, and he always kept a supply of SOC suits in there. Smith found one that looked like it wasn't too tight and put it on. He walked over to the cordon that had been set up outside the house and slipped on a pair of latex gloves. After greeting a PC he didn't know inside the cordon, he put on the protective shoe covers and went inside the house.

Billie Jones was inside the kitchen. Webber's assistant was taking photographs of something on the counter.

"Billie," Smith said.

"How are you?" she said.

"Same old, same old. What do we know so far?"

"Webber is busy upstairs in the bedroom. It's a bloodbath in there, and the perpetrator will not have come away clean."

"Do we know how he got into the house?"

"Are we working on the assumption that the killer is a man?" Billie said.

"They usually are," Smith said.

"The back door was locked. And we only have the husband's word that the front door was too."

"Any evidence of a break-in?"

"Nothing yet. The window in the bathroom upstairs was open but unless we're looking for someone who can climb up walls, I don't think that's how he got in."

Smith walked over to the double-door fridge. There was nothing on either of the doors.

"Don't you think that's odd?"

"My fridge at home is plastered with all kinds of stuff," Billie said.

"Ours is too," Smith said. "It's got reminders about appointments, magnets and other crap that's been there for years. There's no calendar in here either."

"Perhaps the Snows are techie types. Maybe they keep all their to-do stuff electronically. We found a tablet in the bedroom and there's a laptop on the desk in the living room. We'll take a good look through them."

"What about mobile phones?" Smith said.

"Just the one. Also, in the main bedroom."

"It's probably Christine's. It was their wedding anniversary today, and the husband decided to spend it running around a field with a whole load of other blokes in shorts."

"Men," Billie said. "Do you think the anniversary could be significant?"

"I don't see how. How soon before we know what's on the mobile devices?"

"Not anytime soon. What are you thinking?"

"Peter Snow is hardly a model husband," Smith said. "He plays football five times a week. He's an accountant and I don't know when he finds the time to spend with his wife. That to me is a perfect recipe for disaster. He may as well have given his wife permission to indulge in an affair. He has a routine, and that routine doesn't change. I think Mrs Snow was cheating on him and somehow the affair ended badly for her. This is a really cold house."

"The heating is on full blast."

"I don't mean the temperature," Smith said. "There's no love in here – it's a sterile place. And it's far too clean."

"Perhaps Mrs Snow liked to keep it that way."

"Perhaps," Smith said. "I'm going to say hello to Webber."

"I have to warn you," Billie said. "He's in a foul mood today."

"When isn't he in a foul mood?"

Smith went upstairs and headed straight for the main bedroom. He stopped halfway when he reached the open door of the bathroom. He peered inside and noticed that this room was also spotless. There was a brisk breeze outside and the shower curtain was blowing in the wind coming in through the open window. Smith walked over to the window and looked out. He decided that it would be possible for someone to fit through the window, but he didn't think this was how the killer got in and out. Outside the bathroom there was a sheer drop to the concrete in the back yard. There was a downpipe attached to the wall, but Smith didn't think it was humanly possible for anyone to climb up without the help of a ladder.

He coughed to announce his presence in the doorway of the main bedroom. Grant Webber was examining something on the carpet next to the bed. He didn't look up when Smith came in. Christine Snow was lying on the bed, and she'd been covered with a white sheet. Blood had stained most of it red, and it was clear that she'd been badly mutilated. Smith wondered why Webber had covered her up. He asked him.

"It wasn't my doing," Webber said. "She was like that when we got here."

"The husband?"

"You're the detective."

"Have you taken a look at her?"

"Of course. It looks like she was stabbed multiple times. Pathology will tell us more. I'm more interested in the room itself."

"Was she definitely killed here?" Smith said.

"Without a shadow of a doubt," Webber confirmed. "The amount of blood on the sheets and the carpet next to the bed suggests that this is where she died. There isn't a spot of blood anywhere else in the house."

"I think she knew her killer," Smith said.

"I'm inclined to agree. We couldn't find any evidence of a break-in – there are no broken windows and both doors into the house were locked when the husband arrived home."

"She invites her killer in," Smith said. "Something happens that results in him killing her and he leaves through either the front or the back door. We need to ask the husband about the keys. The killer must have locked the door and taken the key with him."

"I assume you're thinking out loud again?"

"Of course. What about the bathroom? The window is open. Do you think it would be possible for someone to gain access that way?"

Webber shook his head. "Not only were there no indications that anyone came in through the bathroom window – no footprints or fingerprints, unless we're dealing with *Spiderman*, it's just not possible to get in and out that way."

CHAPTER FIVE

"Christine Snow." DI Smyth wrote her name on the whiteboard in the small conference room. "Thirty-four years old. Her husband arrived home after playing football and found her in the bedroom. Early indications suggest that she was stabbed multiple times and she bled out where she was found."

"I want to bring in the husband," Smith said. "There are still a lot of questions we need answers to."

"Hold your horses," DI Smyth said. "Mr Snow has suffered a terrible shock, and he needs time to process what's happened."

"I appreciate that, boss but we need those answers now."

"What were your impressions of him?"

"I didn't like him," Smith said.

"You don't like anyone."

"It's not that. There's something *off* about him. What sort of bloke goes out and plays football on their wedding anniversary?"

"Not everyone can be a model husband like you," Bridge said.

"Shut up," Smith said. "I say we haul him in sooner rather than later. The way the killer got into the house is bugging me and I want to know if there are any keys unaccounted for."

"Are you sure he came in through one of the doors?" DC King said.

"It's the only way he could have got inside, Kerry," Smith said. "There were no signs of a break-in and unless he has some kind of superpower, there's no way he could have got in through the bathroom window. I think Christine Snow invited him in, they had a fight and he killed her. He left her in the bedroom and exited the house via either the front or the back door."

"Are we working on the assumption that Mrs Snow knew her killer?" DC Moore said.

"Did you not sleep well last night, Harry?" Smith said. "I would have thought that was obvious. Her husband plays football every Saturday morning. You can set your watch by him. Christine knows she'll have the house to herself; she arranges to meet her lover there and for some reason he ends up killing her."

"Did Webber retrieve the murder weapon?" DC King asked.

"Not as far as I'm aware," Smith said. "There was a knife block in the kitchen and one of the knives is missing. It looks like the killer took it with him."

"It's early days," DI Smyth said. "And it's going to take time to get some answers from Forensics and Pathology, so I suggest we look into the lives of Mr and Mrs Snow. Speak to their friends and family. We're not absolutely certain of the timescale involved in the murder, but we can say for sure that it happened sometime between eight this morning and noon when the husband returned home. That means the killer left the house in daylight, and we might get lucky with the door-to-door. Uniforms are speaking to the neighbours right now. Somebody may have seen something."

"What about CCTV?" Bridge said. "Do any of the neighbouring properties have cameras?"

"None," DI Smyth said. "Right – this is the plan of action. Smith, you and Kerry can do a bit of digging into the lives of Mr and Mrs Snow. If Christine was having an affair, it's possible she might have confided in a friend about it."

"On the surface," Smith said. "It appears that theirs was a loveless marriage. Christine will have talked to someone about it."

"Find out. Bridge, I want you and Harry to work on possible points of exit."

"The house is in the middle of a row of terraced properties," Bridge said. "There's an access road at the back and from the front there are only two possible directions to go in."

"Look into it. We have no way of knowing if there was a vehicle involved, but that can't be helped. Check to see if any of the nearby shops and businesses have CCTV."

"There are very few shops around there," Bridge pointed out. "You've got the hospital three streets back, but other than residential properties there's nothing much else."

"Any questions before we make a start?" DI Smyth said.

"Motive," Smith said. "What's the motive here?"

"Here we go," Bridge said.

"It needs to be considered. We've checked the husband's alibi, and he was where he said he was. More than one person has confirmed it, but it still doesn't rule him out."

"He could have arranged someone to kill Christine," DC King said.

"He finds out about the affair," Smith speculated. "And he pays someone to kill his wife while he's playing football, thus giving him the perfect alibi."

"He could have given the killer a key," DC Moore said. "What kind of locks were they?"

"Bog standard door locks," Bridge said. "On both the front and back doors. They're the kind of locks you can buy at any hardware shop."

"And the keys are easy to replicate," DC King said. "The husband could have got another key cut for the killer, and there's no way of checking."

"Whitton will be back with us tomorrow," DI Smyth said. "And we'll have a full team, but in the meantime there's plenty for us to be getting on with. I'm due in a meeting in ten minutes and it's a meeting I can't get out of."

"What is it now?" Smith said.

"Budget stuff."

"Rather you than me, boss."

"You all know what to do," DI Smyth said.

"I want to bring Peter Snow in for a formal interview," Smith said.

"You're like a stuck record sometimes."

"Is that you giving me the green light?"

"Do it then," DI Smyth said. "Be gentle with him."

"You know me, boss."

"That's what concerns me. Get to work."

CHAPTER SIX

Not all spiders sleep in the same way that humans do, but in certain species of our eight-legged friends the similarities are striking. It's been documented that jumping spiders exhibit traits remarkably similar to people. Jumping spiders have been observed to enter a REM-like sleep phase which suggests they may experience dreams. They exhibit rapid eye movement, and they have also been known to display uncoordinated body movements such as leg twitching and curling.

The man who called himself *The Spider* was entering the REM phase now and for him it heralded the beginning of a dream he'd had since he was a child. It was always the same setting in the dream. A summer's day on a beach in a place he'd forgotten the name of. It's warm and the beach is crowded. Children are playing in the sand. Parents are bringing ice creams from the kiosk on the esplanade. Everyone is smiling. Some people are floating on inflatable boats close to the shore. The sound of laughter can be heard. Everyone is happy.

The Spider is all alone. There are no ice creams for him today. He doesn't play in the surf, and he has nothing to make a sandcastle with. He's been left alone – he can't find his sister, and he doesn't know how to find his way back. A young girl asks him if he's alright and he tells her to go away. She doesn't listen. She asks him if he wants to play with her and that's when the sky darkens. The girl's face is changing – the smile is still there, but it's a different smile now. *The Spider* reaches out with his bony little hands and grips her around the neck. He's surprisingly strong and the girl can't make him stop. Before she dies, she tells him that he's not really alone, but he doesn't believe her.

This is when he always wakes up.

The Spider leapt off the bed and waited for his breathing to slow. His heart was beating dangerously fast, but it always did after the dream. He picked up the glass of water from the bedside table and took a sip. His tattoo was starting to itch, and he couldn't reach it with either of his hands. He put his back to the wall and moved up and down. The relief was instant.

He switched on his laptop and went to the bathroom while it was booting up. He came back and sat down at the desk. After logging on to one of his social media accounts he got to work. He'd been alerted to a promising project last night, but he'd been tired and he wanted to make sure that the criteria were met. This was a woman who needed to learn a hard lesson, and he was going to be her teacher. After scrolling down *The Spider* determined that his instincts had been correct last night. He had work to do.

* * *

Smith had two hours to spare before Peter Snow was due to arrive at the station. Peter had been reluctant at first, but Smith had persuaded him that it was in everybody's best interests if he made himself available at the earliest opportunity, and he'd agreed to come in at five that afternoon.

In the meantime, Smith wanted to speak to one of Christine Snow's friends. He'd tracked down Natalie Mitchell from Christine's Facebook page. Her privacy settings were minimal, and Smith had no problem gaining access to her friends list. Natalie featured often in Christine's posts, and it was clear that the women were good friends.

Natalie lived in a semi-detached property in Rawcliffe. It was in the north of the city, adjacent to Clifton Moor, and Smith knew that the houses in this part of town didn't come cheap. He parked his car outside and he and DC King got out.

"Nice place," DC King said.

"It's a far cry from Christine Snow's terraced house," Smith said. "And I've been wondering about that. Peter Snow must do alright for himself. He's a partner in an accounting firm so why does he choose to live in a terraced house in Bootham?"

"Maybe he likes the area."

"Who knows?" Smith said.

"Is she expecting us?" DC King asked. "Natalie, I mean."

"She is. I called ahead and she's happy to speak to us. Hopefully that means she has something to tell us."

Natalie Mitchell was a short woman with long black hair. Smith noticed that her eyes were two different shades of blue. It was a subtle difference, but her left eye was definitely darker in colour than the right one. Smith introduced himself and DC King, and Natalie invited them in. She asked them to take a seat in the living room.

"It's not every day I get a celebrity in my house," she said.

Smith sat down on the three-seater. "I wouldn't go that far."

"You were incredible in the Vanessa Sweetman interviews."

"I'd prefer to forget about that," Smith said.

This was an understatement. *The Optician* investigation had taken its toll on him, and he wanted nothing more than to put it behind him and leave it there.

"We're very sorry about Christine," Smith said.

"It still hasn't sunk in," Natalie said. "I couldn't believe it when I heard."

"How did you find out?" DC King said.

"It was on Christine's Facebook page."

Smith had seen it too. It always amazed him how people chose to post on the wall of a dead person, but when he'd checked Christine's Facebook there were already dozens of messages of condolence.

"Were you and Christine good friends?" Smith said.

"We were at school together," Natalie said. "And we stayed in touch afterwards. I still can't believe she was murdered."

"Did she have many friends?"

"Not as many as she used to."

"Why do you think that is?" DC King said.

"Peter," Natalie replied without hesitation.

"Do you know her husband well?" Smith said.

"As well as I choose to."

"You're not a big fan of his?"

"Is it that obvious?"

"It is," Smith said. "I spoke to him earlier and I got the impression that the marriage wasn't a normal one."

"You can say that again."

"They didn't spend much time together, did they?"

"Christine was always moaning about it," Natalie said.

"What do you mean?" DC King said.

"They slept in the same bed, but that's about as far as things went. Peter is either at work or playing football."

"Why did she stay with him?" Smith wondered.

"Money. Peter has always held her back – he goes out to work, and she keeps the house in order. She's scared of what she'll do if she leaves him. She left school with no qualifications, and it's not easy to find work without them."

"Did Christine confide in you about her relationship?" Smith said.

"Sometimes," Natalie said. "I knew she was unhappy."

"Do you know if she ever considered seeking comfort elsewhere?"

Natalie laughed. "Sorry, but that's a really old-fashioned way of putting it. Was she cheating on Peter? The answer is no."

"Are you sure?" DC King said.

"Absolutely. Christine is probably the most loyal person I've ever met. She would never do something like that. If she was thinking about entering into another relationship, she would definitely end the current one first. That's just the sort of person she is."

"Is it possible that Peter's behaviour pushed her over the edge?" Smith said. "Perhaps she'd had enough of the way he was treating her, and she started an affair."

"I know Christine better than anyone," Natalie. "She doesn't have a dishonest bone in her body and if she was planning on doing something like that, she wouldn't have kept quiet about it – she would have told me."

Smith got the impression that Natalie Mitchell was telling them the truth but if that was the case it meant the theory that Christine was in a relationship with her killer had no weight to it. He was running out of questions to ask so he opted for an old favourite.

"Can you think of anyone who would want to hurt Christine? Did she have any enemies?"

"None that I'm aware of. She was a sweet soul."

"When was the last time you saw her?"

"I popped round there last week," Natalie said. "On Wednesday. Peter was out, as usual and we shared a bottle of wine and had a chat."

"Did you get the feeling that anything was bothering her?" DC King said.

"No more than usual. She was in a miserable relationship, but that's been the norm for years. Perhaps Peter will have a long hard think about what he actually had with Christine now. You don't know what you've got until it's gone, do you?"

CHAPTER SEVEN

Smith had some time to kill before Peter Snow was due to arrive, so he called Whitton. He'd forgotten about the unexpected visit from Fran's biological father earlier and he wanted to warn Whitton about him. He wasn't sure if Robert Rogers would make another appearance at the house, but he suspected that they hadn't seen the last of the man who abandoned his wife and child all those years ago.

"What did he want?" Whitton asked when Smith had explained about the visit.

"He said he wants what's his," Smith said. "I told him to fuck off."

Whitton sighed. "Of course, you did. What if he comes back?"

"I'll tell him to fuck off again. He doesn't have a leg to stand on. He was made aware of the adoption, and he voiced no objections. You and me are Fran's legal guardians and nothing will change that."

"Robert is Fran's father, Jason."

"Only in a biological sense," Smith said. "There's more to being a father than DNA. I'm not stressed."

"Well, I am. I'm going to do some research. What if he petitions the courts."

"That's not going to happen," Smith said. "We adopted that little girl in accordance with the guidelines set out in law. Everything was done by the book and Robert bloody Rogers has no claim on Fran."

"What if she wants to see him?" Whitton said. "What then?"

"We'll worry about *what ifs*, if and when they happen. I have to go – I'm interviewing the dead woman's husband in a bit. Don't worry about Robert Rogers – I won't let anyone take Fran away from us."

"Why now?" Whitton said. "Why has he come back after all these years?"

"I don't know and I don't care, Erica. As far as I'm aware, once an adoption order is made it legally terminates the relationship between the birth father and the child, and he cannot claim the child. It's a legally binding decision and it cannot be undone, no matter how hard the father petitions the courts. Fran isn't going anywhere. I'll see you later."

He had time for a quick cup of coffee so he headed up to the canteen, selected the strongest one on offer and took it to his usual table by the window. It was still light outside, and Smith knew that soon the days would stretch out until late at night. He liked this time of year.

DC Moore came in and sat down opposite him.
"Any joy with the exit route stuff?" Smith said.
"Dead end, Sarge," DC Moore said. "He didn't have much choice as far as getaway options were concerned, but it doesn't help us."
"What about the door-to-door?"
"Nada. None of the neighbours can remember seeing anything out of the ordinary."
"Shit happens," Smith said. "Something is really bugging me about how he got in."
"I thought we'd established that he was invited in by Mrs Snow."
"We haven't established anything," Smith said. "It's all speculation at this stage. Is Kerry around?"
"She's waiting for you in the interview room," DC Moore said. "Peter Snow has arrived with his lawyer."
Smith finished his coffee. "Why the hell didn't you tell me that when you came in?"
He didn't wait for a reply. He got up and left the canteen.

He went inside the interview room and apologised for keeping them waiting. Peter Snow was sitting next to a woman who looked to be close to the age of retirement. She introduced herself as Olga Pitt and asked him if he could get started. Smith obliged. He stated the details for the recording device and looked across at Peter Snow.

"I'd like to offer you my condolences again, Mr Snow. I'll try to keep this as brief as possible."

"I did not kill my wife," Peter said.

"Let's talk about keys," Smith said.

"What?"

"When you arrived home after playing football," Smith said. "You claim that the front door and the back door were locked. Is this correct?"

"Yes."

"Who has keys for the doors?"

"What has this got to do with what happened?"

"How many keys are there?" Smith said.

"Three," Peter replied. "For both the front and back door."

"You have one," DC King said. "Christine had another, and there's one as a spare. Is that right?"

"Something like that."

"Are any of the keys missing?" Smith asked.

"Not that I'm aware of."

"I need you to think hard," Smith said. "Are any of the keys unaccounted for?"

"I still have mine," Peter said.

He took them out of his pocket to show them.

"Where are the spare keys kept?" Smith said.

"In a drawer in the kitchen. The top drawer under the worktop."

"Kerry," Smith said to DC King. "Could you get hold of Webber and ask him to check please. He and Billie are still busy at the house."

DC King got up and left the room. Smith documented it for the tape.

"When will I be allowed back inside my house?" Peter said.

"When our Forensic team has finished," Smith said. "They're very thorough and they won't leave any stone unturned."

"Why am I being treated like a common criminal? My wife has been murdered, and I'm being made to feel like dirt."

"I'm afraid it can't be helped. In crimes like these we always look at the people closest to the victim first."

DC King came back in.

"Mrs Snow's keys were in her handbag," she said. "And the spares are where Mr Snow said they would be."

"Can we please move on?" Olga said. "My client has been through enough today, wouldn't you agree?"

"Mr Snow," Smith said. "There's a knife block in the kitchen. One of the knives was missing. Do you know anything about that?"

"The paring knife," Peter said. "The tip of the blade broke off months ago, and we threw it away."

"Are you sure?"

"Of course, I'm sure. I'm not an idiot."

"So, there's not much paring going on in the house anymore."

"What the hell is that supposed to mean?" Peter said.

"I have no idea," Smith said.

"Could you please keep this relevant?" It was Olga.

"Point taken," Smith said. "Mr Snow, was Christine having an affair?"

"What the hell?" Peter said.

"Well?" Smith said. "Do you believe that your wife was cheating on you?"

"No. She was not."

"I don't believe you. I think you found out about the affair, and you had her killed."

"Detective Sergeant," Olga said. "This is outrageous."

"You paid someone to kill her," Smith said. "You timed it so you would be playing football, thus giving you a solid alibi. Would you have any objections to us taking a look at your bank accounts?"

"Not without a warrant," Olga said.

"I was hoping we could bypass that," Smith said. "Mr Snow. Peter, I want to take a look at your banking records."

"Go for it," Peter said. "I've got nothing to hide."

"I would advise you against that," Olga told him.

"I don't have a problem with it. I did not pay someone to kill Christine. There's nothing in my bank records that will tell them otherwise."

"OK," Smith said. "Let's wrap things up there. I just have one more question."

"And then can I go?" Peter said.

"You've been free to leave at any time since the start," DC King said.

"Now you tell me."

"You told us you arrived home at around noon today," Smith said. "You found Christine in the bedroom. Why did you cover her with a sheet?"

"I did no such thing."

"When I was there earlier," Smith said. "Christine was on the bed, and she'd been covered in a sheet."

"I didn't touch her. It wasn't me."

"Are you sure?"

"Of course, I'm sure. I wasn't the one who covered her with the sheet."

CHAPTER EIGHT

Brian James checked his face in the mirror in the bathroom. The bruises on his cheek had faded but they were still apparent. Brian was brought back to the events that led up to the attack two nights ago. The evening had started well – he'd had a great day at work, and he'd booked a table at a new restaurant in the city to celebrate. Georgia loved Indian food, and he'd chosen the restaurant for her.

They'd been in high spirits. Georgia's frame of mind was upbeat, and nothing could have prepared Brian for what was to come. Two bottles of wine at the restaurant were followed by two more back in Brian's flat, and he didn't see the fury that was building inside his fiancé. It came from nowhere, and there was a familiarity to it. It hadn't happened for quite some time, and Brian had wondered if it was a thing of the past.

The conversation had turned to work, and Georgia had questioned Brian about one of his colleagues. Valerie Norman was the person he worked closest with and he liked her. Georgia was aware of this, and it became apparent that she didn't like it. In hindsight, Brian realised that he ought to have steered the conversation in another direction, but hindsight is rarely helpful.

Georgia had hit him hard. Her fist was closed and there was real anger in the first blow. The second punch had caused an explosion of light inside Brian's head, and he was almost knocked out. He'd managed to lock himself in the bathroom before she had the chance to hit him a third time and he'd waited until everything outside was silent. Georgia had apologised the next morning. She deeply regretted what had happened, and she promised that it would never happen again. Brian had heard it all before, but as he had done many times, he took her at her word. It was a cycle he couldn't seem to break, and he was willing to believe that she would change.

He touched his cheek and winced. His face was going to be sore for a while. He turned away from the mirror and left the bathroom. It was late Saturday afternoon, and he had no plans for the evening. Georgia was visiting her parents in Newcastle and Brian decided to occupy his time with work. He was a literary agent, and he'd received a manuscript that looked promising. He would open a bottle of wine, put on some music and read through it.

He checked to see if the door to the flat was locked and selected a CD from the rack. He was in the mood for something mellow, so he took out a Fiona Apple album and slotted it into the CD player. He turned up the volume and woke his laptop up. He opened a bottle of red wine and left it on the desk to breathe. Fiona Apple stopped lamenting about shadowboxing and in the silence before the next track something caused Brian to turn around. It was a noise that shouldn't be there. It sounded like someone was in the bathroom.

He got up and paused the CD. He heard the sound again – it was a light tapping noise and it was definitely coming from the bathroom. Brian was instantly alert. He knew there was no way anyone could have got inside the flat. The door was locked, and he was three floors up, but the strange sound couldn't be ignored. He walked down the corridor to the bathroom and stopped outside the door. The flat was silent now and Brian wondered if he'd imagined it. His phone started to ring in the living room.

He turned around and he didn't hear the bathroom door opening. Shortly afterwards he experienced an intense pain in his lower back and he cried out. The second stab silenced him in an instant and when the knife went in a third time Brian's senses began to fail, one by one. The blade had pierced the heart from behind and the last thing that he registered was the stain in the carpet as he was helped to the floor. He was dead before he could recall what had caused the stain. He didn't hear the soft footsteps as *The Spider* retrieved a sheet from the bedroom, and he wasn't aware of the scent of the freshly washed sheet as it was placed over his body.

* * *

"He covered her with a sheet."
Smith wrote this new information on the whiteboard in the small conference room.
"Webber has been informed," he said. "And the sheet has been taken into evidence."
"Why cover her up?" DC Moore wondered.
"Compassion?" DC King suggested.
"He stabbed her multiple times," Bridge pointed out. "There was no compassion on display there."
"I think Kerry might have a point," Smith said. "He showed a lot of fury during the attack itself, but afterwards… Afterwards, he covered her up. Why does someone do that? He's showing some kind of remorse and I don't believe he took any pleasure in the murder."
"You've lost me there, Sarge," DC Moore said. "What's the point in killing someone if you're not enjoying it?"
"Perhaps the murder was necessary," Smith said. "And that would tie in with the theory that it was a hired gun who carried out the killing. It's a job to him – nothing more, but there was a certain respect shown afterwards. He didn't leave her on display – he covered her with a sheet to ensure that a modicum of dignity remained intact."
"I'm not buying it," DC Moore said. "And how do we even know the husband was telling the truth?"
"I believed him," Smith said. "He wasn't lying to us when he said he wasn't the one who covered her up when he got home."
"Why lie about something like that?" DC King said.

DI Smyth came in and asked to be brought up to date. Smith told him about the interview with Peter Snow and the mystery surrounding the sheet. "He's giving us full access to his bank accounts," he added. "Which throws some doubt on the theory that he paid someone to kill his wife."

"There are more ways than you think to pay someone," DC Moore said. "He could have used a virtual currency."

"Not that bollocks again," Bridge said, rather eloquently. "They should make Bitcoin illegal."

"We'll examine Mr Snow's financial history," DI Smyth said. "But I'm inclined to agree with Smith. He was under no obligation to allow us access without a warrant and that makes me think he's got nothing to hide. Have we had any other developments?"

"Nothing, boss," Smith said. "All the keys are accounted for. Mr Snow has a set, his wife's keys were in her handbag, and the spares were where he said they would be, in the drawer in the kitchen. So, unless he had extra keys cut, it looks like the killer didn't get in through either of the doors."

"Mr Snow could have been lying about the doors being locked," DC Moore said. "We only have his word that they were locked."

"I don't believe spending time speculating about this will be time well spent," DI Smyth said.

"It's bothering me, boss," Smith said. "The only other possible point of entry into the house was through a window twenty feet up in the air and I don't see how that's physically possible."

He was about to get a bit closer to the truth and it was going to come from an unexpected source.

PC Angie Bowler came inside the room. She apologised for the interruption. "We've had a report of an intruder over in Scarcroft."

"Uniforms can deal with it," DC Moore said.

"They did deal with it," PC Bowler said. "And when they arrived on the scene, they saw the intruder as he made his escape."

"And?" Smith said.

"You're not going to believe this, Sarge," PC Bowler said. "When PC Griffin called it in, he described the man as something akin to an insect. The flat is on the third floor, and the intruder came down the wall like a spider. He was down and gone before the officers had chance to blink."

CHAPTER NINE

"The owner of the flat is a man by the name of Brian James," DI Smyth told Smith.

"He's dead," Smith said.

"We don't know that."

"He's dead," Smith said once more. "And I think the mystery of how the killer got into Christine Snow's house is about to be cleared up too."

"Let's not jump to conclusions. According to the caretaker, Brian James is home. Mr Golding has been the caretaker here for ten years – he has a flat on the ground floor, and he bumped into Brian at around five. He went up to his flat and he hasn't left."

"That's because he's dead, boss."

The caretaker had spare keys for all of the flats and Smith was glad. The door was strong, and he didn't envy the person who would have had to break it down. Webber had been informed but the Head of Forensics had put his foot down. He wasn't about to cut his Saturday evening short based on a feeling in the pit of Smith's stomach. He told him to give him a call as soon as he knew something concrete.

It didn't take long. Smith didn't even have to set foot inside the flat to get confirmation. A man he assumed to be Brian James was lying face down in the hallway. He wasn't moving and the amount of blood on the sheet covering his body, and on the carpet told Smith everything he needed to know. He closed the door and phoned Webber.

While he waited, he smoked a cigarette outside. He walked around the back of the block of flats and looked upwards. One of the windows of flat 3D was open. Smith estimated that the window was at least twenty-five feet up, and if the officers first on the scene hadn't witnessed the remarkable getaway of the intruder, Smith wouldn't believe it was possible to get out of the flat that way.

There was no garden and the back of the flats looked straight onto Nunnery Lane. Something occurred to Smith. This was a risky murder. The sun was low in the sky, but it was still light outside. The killer was taking a huge chance breaking in during the day and Smith wondered why he hadn't waited for the cover of darkness. He didn't know why but he got the feeling that this was the start of something – something nasty. The fact that Brian James had been covered with a sheet also told him that this murder was definitely linked to the slaying of Christine Snow.

His phone started to ring while he was lighting his second cigarette. The ringtone told him it was Whitton. Meatloaf was wailing about a bat out of hell. Smith shut him up quickly.

"We've got another body," he told his wife.

He gave her the details of what they knew thus far. That wasn't why she'd phoned.

"Robert Rogers came back," she told him.

"When?"

"I've just got rid of him."

"Did Fran see him?"

"Luckily, Fran and Laura are spending the night at my mum's house," Whitton said.

"What did he say?"

"The same as he said to you. He's Fran's real father and he's going to get her back."

"That's never going to happen," Smith said. "Was his tone threatening?"

"Not particularly. I wasn't scared, if that's what you mean."

"Yes, you were," Smith said.

"I really wasn't. He's not exactly what you'd describe as menacing."

"We won't mention that when we apply for the restraining order."

"You can't be serious."

"I'm deadly serious," Smith said. "He's come to the house twice now and he's made veiled threats. We're worried that he'll take drastic measures and go as far as abducting Fran. It'll work."

"A restraining order?"

"It's the perfect solution. If he comes anywhere near us, he gets arrested. The law has to work in our favour sometimes."

"I don't really know what you mean by that."

"We'll sort him out," Smith said. "It's either a restraining order or more drastic measures, but I'm getting a bit old for drastic measures. I'd better get back to work – Webber has arrived."

Smith intercepted him before he went inside the block of flats.

"You were right," Webber said.

"I was right. You need to take a look at the outside of the flats first."

Webber nodded. "I was given a brief heads-up on the way."

"If the officers first on the scene hadn't witnessed the getaway," Smith said. "I wouldn't have believed it, but two PCs both saw the same thing, and we can't ignore it. Have you got a ladder?"

"Do I look like a window cleaner?"

Smith nodded. "I reckon the caretaker will have one you can borrow."

"Pete is on his way," Webber said. "Me and ladders don't really get on."

"He got in and out through the bathroom window. And he covered the body with a sheet. Ring any bells?"

"Loud ones. What's going on here, Smith?"

"We're going to find out. I need to have a quick word with the boss. You'll let me..."

"As soon as I have something for you."

Smith found DI Smyth by the entrance to the block of flats. Bridge and DC Moore had arrived, and the DI was bringing them up to date.

"Boss," Smith said. "Can I have a quick word?"

DI Smyth walked towards the parking area. Smith followed him.

"What's on your mind?" DI Smyth asked.

Smith took out a cigarette and lit it. He told DI Smyth about Robert Rogers.

"When was the last time you saw him?" DI Smyth asked when he was finished.

"I'd never met the bloke before until today," Smith said.

"Why do you think he's come back now?"

"God knows. He wasn't interested in Fran when her mother died, and I don't know why he's back now. I was considering a restraining order."

"That's a bit drastic. As far as I'm aware, you and Whitton are Fran's legal guardians. Nothing can change that. When the adoption was granted the birth father forfeited all claims on his daughter."

"I know all that," Smith said. "But I don't think that's going to stop a man like Robert Rogers. He's been to the house twice today, and surely that's grounds for a restraining order."

"Has he made any threats?"

"Nothing obvious," Smith said. "Everything he said was implied, but the courts don't need to know that. I was thinking of bending the law a bit."

"Why don't I like the sound of this?"

"For a restraining order to be granted," Smith said. "There has to be reasonable grounds. As far as I know, Robert Rogers has never been convicted of an offence so that's off the table. But and this is a big but – his conduct could be construed as threatening, and we could petition that the persistent harassment could escalate to violence."

"You're going to need more than a few veiled threats for that to stick," DI Smyth pointed out.

"I'm aware of that, boss," Smith said. "And that's why I want to give the courts more than that. Surely the testament of two long-serving police officers will count for something. It doesn't necessarily have to be the truth."

"I would advise against this, Smith."

"It's either that or more, drastic measures."

DI Smyth didn't get the chance to voice his opinion on this. DC Moore approached and the wild expression on his face told them that he had something important to tell them.

"Are you on drugs?" Smith asked him.

"What?" DC Moore said. "No, Sarge. I took a look round the back of the block of flats and I think I might have something. There's a small hotel on Nunnery Lane and they have a camera facing the flats. DS Bridge is in there now speaking to someone who can access the CCTV stuff. We might have footage of the killer getting in and out of flat 3D."

CHAPTER TEN

They were in luck. The CCTV camera on the hotel opposite the block of flats did capture the entry and exit of the man they believed to have murdered Brian James, but after watching the footage for the second time it only proved what the officers first on the scene had claimed. And when the footage stopped none of the detectives inside the briefing room said a word. What they'd just witnessed didn't seem possible.

"What the hell are we dealing with here?" Smith was the first to find his voice. "Play it once more."
DC Moore started the footage from the beginning. At 17:36 a figure appeared in the shot.
"Can you pause it there?" Bridge said.
DC Moore obliged.
"It looks like a man," DC King said.

The CCTV camera was top quality, and the image was clear, but it didn't really help them. The figure was dressed in black tracksuit pants and a dark-coloured hooded top. The camera angle meant that they could only see him from behind. He paused in front of the block of flats and stopped stock still for more than thirty seconds.
"What is he doing?" DC Moore wondered.
"Planning his climb," Smith said without thinking.
"Planning his climb?" Bridge repeated.
"Like an extreme mountain climber," DC King joined in.
"Exactly like a mountain climber," Smith said.

At 17:38 the real action started. Everyone watched as the man on the screen ran towards the block of flats. His initial leap didn't seem humanly possible. His right foot landed on the windowsill of the ground floor flat, and he pushed himself upwards. He gripped the downpipe next to the window and flung himself further upwards. He was now halfway up. He grabbed the sill of the window on the second floor flat and pulled himself up. From here it was a simple task of reaching the windowsill of the bathroom belonging to Brian James. He stopped for a moment and with his body blocking the window they couldn't see what was happening.

"I think he's getting to work on the window latch," Smith guessed.

They watched as he slid through the open window with ease.

DC Moore paused the footage again.

"I still can't figure out how he climbed up there," he said.

"He's done this before," Smith said. "And I'm not just talking about Christine Snow. You do not achieve that level of agility without practice."

"We need to look into climbing clubs, don't we?" DC King said.

"Definitely. This is a specialised skill. There aren't many people capable of something like this. Start the footage again."

At 17:52 there was movement inside the bathroom again.

"Surely this is illegal," DC Moore said, and paused the footage.

Smith turned to look at him with a deep frown on his face.

"I fucking hope murder is still illegal, Harry."

"I'm not talking about that, Sarge," DC Moore said. "The hotel camera is pointing right at the back of the flats. They're not allowed to do that."

"Who cares?" Bridge said. "This is a development. I'm not worried about the legal implications of the positioning of a CCTV camera."

"Can we get back to the important stuff?" Smith said.

DC Moore resumed the footage. It was 17:53.

"He's coming back out," DC King said.

"He was inside for less than fifteen minutes," Bridge said. "According to PC Griffin, they arrived on the scene at 17:52."

"They just missed him," Smith said. "But I don't think they would have been able to apprehend him, even if they'd got there sooner."

After watching the man's skilful descent, none of the team disagreed. He was on the ground in seconds. And he was out of the camera shot soon afterwards.

"Which direction did he go in?" Smith said.

"According to PC Griffin's notes," Bridge said. "He legged it up Nunnery Lane and then headed north. We've since had a witness report saying they saw someone matching his description hopping over the city wall and Victoria Bar like they were three-foot hurdles."

"What's Victoria Bar?" DC Moore said.

"It's a famous landmark," Bridge said.

"A three arched bridge," Smith elaborated. "And it's about twenty feet high."

"Who is this creature?" DC King said.

"He's not a creature," Smith said. "He's a murderer, and we'll catch him, just like we've caught every other sick fuck who thinks they can kill people in this city."

"Why do you think he's doing it?" DC King put forward.

"We won't have a starting point there until we know more about the victims," Smith said.

"Are we working on the assumption that the two murders today are connected?" DC Moore said.

"Definitely. The MOs are identical. He gets in by somehow scaling the wall, he kills with a knife, and he covers his victims with a sheet afterwards. It's definitely the work of the same killer."

"How do we catch someone like this?" Bridge said. "We stand no chance in a chase. The man can do things that don't seem possible."

"We'll come back to that," Smith said. "Let's go through what we know first."

"I get the feeling he's in a hurry," DC King said. "Two murders in the space of a few hours suggests he's in a rush to carry them out."

"You're right," Smith said. "Christine Snow was killed sometime between eight and noon this morning and Brian James was murdered late afternoon."

"And he's done some homework," Bridge added. "Christine's husband plays football every Saturday morning and we now know that Brian James's fiancé was visiting her parents in Newcastle. I think he was aware of this."

"How do we know about Brian's fiancé's plans?" Smith asked.

"Billie," Bridge said with an inane grin on his face. "It was on the calendar in the kitchen."

"Has she been informed?" Smith said. "The fiancé, I mean."

"She has."

"We need to speak to her."

"She'll be back tomorrow," Bridge said. "And I suggest we call it a day until tomorrow too. I happen to have a date with the forensics officer with the finest arse in Yorkshire, and I plan to keep that date."

"I wouldn't say Webber's arse is that special," Smith said.

"Urgh," Bridge said. "Now I can't get that image out of my head."

Smith grinned. "On that note, I agree with Bridge. I need a beer."

"I thought you were doing a fitness thing, Sarge," DC King said.

"Baby steps, Kerry. Too much drastic change in lifestyle can be dangerous. I'll see you all tomorrow."

CHAPTER ELEVEN

The house was quiet when Smith got home. The door was locked, and this was unusual when Whitton was home, so he assumed she'd gone out somewhere. He grabbed a beer from the fridge and sat down at the table in the kitchen to gather his thoughts. Two murders in one day was almost unprecedented. He'd come across it before, but it was extremely rare. The man who'd killed Christine Snow and Brian James had acted with haste and Smith knew instinctively that there was a reason for this.

The footage of the entry and exit into Brian James's flat played out on repeat inside Smith's head. He was certain that the killer had trained extensively to reach that level of fitness and it was somewhere to start. Smith could barely manage to get over the wall at the back of his house and that was only six feet high. He couldn't imagine scaling a wall and managing to gain access to a window twenty-odd feet up.

A noise upstairs interrupted his thoughts. Smith knew exactly what it was. It was the sound of Theakston announcing his presence. It was a pointless bark, and it rarely amounted to anything. Usually, the fat Bull Terrier couldn't be bothered to voice his opinion, but this time it caused Smith to take notice. He wondered what Theakston was even doing upstairs.

He got his answer shortly afterwards. Whitton came into the kitchen and her wet hair and the fresh scent that came with her told Smith that she'd taken a bath.

"I thought you'd gone out," he said.

"I felt like a long bath," Whitton said.

"Is that why you locked the door?"

"You can't be too careful these days," Whitton said. "Although I had protection up there."

The *protection* came into the room in the form of Theakston and Fred. Both of them gave Smith a perfunctory glance and headed for their respective food bowls.

"Protection, my arse," he said. "Any intruder with a pocket full of treats will be allowed free rein in this house."

"You'd be surprised," Whitton said. "I didn't ask them to follow me to the bathroom. I think they sensed that I was a bit stressed."

"Robert Rogers?" Smith guessed.

"I'm worried about him, Jason."

"Me too," Smith admitted. "But I'm not going to be bullied by a man like him. We have solid grounds for a restraining order."

"Do you know what that will entail?"

"Not really."

"We'll have to lodge a formal complaint," Whitton said. "And apply for the order. And only when the courts have considered all the details will they approve or deny the order. It's a serious procedure and we also have to consider the press."

"You know how I feel about the press," Smith said.

"It'll be a newsworthy story," Whitton said. "Two detective sergeants have to resort to a restraining order because they can't protect their adopted child."

"Why are you so anti this, Erica?" Smith said.

"I don't know. It just feels unfair on Fran's biological father."

"I'm going to stop you right there. Do not even think about feeling sorry for that bastard."

"We don't know the full story."

"I know enough," Smith said. "Robert left Sheila when Fran was barely out of nappies. The man deserted his wife and daughter, and whatever his reasons, I don't want to hear them. He got another chance to make things right when Sheila died and he was asked if he had any objections to us adopting her. He had every opportunity to step in and be a father, but he chose not to. As far as I'm concerned, he is as dead to Fran as her biological mother is."

"I'm just seeing it from his perspective."

"Don't," Smith said. "It won't do anyone any good to think like that. Fran has settled here – we're doing alright with her, and if we reintroduce Robert Rogers into her life, it will only end badly. Do you want a beer?"

She did. Smith got two more out of the fridge and brought up the developments in the investigation instead. The details of the double murder were infinitely more preferable topics of conversation than a bottom feeder like Robert Rogers. He told her about the extraordinary agility the killer displayed and the way the murders were carried out. He also mentioned the sheet that was placed over the bodies afterwards.

"He was in a hurry," Whitton said.

"We discussed that," Smith said. "Two murders in one day is no mean feat. And he's definitely done some homework. He knew that the victims would be alone, and he knew how to get in and out of the properties quickly."

"Tell me about the victims?"

"Christine Snow was thirty-four. She didn't work and from what we've gathered about her, hers was a pretty miserable existence. Her husband is an accountant, and he'd much rather kick a ball around a field than spend time with his wife. It was their wedding anniversary today and he chose to spend it playing football.

"Is he a suspect?"

"For what it's worth," Smith said.

"You don't think he's involved?"

"I don't. I did consider a scenario where Christine was having an affair and he found out about it and had her killed, but after seeing the footage of the killer today, he didn't strike me as a killer for hire. And the husband had no qualms about letting us into his bank accounts. I think the killer knew about Christine's husband's routine and he broke in when he knew she would be alone in the house."

"What about the second victim?" Whitton said.

"Brian James," Smith said. "We know very little about him. He too was alone in the house because his fiancé was in Newcastle visiting her parents. We'll be speaking to her tomorrow. Brian was also stabbed multiple times and covered with a sheet."

"Have you thought about why he does that?"

"We've tossed a few theories around," Smith said. "But it's all speculation right now. He showed a certain amount of compassion by doing that and that makes me wonder if he feels remorse afterwards. The killing is necessary, but he takes no pleasure in it."

"Do you think he's finished?"

"That's a question we'll only ask when it becomes necessary," Smith said.

"You must have a sense one way or another."

"In that case, no," Smith said. "No, I do not think he's finished. In fact, I get the feeling that he's barely started."

CHAPTER TWELVE

Smith was the last one to work the next day. When he'd got inside his car and turned the key, nothing happened. It was only after uttering a few words of encouragement followed by a number of impressive expletives that his old Sierra had taken the hint and spluttered into life. Smith was relieved – he knew that Whitton had been telling him to buy a new car for years, and he didn't want to get rid of his old friend just yet. He would have a quiet word with Darren Lewis. Darren's brother was a decent mechanic, and he knew the car inside out. He ought to – not so long ago, Gary had replaced just about every possible part in the car and given it a new lease of life.

Even though he was late, Smith's first port of call was the canteen. He didn't want to start the day without a cup of his favourite coffee from the machine in there. He took it with him to the briefing room.

"It's nice of you to join us," DI Smyth said.

"Sorry, boss," Smith said. "I would have been here earlier, but I got caught behind a dickhead on the A19 and I had to drive at twenty all the way."

"What were you doing on the A19?" Whitton said. "That's miles out of the way."

"I took the long way round," Smith lied. "What have I missed."

Whitton's eyes narrowed, but she remained silent.

"We've got the results from the post-mortem on Christine Snow," DI Smyth said. "Mrs Snow died as a result of massive blood loss. She was stabbed six times in the chest and stomach and any one of those wounds probably would have proved to be fatal."

"He definitely wanted her dead then," DC Moore concluded.

"You're in fine form this morning, Harry," Smith said.

"I was just…"

"Unfortunately," DI Smyth carried on. "From a forensics perspective we've got very little to look at. But Webber can say with ninety-five percent certainty that the killer did in fact gain access to the property through the bathroom window. There was nothing in the bathroom itself – no fingerprints or scuff marks, but there were definite shoeprints on the downpipe on the side of the house. And this looks promising – they're very unusual shoeprints."

"In what way?" Smith said.

"Webber believes the tread is designed to offer maximum purchase."

"Makes sense," Smith said. "To perform a climb like that, you'd make sure you're wearing the correct gear. The footwear is definitely worth looking into. Anything else?"

"That's it for now. It was starting to get dark by the time Forensics got round to the outside of Brian James's flat and Webber decided to wait for daylight to take a look at possible routes up to the bathroom."

"Health and safety?" Smith said.

"This is Webber we're talking about here," Bridge said. "Since when does he give a hoot about health and safety?"

"It's simply a question of visibility," DI Smyth said. "He's promised to make an early start and hopefully we'll have some answers before the end of the day."

"Today is all about the victims," Smith said. "Who were they and why did this freak of nature want them dead?"

"Brian James's fiancé should be back sometime this morning," DI Smyth said. "Her name is Georgia Francis and that's all we know about her. I want you to speak to Brian's friends and other family members too."

"What did he do for work?" DC Moore said.

"He was a literary agent," DI Smyth said.

"Lucky bugger," DC Moore said. "I wish I could get paid to read books all day."

"I think there's a bit more to it than that," Smith said. "And when was the last time you read a book – apart from the Christmas Beano annual, I mean?"

"I happen to read a lot. I can't recall ever seeing you with your face in a book."

"I have my moments."

"Children," DI Smyth said. "Could we carry on please?"

"Sorry Dad," Smith said.

"We found nothing untoward in Peter Snow's bank accounts," DC Moore said. "He was happy to give us full access, and I'm only talking about what I could find in the statements, but there was nothing there that sounded any warning bells. It's possible he has accounts he hasn't made us aware of, but I don't get the impression that we're going to find anything suspicious. He seems like a spectacularly boring man."

"You got that feeling from his bank accounts?" Bridge said.

"It's amazing what you can learn about a person by sifting through what they spend their money on. For example, Mr Snow has subscriptions to no fewer than three online football manager forums."

"I have no idea what you're talking about," Smith said.

"It's big business," DC Moore said. "You're a virtual manager and you have virtual players in virtual leagues. Apparently, it's quite addictive."

"And totally irrelevant to the investigation," Smith decided.

"All I'm saying is there's nothing in Mr Snow's financials that hinted that he may have paid someone to kill his wife."

"For what it's worth," Smith said. "I don't think he's involved. I think Christine was married to a dickhead, but her murder isn't connected in any way to said dickhead."

"We won't spend time discussing Brian James until we have more information at our disposal," DI Smyth said. "Any final thoughts before we wrap up?"

"Something connects the victims," Smith said.

"It usually does," DI Smyth agreed.

"A man and a woman," Smith said. "Which means we can rule out a gender-focused serial killer."

"Serial killer?" Bridge said. "Technically…"

Smith held up his hands. "OK, potential serial killer. He's not finished."

"There's no such thing as a potential serial killer," Bridge said. "Even the FBI have admitted that they made mistakes in their early attempts at profiling men and women who displayed traits that could indicate they were future serial murderers."

"Enough." DI Smyth had seen discussions like these last for hours. "This briefing is officially over."

CHAPTER THIRTEEN

Smith was feeling annoyed. He was supposed to be meeting Georgia Francis at the block of flats, but a phone call to her told him that she hadn't even left Newcastle yet. Webber and Pete Richards were still busy at the back of the flats. They'd finished inside the flat, but they still needed to take a look at the place where the killer gained access to the property. Smith didn't think it was worth waiting for Georgia there – he had better things to do, but when he spotted a familiar figure walking back to the entrance, he decided he might as well stay a bit longer.

They learned that Mr Golding's name was Otto and when the caretaker asked them if they wanted a chat and a cup of coffee, Smith thought it couldn't hurt. Otto had been the caretaker at the flats for a decade, and experience had taught him that people like Otto were often useful sources of information. He invited Smith and DC King into his flat, and the first thing that struck Smith was how neat and tidy the place was. There wasn't a speck of dust to be seen, and everything seemed to have its place. The flat even smelled clean.

Otto told them to make themselves comfortable in the living room while he made the coffee. This room was spotless too, and when Smith looked at the framed photographs on the wall it sort of made sense. Otto Golding was clearly ex-armed forces. All of the photos depicted a much younger Otto in uniform. The photographs looked to have been taken in various places around the world and Smith didn't recognise any of them. Smith's attention was caught by one photo in particular. In it was a bunch of young men somewhere in the desert.

"Good times," Otto said. "To begin with. Help yourself to milk and sugar." He placed the tray of coffee on the table.

"You're ex-army?" Smith said.

"Aye," Otto said. "39 Engineer Regiment. That one was taken just before Operation Telic. Basra 2004."

"Iraq?" DC King said.

Otto nodded. "The 39 Engineers were one of the first regiments to have the pleasure. I did four tours in Iraq. It was hot as hell. A Yorkshireman is not designed for desert life, but I have some good memories."

"When did you leave the armed forces?" Smith said.

"I didn't leave the army," Otto said. "The army left me. Like I said, it was great to begin with. And then it wasn't. Blair fucked up there – he really did. You'll have to excuse my language, love."

He smiled apologetically at DC King.

"I've heard worse," she said.

"Once a squaddie, always a squaddie. You haven't touched the coffee."

Smith poured a cup for himself and DC King.

"You've been caretaker here for ten years," he said to Otto.

"Thereabouts," Otto said.

"It's a far cry from army life," DC King said.

Otto nodded. "I was like a lost fart when I left the army – a lot of us were, and I tried my hand at a few things. I've always been good with my hands, and I got a few jobs doing basic plumbing and electrics. I've got all my qualifications if you're bothered about that."

Smith wasn't. In truth, he couldn't care less.

"How did you end up here?" he asked.

"A mate told me about it. The flats are owned by a young couple. The husband inherited it, and he doesn't have any idea about how to be a landlord. It was his missus who hired me. She's the savvy one. Nice with it, though. She explained that it made business sense to have a caretaker on site. Getting a plumber in or someone to fix a broken window can be costly in the long run."

"Makes sense," Smith said.

"I didn't have to think twice about it," Otto said. "It pays OK and the job comes with this place. Win, win. Most of the tenants are alright."

"What can you tell me about Brian James?" Smith said.

"He's a decent bloke," Otto said. "Quiet as a lamb. Proper intellectual type. He's got a job in the book world."

"He's a literary agent," DC King said.

"Whatever that is when it's at home."

"You haven't had any trouble with Mr James in the past then?" Smith said.

"Never. I've fixed a few things in the flat. And I always got the impression that Brian was reluctant to complain. He was a good man. He wouldn't be my choice of friend, but we're not all the same, are we?"

"What do you mean by that?" DC King said.

"When you spend years in the company of men and women trained to fight you get used to it. When you get out, everyone you meet seems a bit wet somehow. I'm not passing judgement – that's just the way it is."

"Brian's fiancé doesn't live with him, does she?" Smith said.

"That's right," Otto confirmed. "She stays here a lot, but I think she has her own place."

"What's your opinion of her?" DC King said.

"Honestly?"

"You can be as honest as you like," Smith said.

"I don't like her. And before you ask, I don't know why I don't like her. It's just something about her that makes me wary. Some people have that effect on me."

"Does she stay over a lot?" Smith said.

"A few times a week. I usually know when she's here because of the change in volume in the flat."

"They make a lot of noise?" DC King said.

"It's hard to miss it."

"Do the other tenants complain about it?" Smith said.

"Sometimes."

"Can't you just ask them to turn it down a bit?" Smith said. "Tell them to tone it down with the music."

Otto took a sip of his coffee. "I'm not talking about music. I'm talking about them making the noise. Shouting and screaming. And more than once I've got the feeling that they're not stopping there. I've heard stuff being broken and sometimes worse."

"Worse?" Smith said.

"I'm no stranger to violence," Otto said. "And I know what it sounds like when someone is getting a few slaps."

"Are you telling us that Brian was violent towards his fiancé?" DC King said.

"I'm telling you nothing of the sort. I've seen the bruises on his face. He tried to hide them, but I'm not stupid. That poor bastard was being knocked about by his woman, and it had been going on for a very long time."

CHAPTER FOURTEEN

Smith decided not to stick around at the block of flats in Scarcroft. Another phone call to Georgia Francis confirmed that it would be a waste of time. She wasn't coming back today. She told him she wasn't in any state to drive and she was going to stay another night at her parents' house. Smith wasn't too put out. Otto's revelation about her violent nature was interesting but they knew that Georgia was already in Newcastle when Brian was murdered, and he didn't think she was involved in his death.

"We're still going to speak to her though," DC King said.
"We will," Smith said. "But it's not urgent. Something tells me that this investigation is much more complicated than it appears to be on the surface. Christine and Brian were killed for a specific reason, but it won't be something that's easy to unravel."
"What did you make of what the caretaker told us about Brian's fiancé? Do you think it's true?"
"Do I believe a woman is capable of abusing a man?" Smith said. "Definitely. It's not as common as a bloke knocking his wife about, but it happens. You of all people know what level of violence a woman is capable of."
"Do you think it's something we need to discuss at the afternoon briefing?"
"It can't hurt to bring it up," Smith said. "But I don't think it's relevant to the investigation."
"What if it is?"
"What are you thinking?"
"I'm just considering the victims," DC King said. "Christine Snow was in a miserable marriage. Her husband's behaviour was bordering on neglect. He worked long hours and when he was off, he spent his time playing football. Brian James was abused by his fiancé. Both of them were victims in a way."

"Are you suggesting the victims were targeted because of precisely that?" Smith said. "Because they were *victims*? That has to be the most far-fetched theory I've ever heard come out of your mouth, Kerry. I thought I was the master of the fanciful suggestion, but it's clear that I've got a contender vying for my position. No, what you're saying makes no logical sense whatsoever."

"Where are we going?" DC King changed the subject very obviously.
"Hospital," Smith said. "Kenny should have finished the PM of Brian James. I want to see if there's any evidence of what Otto Golding told us."
"Why?" DC King asked. "A minute ago, you said you didn't think it was relevant to the investigation."
"Curiosity, I suppose," Smith said. "And it's been a while since I've seen Kenny. What the hell is that noise?"
"What noise?"
"Listen."
DC King could hear it now. It was a faint whirring sound that seemed to get louder when Smith increased his speed."
"Sounds like your starter is about to go, Sarge," she said.
"My what?"
"The solenoid sounds like it's sticking. You'd better get it checked out. The starter is definitely about to die."
"How come you know stuff like this?" Smith said.
"Older brothers. I used to watch them tinkering on their cars."
"Let's hope it gets us to the hospital."
"It will," DC King said. "Whether the car will start afterwards is a different story."

Smith got out of the car and patted the roof in encouragement. DC King got out of the other side. "I don't think that will help, Sarge."
"You don't know this car, Kerry. She's like an old friend."

"Why do you hang on to it? Surely you can afford a new one."

"Some things can't be replaced," Smith said. "Women will never understand."

After speaking to Dr Bean's assistant, they were informed that the Head of Pathology was writing up some notes in his office. Sarah Monk asked if they had an appointment and Smith replied in the negative.

"Kenny wouldn't expect me to make one," he added.

"You like him, don't you?" DC King said. "Dr Bean, I mean?"

"He's not everyone's cup of tea," Smith said. "But, considering what he does for a living I wouldn't expect him to be a normal bloke. You should have met the pathologist who worked here before Kenny arrived. Paul Johnson was his name, but we called him The Ghoul."

"Why *The Ghoul*?"

"Because he was a proper creature of the night, Kerry. He was exceptional, and he suffered fools even less than I do."

"That's not possible."

"The Ghoul did. Not only was he the best pathologist I've ever met, but he was also a financial expert. He played the markets, and he made a lot of money out of it."

"What happened to him?" DC King asked.

"We were working a case," Smith said. "A complicated one. Football players were being taken out. A sniper was assassinating them on the football pitch, but that wasn't the end of it. At the heart of it were some very nasty people. They were phantoms and when we started to make headway it turned out that I shared a history with one of them. It's a long story, but it was personal for me, and they made it even more personal when they murdered my best friend. The Ghoul died when a car bomb obliterated his car."

"Oh my God."

"I'll never forget him," Smith said. "The crazy bastard wrote his own eulogy, and his funeral took place on Friday the thirteenth."

"He sounds like a real character."

"He certainly was," Smith said. "Kenny is special, but The Ghoul was one in a million. After you."

CHAPTER FIFTEEN

Smith pushed the door open and followed DC King into the office. Dr Bean was tapping away on a laptop on his desk. He stopped when he heard the door close.

"The ward with the mental patients is on the other side of the hospital, Smith," he said without looking up.

"That's not very PC, Kenny," Smith said. "And how did you know it was me? It could have been anyone."

"Most people tend to knock," Kenny said. "And I sensed your presence. You have a particular aura about you."

Smith sat down opposite him without being asked to. DC King sat next to him.

"How are you?" Smith said.

"Always good. I don't have anything to tell you. Everything pertaining to the post-mortem of your first victim was sent to your boss."

"The DI mentioned stab wounds," Smith said. "But if he elaborated further, I wasn't paying attention."

Dr Bean sighed. He closed down the report he was working on and opened another one. "Christine Snow."

"That's her," Smith said.

"Thirty-four years old. She was in good health until she wasn't."

DC King frowned at Smith. He shook his head.

"Go on," Smith said.

"Mrs Snow suffered six stab wounds to her chest and stomach. Her liver was pierced as was her spleen. One of the jabs nicked her right lung and another went straight through her heart. Any one of the wounds could have been fatal. She lost a lot of blood and if I were to hazard a guess I would say she died quickly."

He looked up at Smith.

"Anything else?" Smith said.

"If there was, I would have told you."

"What about Brian James?"

Dr Bean reopened the file he'd been working on.

"Mr James had his back to his attacker when he was stabbed. All of the wounds were on the lower back with the exception of the one that killed him. A money shot to the heart."

"Money shot?" Smith repeated.

"Dead centre. Certain death, hence, money shot. I would suggest that your perpetrator knew exactly what he was doing. And, before you ask if there's anything else, I can save you the time and answer in the affirmative. Mr James had a number of old injuries."

"What kind of injuries?" Smith said.

"We found discolouration in the skin that suggests past trauma. He had a few more recent injuries on his left cheek, but the rest were weeks, if not months old."

"A witness claims that he was being physically abused by his fiancé," DC King said.

"That would tie in with what we found. Is this fiancé a suspect?"

"Since when did you care about stuff like that?" Smith said.

"Since I discovered the joy of crime thrillers," Dr Bean said. "Of course, they always get the pathology wrong and in most of them the pathologist is portrayed as a socially inept miscreant, but you can't have everything. The wounds that killed Mr James are a far cry from a few bruises caused by a woman's fist. I don't believe the fiancé did this."

"Me neither," Smith said. "Besides, she was sixty miles away at the time."

"Moving on to the type of knife that was used," Dr Bean said. "I can tell you that it was some kind of hunting knife with a blade roughly six inches long. It is a double-bladed knife and one of the blades is serrated – an effective killing weapon."

"Both victims were killed by the same knife, weren't they?" Smith asked, even though he already knew the answer.

"Correct. Without a shadow of a doubt. Unless you happen to have two killers whose choice of weapon is identical, you're looking at the same murderer."

"Is there anything else you can tell us?" Smith said. "Mrs Snow was found in the bedroom, and Brian James was face-down in the hallway."

"I didn't attend the scenes," Dr Bean said. "But the positioning of the stab wounds on Mrs Snow suggest that she was stabbed while she was lying on her back. Was she found in bed?"

"She was," DC King said.

"Her husband went to play football," Smith said. "And he told us she was in bed when he left."

"There were no defensive wounds on Mrs Snow," Dr Bean said. "Which suggests the attack was quick."

"He crept into the bedroom and stabbed her repeatedly in quick succession."

"Mr James was definitely surprised from behind," Dr Bean said. "He was standing up when he was attacked and, once more the attack was rapid. Three quick stabs to the lower back and heart. He will have died before he fell to the floor. You're dealing with an exceptional killer."

"You're not wrong there," Smith said. "And killing is not the only thing he's extremely adept at. The bloke climbed up a wall to a flat on the third floor without a ladder. He was up and inside in seconds."

"He's like a spider," DC King said.

"And that must have taken a lot of practice," Smith said.

Dr Bean looked at him. He turned his attention to his laptop and tapped the keypad.

"I think you might find this interesting."
He turned the laptop so Smith and DC King could see the screen.
"What are we looking at?" Smith asked.
"I've become somewhat addicted to this," Dr Bean said. "I find it incredible what a human being can train the body to achieve."

He tapped the keypad again and a video clip started to play. It was a series of short videos depicting men and women overcoming obstacles. Smith watched as they jumped and scrambled over seemingly impossible barriers. The final clip was incredible. A tall, thin woman ran across a metal railing fifty feet up in the air. She jumped across the gap to another rail four metres away. Then she began her descent. This involved making use of anything she had at her disposal, and there wasn't much to choose from. She finished off by leaping ten feet to the ground and performing a roll that would make any paratrooper proud."

"What is this stuff?" Smith asked.
"Parkour," Dr Bean said. "It's incredible, isn't it?"
"It certainly is," Smith said. "Kenny, I owe you a drink."
"I'll take you up on that."
"Where do these parkour people like to hang out?" Smith said.
"Wherever there are walls to climb and buildings to jump off," Dr Bean said.
"This is a breakthrough. Come on, Kerry – I reckon we've taken up enough of the good doctor's time."
He stood up.
"Scotch whisky," Dr Bean said.
"What?" Smith said.
"It's what I like to drink these days," Dr Bean said. "Single malt is vastly overrated."
"Scotch it is then. I'll have a bottle delivered."
"Parkour," Dr Bean said. "Do you want me to write it down?"

"I think I'll remember it," Smith said. "Thanks again, Kenny."

CHAPTER SIXTEEN

DC Moore would be seeing footwear when he closed his eyes that night. The man from London had spent the past two hours trawling the Internet for shoes with treads that matched the imprint on the downpipe at the scene of the Christine Snow murder, and he was feeling somewhat overwhelmed.

Webber had provided photographs of the imprint, and DC Moore had managed to narrow down the search to a few dozen shoes. There were more specialised climbing shoes than he thought, and he wondered if this was going to be a task that would beat him. Not only were there numerous shoes with grips that matched the ones on the downpipe, but the list of suppliers was also huge. There were no fewer than eleven specialised footwear distributors in York alone and the number of online shops ran into the hundreds.

"I don't think we're going to get anything from the shoes," DC Moore told Bridge.

"Keep looking," Bridge said.

"Do you know how many outlets for sports footwear there are? He could have got them from overseas for all we know. This is a waste of time."

"The DI told you to look into it."

"And I have looked into it," DC Moore said. "To go through this lot will take weeks."

Bridge moved closer to the laptop and clicked on one of the photographs of the imprint. The tread was diamond shaped and he could see that the diamonds were split in two with what appeared to be differing depths. It was clear that these treads had been designed with maximum traction in mind.

"Loads of shoes have those treads," DC Moore said.

Bridge clicked on another photograph. This one showed the tread in more detail.

"What's that?" He pointed to what appeared to be some kind of logo. It looked like a mountain superimposed with the letter S. Bridge zoomed in and cropped the part of the photo with the logo in it.

"I don't recognise it," DC Moore said.

"I wouldn't expect you to," Bridge said. "You're not an expert in extreme sports shoes."

He right clicked and copied the logo, then he pasted it into the task bar.

"Five seconds," Bridge said.

"Sarge?" DC Moore said.

"That's how long it took me to find out the make of the shoes the killer was wearing."

"Sherpa," DC Moore read from the screen. "I'm losing my touch."

"You can't win them all. Let's see where you can buy these things."

A few taps on the keypad told him that these particular shoes were not widely available. In fact, there were only three outlets – one an online store based in China, another a store in America, and one less than three miles away.

"Bingo," Bridge said. "Outdoor King. It's a shop on Stockton Lane in Heworth. According to their website, they cater for the outdoor enthusiast who likes to take things to the extreme."

"Sounds promising," DC Moore said. "It's a shame it's Sunday."

"They're open on Sundays. The opening hours are on the website. We're onto something here – I can feel it."

* * *

The Spider opened the box and took in the smell of the new shoes. He inhaled deeply and he could feel the contentment rush through him as the scent brought back a rare happy memory. There weren't too many of these stored in his memory bank, and he relished the recollection as it came to him now.

The climbing spikes had been a present from his father, back when his dad knew what kindness was. They weren't expensive – they were entry-level climbing shoes, but *The Spider* didn't care. He recalled the feeling he got when he put them on and stood below the climbing wall. He was too hasty that day and he barely made it halfway up, but he persevered and got to the top on the third attempt. It was a beginner's climb, but it was a start.

He kept those spikes even when his feet grew too big for them. He even went so far as to slit open the front of the shoes, so his toes had some freedom, but eventually they fell apart and became useless.

Since then, he'd lost count of how many different climbing shoes he'd gone through. He'd been climbing for sixteen years now, and it soon became second nature, but then he woke up one morning and wanted something more. He could scale seemingly impossible heights, but it wasn't enough. He needed a new challenge and that's when he'd discovered parkour. With its roots in extreme military training, incorporating various martial arts it is a sport that requires absolute discipline. The participants interact with their environment, and the aim is to move through the obstacles artistically. *The Spider* believes a true master of parkour is a joy to behold. Nothing is too high or too far away if you focus on new ways to perceive your environment. It's exciting and it's extremely addictive.

The Spider unwrapped the new shoes and inspected them. They were a brand called *Barefoot* and they were expensive. The reviews were positive, and *The Spider* was looking forward to testing them out. The first thing he checked was the tread. It was a different mould to the soles of the Sherpa Ultra's he'd picked up during a recent trip to America, but the concept was the same. Thin rubber with ridges designed to offer maximum purchase. He put them on and walked up and down the room. They felt wrong somehow, so he removed them and put on the Sherpas instead. He still had the receipt from the shop in Heworth for the *Barefoots*, and he would return the new pair as soon as he had the chance. He recalled that Outdoor King had a reasonable returns policy.

CHAPTER SEVENTEEN

Outdoor King wasn't what Bridge had been expecting. He'd been in plenty of stores that sold outdoor gear but the shop on Stockton Road wasn't like any of them. There wasn't a great deal of products on offer inside and he wondered if they did most of their trade online. It was quiet – in fact Bridge and DC Moore were the only customers today.

They got the attention of a man engrossed in his phone behind the counter and explained who they were. The name on the man's badge was Luke.

"I didn't think you were here to buy anything."

Bridge guessed his age to be somewhere in the mid-twenties. He was tanned and he didn't get that tan in Yorkshire. He looked like he'd recently been abroad.

"Your website said you stock a brand of footwear called Sherpa," Bridge said.

"Great shoes. Which ones are you interested in?"

"I'm not sure," Bridge said.

He took out his phone and found a photograph of the tread imprint.

"Does this help?" He showed Luke the photo.

"Sherpa Ultra pro-grip," Luke said after a few seconds.

"Do you sell them here?" DC Moore said.

"Not for a while."

"Would you be able to check the sales for us?" Bridge said.

"Don't you need a warrant or something?" Luke said.

"You'd be doing us a big favour," DC Moore said. "We could come back with a warrant, but that can take time."

"I'll have to ask the boss," Luke said.

"Could you do that please?" Bridge said.

"I'm messing with you. I am the boss – I own this place. Give me a few minutes."

He got up and walked towards the room at the back of the shop.

"He should do standup comedy," DC Moore said.

Bridge took a look around the shop. There were posters of various outdoor activities on the walls and the products on offer were displayed on shelves attached to the walls.

"There isn't much here, is there?" DC Moore said.

"I wonder why they even bother having a showroom," Bridge said. "It's obvious they do most of their trade online so why spend all the money on shop space."

Luke came back and Bridge asked him.

"The rent isn't too bad in this part of town," Luke said. "We do make most of our money from online sales, but there are still a lot of people who like to see what they're buying before they take the plunge. Most of the business is done on a pay first basis. I get the cash and then I order the stock."

"Where do you get your products from?" DC Moore said.

"China mostly," Luke said. "But you didn't hear that from me. You were interested in the Sherpa Ultras."

"When was the last time you sold a pair of those shoes?" Bridge said.

"Last year. In June."

"Do you have the details of the transaction?" DC Moore said.

"It was a woman by the name of Francesca. Francesca Hogan. She actually bought two pairs. Both size five."

Bridge didn't know why, but he suspected that this wasn't connected to their killer. The person in the CCTV footage at the block of flats was definitely a man and it was rare for a man to have such small feet.

"And you haven't had any other sales of that make of shoe?" he said.

"That's the only recent one," Luke said.

"What about older sales?" DC Moore said.

"Impossible," Luke said.

"Why's that?"

"Because the Sherpa Ultra pro-grips only came out last year."

"And the soles I showed you are definitely from that make of shoe?" Bridge said.

"No doubt about it. You can't miss the Sherpa logo, and the grips are unmistakable. I'm sorry I couldn't help you."

"Perhaps you can," Bridge said. "You must know a lot about extreme climbing."

"I still do a bit," Luke said. "Not as much as I used to, what with this place to look after, but I still get up the walls when I can."

"Where do you climb?"

"I do some outdoor stuff," Luke said. "Yorkshire is full of decent crags, but most of the time I practice on the climbing walls."

"What are they?" DC Moore said.

"Artificial rock faces. They're designed to offer various levels of difficulty."

"Are there any of these in the city?" Bridge said.

"Quite a few."

Luke reached behind the counter and pulled out a brochure.

"They're all on there."

He handed it to Bridge.

"Thanks," Bridge said.

He scanned the page, and he was surprised how many climbing walls there were nearby.

"You must know most of the local climbers," he said. "Working in the industry, I mean."

"Pretty much," Luke said.

"Are there any legends in the field?" Bridge said.

"Legends?"

"People who stand out from the others," Bridge elaborated. "Particularly men."

"What exactly is this about?" Luke said. "Why are you looking for a climber?"

"We're just following up on a lead," Bridge said. "Can you think of anyone you know who is a cut above the rest when it comes to climbing?"

"There's a bloke I sometimes see at the Murton climbing wall."

"And he's good?"

"He's better than good, "Luke said. "Most people tackle the extreme wall there to see if they can actually get to the top, but this guy climbs to see how quick he can do it. I think his record is thirty-two seconds. That wall is insane. I'd be lucky to get up in five minutes. If you're looking for a legend climber, he's the closest you're going to get. He climbs that wall like a frikkin' spider."

CHAPTER EIGHTEEN

Bridge and DC Moore were surprised when they arrived at the climbing wall in Murton to see a familiar car. It was Smith's old Ford Sierra.
"I wonder what he's doing here?" DC Moore said.
"Great minds think alike, I imagine," Bridge said.
"I wouldn't admit to having a mind like Smith's, Sarge."
"It is an acquired taste," Bridge agreed. "Hopefully we're going to find some answers here. It looks like it's busy."
The car park was almost full, and it had taken them a while to find a parking space.

They found Smith and DC King by one of the climbing walls. They were standing with a woman who looked to be in her mid-twenties. DC King spotted them first.
"What are you doing here?" she asked when they walked over.
"I could ask you the same question," Bridge said.
"It was something Kenny showed us," Smith said. "He reckons the bloke we're looking for might be into parkour. It's a discipline that involves negotiating obstacles in an urban environment, and I figured he might do a bit of climbing too. This is the best climbing wall in the city, and some of the climbs are pretty tough. What about you – what brings you here?"
"Something similar," Bridge said. "We managed to identify the shoes the tread on the downpipe at Christine Snow's house came from, and the owner of the shop suggested we ask around here. There's a climber who stands out from the rest, and I thought it was worth a bash."
"Did you have any luck with the shoes?" DC King said.
"It was a dead end," Bridge said. "The only sales of those particular shoes were to a woman last year. She bought two pairs of size fives."
"The tread on the downpipe came from bigger shoes than that," Smith said.

"Hence, dead end," Bridge said.

Smith looked at the woman standing next to him and apologised to her for their rudeness.

"This is Bonnie Maddox," he said. "She's one of the instructors here."

"The owner of Outdoor King mentioned a climber," Bridge told her.

"Luke knows most of them," Bonnie said.

"This climber is a real pro," DC Moore said. "Apparently you have an advanced wall here and he gets up in no time."

Bonnie nodded. "That will be Warren."

"Does he have a surname?" Smith asked.

"Probably, but I don't know it."

"When was the last time you saw him?" Bridge said.

"About ten minutes ago," Bonnie said. "He's here now."

"Where can we find him?" Smith said.

"Look for the crowds. He always attracts an audience when he's in the mood to try and beat his personal best."

It wasn't difficult to find him. A small group of people were gathered at the bottom of the wall Smith assumed was the advanced climb. A man was halfway up, and he wasn't holding back. Smith watched as he navigated an overhang as though it wasn't there. He reached for one of the multicoloured handholds and flung himself upwards. His right leg connected with another handhold, and he was up on the final stretch. He got to the top and looked at his watch. Smith gasped as he stood on the edge and fell backwards. He dropped a few feet and the safety rope attached to his harness did what it was supposed to do. He was on the ground in seconds.

"Thirty-eight," he said, and unclipped the rope. "My heart isn't in it today."

Smith walked over to him. "Can I have a word?"

"I don't do instruction," Warren said. "If you're after a teacher, you can enquire at the desk."

"I'm not looking for a teacher," Smith told him.

He took out his ID and suggested they speak in private. A few of Warren's fans were lingering, no doubt hoping to get some free snippets of advice. "We can go to the canteen," he said. "I'm not in the zone today, so I think I'll call it a day."

"What's this all about?" he asked.

He was sitting opposite Smith at one of the plastic tables.

"You're good," Smith said. "How long have you been climbing?"

"Since I was a kid. About fifteen years."

"I imagine you need special shoes to climb in."

"Definitely."

"What shoes do you wear?" Smith said.

Warren showed him. They were luminous yellow with black soles. There was a logo Smith didn't recognise on the sides."

"What brand are they?" Smith said.

"Sherpa," Warren said.

Smith heart started to beat more quickly. He wondered if this was their lucky day. He was about to be disappointed.

"I got them direct from the factory in China."

"How long have you had them?"

"A few years. A lot of climbers replace their footwear regularly, but I like to keep mine for a while. They take some time to wear in, and the good ones mould to the shape of your feet. Why are you interested in my shoes?"

Smith didn't reply. Bridge had told him that the tread marks on the downpipe came from shoes that only became available last year, so unless Warren was lying to him, his shoes didn't match.

"I imagine you know about parkour," he said instead.

"Of course."

"Do you participate in the discipline?"

"Sometimes. I used to be really into it, but these days I prefer natural climbs. Crags and rock faces. Street climbing isn't really my thing anymore."

"Some of the stuff those people do is quite impressive," Smith said. "Do they train on walls like they have here?"

"Not if they want to master it," Warren said. "If you want to be the best in parkour, you don't want the false sense of security that a safety harness gives you."

"False sense of security?"

"It sends the wrong message to your brain," Warren explained. "You don't have the possible risk factor, and it messes with the chemicals the body produces to make sure you're in optimal shape to carry out the climbs."

"You used a safety harness today," Smith pointed out.

"Regulations. I'd climb without it if I was allowed to, but the idiots who make the rules about health and safety won't let me."

Smith didn't know why, but he sensed that they weren't going to find the man they were looking for at one of the climbing centres.

"Where do I start looking for one of these parkour junkies?" he said.

"In this city," Warren said. "There aren't many places to look. There's a wall by one of the bridges over the river that's quite challenging. It has a railing at the top, and it's quite a leap across to the bridge. And some of them like to train at one of the indoor centres. Is the bloke you're looking for good?"

Smith decided to take a chance. He'd saved the CCTV clip of the man scaling the wall at Christine Snow's house to his phone and he brought it up now.

Warren's reaction left little room for interpretation. His eyes widened as he watched.

"Shit. Holy shit. I thought I was good."

"Do you recognise any of these moves?" Smith said.

"I don't," Warren said. "And this is something you would not forget. Whoever this creature is, I've never seen him before. Why are you looking for him?"

"We've had a series of burglaries in the city," Smith lied. "And we got lucky with some CCTV footage. Are you sure you've never seen this man before?"

"Positive. Like I said, you wouldn't forget someone who can climb like that. He moves like a bloody spider."

CHAPTER NINETEEN

"That's two people who have compared him to a spider today," Bridge said. Smith had brought him up to speed with what Warren had told him.
"The owner of Outdoor King said the same thing," he added. "Did he know who the bloke is?"
"He'd never seen him before," Smith said. "And he reckoned he would have remembered moves like that."
"What now?" DC King said.
"We take a look at some of the popular parkour spots in town," Smith said. "Warren doesn't think our guy would train in places like these. They're too safety orientated, and he believes a man like our spider prefers a bit of risk when he climbs."
"*The Spider*," Bridge said. "It's as good a name as any for the investigation."
"For once," Smith said. "I'm inclined to agree. Where's Harry?"
"He's speaking to a few of the climbers. For what it's worth."

Right on cue, DC Moore came back with a woman who Smith guessed wasn't long out of her teens.
"This is Sharon Billing," he said. "And I think she might have something for us."
Sharon was dressed in a pair of leggings and a sleeveless T-shirt. The muscles in her arms weren't huge, but they were well defined, and Smith sensed she had a lot of upper body strength.
"What can you tell us?" Smith asked her.
"You're the Australian," Sharon said. "The celebrity detective."
"Don't remind him," Bridge said. "His head is big enough already."
"Your colleague was asking about parkour," Sharon said. "Whether I knew of anyone who was a cut above the rest."
"Do you?" Smith said.

"There was this guy the other day over by the bridge on Water End. I was showing a friend how best to get up a wall there and this man came out of nowhere. He was standing far too close to the wall, and I told him he wouldn't make it. His run-up was too short, but he ignored me."

"Did he make it?" Smith said.

"He made it look like he could climb a wall twice as high," Sharon said. "Not only did he get up the wall, but he also danced across the railing and leaped over to the bridge five metres away. I can't even manage five metres in the long jump with a proper run-up. The bloke was an alien."

"Or a spider," Smith said.

"What?"

"Just thinking out loud," Smith said.

He took out his phone and showed her the CCTV footage he'd shown the man called Warren. Sharon's reaction was identical to Warren's.

"Could this be the man you saw?" Smith asked her.

"It is him," Sharon confirmed. "He was wearing the same hooded top."

"Is there anything else about him you remember?" Bridge said. "Did you see his face?"

Sharon shook her head. "He had some kind of bandana over his nose and mouth, and he was wearing sunglasses."

"He didn't want to be recognised," Smith said.

"He's thinking out loud again," Bridge said.

"Had you seen him before?" Smith said.

"Never. I would have remembered someone who climbed like that."

"Have you been climbing for long?"

"A few years."

"And you know most of the top climbers?"

"All of them. This bloke isn't one of them."

Smith took out one of his cards and handed it to her.

"If you do see him again, I want you to call me. Day or night."

"OK," Sharon said. "What's he done? Why are you so interested in him?"

"The footage you just watched was taken at the scene of a serious crime."

"Murder?" Sharon guessed.

"Correct. And if you do happen to see him again, it's important that we know about it."

"He didn't look like a murderer."

"They very rarely do," Smith said. "Thank you for speaking to us."

His phone started to ring, and the ringtone told him that it was DI Smyth. He walked away to take the call.

"Boss."

"Where are you?" DI Smyth said.

"We've just finished speaking to a witness," Smith said. "She recognised the man in the CCTV footage. He was there at the location of a popular parkour climb. She's promised to let me know if she sees him again. Has something happened?"

"We've got another body."

"Go on."

"Another man. His wife found him when she got back from a work trip. It's the same MO as the others. Apartment on the top floor of a block. One of the bedroom windows was left open. It's thirty feet up in the air."

"We're dealing with something special, aren't we?" Smith said.

"I wouldn't use the word special," DI Smyth said. "But it is something we've never seen before."

"*The Spider.*"

"Excuse me?" DI Smyth said.

"That's what we're calling him."

"I thought you hated giving nicknames to murderers."

"I usually do, boss," Smith said. "But *The Spider* has a certain ring to it. Me and Kerry will get right over."

DI Smyth gave him the address. It was in Del Pkye in the city centre. Smith informed the others, and he and DC King headed back to his car.

He knew he had a problem as soon as he turned the key in the ignition. Before there had been a whirring sound as the engine struggled to tick over but now there wasn't even that. Smith tried again with the same result.

"Do you reckon we can jumpstart it?" he asked DC King.

"No, Sarge," she said. "If your starter is knackered, jumpstarting it won't work. It requires a functioning starter motor. You could try push starting it. You might get enough momentum to get a bit of life out of the starter. Or..."

"Or?" Smith repeated.

"You could just admit defeat and buy a new car."

CHAPTER TWENTY

Smith got out of Bridge's Toyota and sighed. He didn't think he'd have to ask someone for a lift to a crime scene today. He'd phoned Darren Lewis and Darren had promised to let his brother know about the car. Halfway to Del Pyke, Gary had sent him a message telling him he'd arranged a tow truck, and he would start work on the Sierra as soon as he could. Smith hoped he would be able to find a replacement starter. The car was a few years old now, and he wondered if spares would still be available. Bridge had dropped the DCs Moore and King off at the station. DI Smyth didn't think it was necessary for all of them to attend the scene and Smith had agreed. There were plenty of other things for them to do.

The apartment block was four storeys high, and the dead man had been found in the top floor flat. Smith decided to let Webber and his team work in peace. His priority was the dead man's wife.
"The man's name is George Baron," Bridge told him. "And that's about all we know."
"Where's the wife?" Smith said.
"According to the uniforms first on the scene she was offered medical assistance, but she declined. She should still be here somewhere. I'll go and find out."

Smith looked up at the apartment block, and something occurred to him immediately. With the exception of the ground floor flat, all of the others had balconies surrounded by safety railings. From the ground it was roughly two metres up to the railing on the floor above, and Smith decided that it would be possible to stand on that railing and pull yourself up onto the balcony on the third floor – ditto the one above on the top floor. This wasn't as difficult a climb as he first thought.

Bridge came back with PC William Griffin in tow. The pig-eyed PC looked nervous.

"According to this idiot," Bridge said. "The wife has gone to her brother's house."

"Whose idea was that?" Smith said.

"Hers, Sarge," PC Griffin said. "She was very insistent."

"Did you get anything out of her?"

"She told me I was possibly the ugliest man she'd ever met."

"I'm sure she didn't mean it," Smith said. "Please tell me you have an address for the brother."

"Of course, Sarge. He's got a house in Holgate."

He took out a notebook and opened it. He tore off a page and handed it to Smith.

"I suppose there isn't much we can do here," Smith said. "We might as well head over to Holgate."

"There was a witness, Sarge," PC Griffin said. "A man saw the perpetrator coming down the wall at the back."

"He came down the back?"

"According to the witness, he did."

Smith thought that made sense. The front of the building was exposed, and it would have been risky to get in and out that way.

"Where is this witness? Please tell me you told this one to stick around."

"Mrs Baron wouldn't take no for an answer," PC Griffin said. "There was no arguing with the woman. I told the witness not to leave his flat. He owns the one directly below the Barons."

They had confirmation that the killer entered and exited the apartment block by climbing the walls and, as such the interior of the flats wasn't considered to be a crime scene, so Smith didn't bother with the usual crime scene protocol before he went in. He and Bridge walked up the stairs to the apartment on the third floor.

The man who opened the door looked to be in his late fifties. He was completely bald and his attempt to compensate for this by growing a beard had failed miserably. Daniel Young was hirsutely challenged in every possible way. Smith introduced himself and Bridge and they were invited inside the apartment. The area consisted of an open-plan living room/dining room with a small kitchen in the corner. Daniel asked them to take a seat. He didn't offer them anything to drink.

"We'll keep this brief," Smith said. "Tell us what you saw earlier."
"I thought I was imagining it at first," Daniel said. "My eyes have never been great, but the more I watched him, the more I realised that my brain wasn't playing tricks on me."
"Could you please answer the question without the irrelevant stuff?" Smith said.
Daniel frowned at Bridge. "Did he get out of the wrong side of the bed this morning?"
"Could you just tell us what you saw," Bridge said.
"A bloke climbing down the wall."
"What time was this?" Smith said.
"Probably around three."
"Probably?"
"It was," Daniel said. "I was waiting for the football to start. The Manchester derby. City walloped United four - one. Mahrez rubbed a bit of salt in the wounds by slotting one in a minute into injury time. Are you a football fan?"
"Definitely not," Smith said. "I think it's a pointless game. Tell us more about what you saw."
"He was down and gone in no time," Daniel said. "It was incredible."
"Did you phone the police?" Bridge said.

"I didn't think it was worth bothering."

"A man was murdered," Smith said. "And you witnessed his killer exiting the scene. You didn't think it was important?"

"How was I supposed to know George was dead? I thought the bloke was a burglar, and before you get all antsy, I'll tell you why I didn't phone the police. I had a break-in a few months back and you lot did sweet FA about it. Nowadays, you only get the police involved for insurance purposes. No, I thought that if anyone was going to phone the police it would be George."

"It's hard to pick up the phone when you're no longer breathing," Smith said.

"I really don't like your attitude."

"I'm working on it," Smith said.

"Did you know Mr Baron well?" Bridge said.

"Well enough to say hello when we passed on the stairs," Daniel said. "We weren't exactly what you would call friends."

"Did you hear anything before you saw the man making his way down the wall?" Smith said.

"Like what?"

"Raised voices," Smith said. "Crashing and banging?"

"I didn't. Although, I had the football on, and I like to watch it with the volume turned up."

"I thought you said the game started at three," Smith said.

"That was the Manchester derby," Daniel explained. "There was the Watford, Arsenal match on before that. It was nowhere near as exciting as the derby."

"Tell someone who cares?" Smith said.

He got up and walked to the window. He opened the curtains and peered out. He opened the window and looked upwards. There was a downpipe running past the window and he decided that Daniel Young wouldn't be aware of someone climbing down it, especially with the curtains closed.

"What made you look outside?"

"Excuse me?" Daniel said.

"You told us you heard nothing because of the football," Smith said. "What made you look outside?"

"The Manchester derby hadn't started yet," Daniel said. "So, I opened the curtains to let in a bit of light. That's when I saw the man coming down the wall."

Smith nodded. It made sense.

"Do you know Mrs Baron well?" he asked.

"I've probably spoken to her half a dozen times since they moved in. I think she works away a lot."

"Do you know what she does?" Bridge said.

"God knows," Daniel said. "But she's always coming in at weird hours with a suitcase."

Smith walked back over to them. "I think that's everything."

"How did he die?" Daniel asked. "George, I mean."

"Same way most people do," Smith said. "A shortage of blood to the brain."

"You really need to work on your people skills, mister."

"He's tried," Bridge said. "But nothing seems to work. Thanks for your time."

CHAPTER TWENTY ONE

"A pattern is starting to emerge."
Smith was standing by the whiteboard in the small conference room. The names of the three victims were staring at him and the rest of the team. Smith had written *The Spider* in bold letters at the top of the board – he couldn't resist it. They'd tried to get hold of George Baron's wife, but Donna's brother had refused to let them talk to her. Smith decided he would do that tomorrow. It was getting late and they would have a final briefing before they called it a day.

"Christine Snow." He tapped her name. "Mrs Snow was an archetypal football widow. When her husband wasn't working, he was out playing football. Five times a week, he left her alone while he was kicking a ball around. As a partner in an accounting firm, I imagine Peter worked long hours. The Snows may as well have not been married – they never saw one another."

"What's this pattern you mentioned?" DC Moore wondered.

"Just bear with me, Harry. Brian James was in an abusive relationship. We have witness statements implying it, and we have physical evidence to confirm it. Brian was being knocked about by his fiancé. And that brings us to the latest victim of *The Spider*. As of now, we know very little about George and Donna Baron, but I sense that their relationship was a miserable one too. We'll be speaking to Donna in the morning, but early indications suggest she was hardly ever home."

"I'm still not seeing a pattern," DC Moore said.

"I am," DC King said. "All three victims were targeted because of their miserable existence."

"Why?" Bridge said. "I don't dispute that their lives were sad and lonely, but what is this spider getting out of it?"

"I haven't figured that bit out yet," Smith admitted.

"Great," DC Moore said.

"He'll let us know when he has," Bridge said.

"This theory of yours is all very well," DI Smyth said. "But how do you suggest we move forward with it?"

"Dig deeper, boss," Smith said. "We have to ask ourselves how *The Spider* became aware of their misery."

"Are we really going to continue to call him that?"

"I like it," Smith said. "How is this creature privy to this information? So far, he's carried out the murders with absolute precision. He strikes when he knows the victims are alone, but how does he know this?"

"Social media?" Whitton suggested.

"It's worth considering," Smith said. "Did the victims vent their frustration on social media? Did they inadvertently advertise their partners' lives for anyone to see?"

"Accessing the social media of a deceased individual could be tricky," DI Smyth said.

"I managed to get into Christine Snow's Facebook," Smith said. "*After* she was murdered. Her page is full of condolence messages, and as far as I'm aware her profile is still active. I didn't look any further than the stuff that was posted after she was killed, and we need to go further back. That goes for the other two victims. Does *The Spider* do his hunting in the realms of the Internet?"

"That's ridiculous, Sarge," DC Moore said.

"It's not," DC King argued. "Social media is an ideal place to select a potential victim. You can stalk them and remain invisible. A killer can compile a profile of a victim without having any contact with them. It's a perfect platform to plan a murder from."

"We'll come back to how he chooses them," DI Smyth said. "It's getting late and I suggest we go through what we know about the latest victim before we wrap things up. George Baron was forty-one. His wife returned home from a business trip to China and found him in the living room. Cause of death is yet to be confirmed, but early reports suggest that he died due to the stab wounds to his torso. He lost a lot of blood and Webber believes he died where he was found."

"Was he covered with a sheet?" Smith said.

"He was. The sheet from the bed in the spare room had been removed and used to cover him up."

"That part of his MO is important."

"I thought we'd established that," DC Moore said.

"Yes," Smith said. "But we haven't yet established why it's significant."

"From a timescale perspective," DI Smyth said. "We know that the man on the floor below witnessed the killer leaving the property at just before three this afternoon."

"If we take the other murders into account," Smith said. "He probably broke in shortly before that. He kills quickly, and he doesn't stick around."

"Do we know if the same weapon was used to kill Mr Baron?" DC Moore said.

"Irrelevant," Smith said. "Let's focus on the important stuff."

"Are you saying the murder weapon isn't important?"

"I am. In this instance, it really isn't. The only thing we need to ask ourselves is why is he doing this?"

"Motive?" Bridge said.

"Motive," Smith repeated.

He wrote this on the whiteboard for good measure.

"Christine Snow," he said. "Suffered serious neglect at the hands of her husband."

"How many times do we have to go over the same ground?" DC Moore said.

"As many times as it takes to see the pattern in more detail," Smith said. "There is something here, and I'm going to find out what it is. Brian James was in a violent relationship and that violence was one-sided. George Baron's wife was never home."

"We can go over this until we're blue in the face, Sarge, but I fail to see how it's relevant."

"Perhaps he's punishing them because they're weak," Whitton said.

"Kerry hinted at something similar," Smith said. "But it doesn't quite fit. Is he murdering them to put them out of their misery? Does he do it to end their suffering? I don't think that's it. The fact that he covers them with a sheet afterwards suggests a certain amount of compassion. And perhaps some guilt too. He's not killing them to put an end to their miserable existences."

"It makes sense to me," DC Moore said. "Perhaps it's a simple case of survival of the fittest. That's how nature works. The weaklings in the herd are cast out. It's the only way a species can survive. He's eliminating the weaklings of society."

Smith scanned the names on the board again. Two men and a woman. All of them with one thing in common. They were victims in one way or another. It still didn't make sense for someone to want them dead because of that. It just didn't feel right. They were missing something vital. It occurred to him without him knowing why. He wasn't a big fan of *what ifs*, but he decided to suggest one now.

"What if," he said. "What if it's not the victims *The Spider* is targeting?"

"You're talking in riddles again, Sarge," DC Moore said.

"I'm not," Smith said. "What if this isn't about the victims at all? What if his goal is to punish the ones left behind?"

"I think you might be onto something," DC King said.

"I don't." It was Bridge.

"It's worth considering," Smith said. "It's a perfect example of the old adage – you don't know what you've got 'til it's gone."

CHAPTER TWENTY TWO

"What the hell is he doing here?"

Smith had got a lift home with Whitton. His beloved Sierra was now parked in the garage where Gary Lewis worked and according to Gary, it could be some time before he managed to source a starter motor for the old car. Whitton had been surprisingly calm about it. Smith had expected a lecture and a load of *I told you so's*, but he didn't get any and he suspected that she had other things on her mind. One of those things was now standing outside their house, and Smith could feel the anger building inside him.

"Don't do anything rash," Whitton warned.

"Robert Rogers needs to learn that he's not welcome here," Smith said.

"Let me speak to him," Whitton said. "I'll see if I can reason with him."

"He doesn't deserve reason, Erica. Just looking at that smug face makes me want to hit him with something hard. He's standing there, bold as brass. What if he's spoken to Fran?"

"Let see what he wants."

She parked in the driveway and told Smith to stay in the car.

"Please," she added. "I know that look of yours."

"What look?" Smith said.

"The one you get, moments before you do something really stupid."

She got out of the car and left him to think about what she'd just said.

She walked over to Robert Rogers.

He held up his hands. "I'm not here to cause trouble."

"What *are* you here for?" Whitton said.

"I just want to talk."

"Talk away."

"I want to see Fran," Robert said. "She's my flesh and blood."

"That little girl has been through enough," Whitton said. "She's only just starting to settle into a routine with us, and I will not let you upset that."

"She's my daughter."

"You no longer have any rights where Fran is concerned. You had every opportunity to reconnect with her, but you chose not to. As far as I'm concerned, this matter is closed."

"It's far from closed."

"I'm warning you, Mr Rogers," Whitton said. "This is tantamount to harassment and if you persist in this bullying, we will take drastic measures."

"You don't scare me," Robert said. "I'm not going to be rattled because you're a couple of police officers."

"That's not what I'm talking about. Don't come here again, because if you do, we will apply for a restraining order, and that restraining order will be granted. Do I make myself clear?"

Robert shrugged his shoulders. "I'll be off then."

"You do that," Whitton said. "And don't come back."

"I just want to give you this before I go."

He reached inside his jacket pocket and pulled out an envelope.

"What's that?" Whitton said.

Robert handed it to her. "Read it. I'm not obliged to let you have a copy of that, but me being a decent bloke, I thought it was the right thing to do."

"What is it?"

"It's a formal application to review the adoption order."

"The decision was a legally binding one," Whitton said. "It cannot be undone."

"Under normal circumstances, yes," Robert agreed. "But according to my lawyer there are a number of anomalies in the original adoption application that need to be taken into consideration."

"What anomalies?" Whitton said.

"I'm not obliged to give you that information, and I'm not going to."

"This is nonsense."

Robert tapped the envelope. "It's all in there. Read it."

"You can't get away with this," Whitton said.

Robert walked away from the house.

"You'll be hearing from my lawyer in due course," he said without turning around.

Smith was out of the car before Whitton reached it.

"What was that all about?"

"I'll tell you inside."

She knew that if she told him in the driveway he would chase after Robert Rogers and he would do something he would regret.

"What did the dickhead want?" Smith said. "Did you threaten him with a restraining order?"

"Let's go inside."

Smith got two beers out of the fridge. He opened them both and handed one to Whitton.

"Well?"

"He's threatening to review the adoption order," Whitton told him.

"He's bluffing," Smith said.

"He gave me a copy of the application. He sounded confident."

Smith sat down at the table. "OK, tell me everything he said."

Whitton sat opposite him. "I explained that the adoption order cannot be undone but he countered with some crap about circumstances. He said there were anomalies in the application that need to be considered."

She ripped open the envelope. It looked genuine enough. She read the words and put the piece of paper down.

"I don't understand half of this."

"We need to get a lawyer to look over it," Smith said. "I still reckon he's trying it on. Everything that we did was done by the book – there were no anomalies."

"Why did he seem so confident?"

"Because that's how bluffs work," Smith said. "You make your opponent think you're holding a high card when you're not. I'm not worried about Robert fucking Rogers. I have more pressing matters to be concerned about."

"Your car?"

"Got it in one. I know it's old, but I'm really not ready to part company with it just yet. Do you feel like a bite to eat at the Hog's Head?"

"Where did that come from?"

"Same place it always comes from," Smith said. "When life throws a load of shit your way, the best way to forget about it is one of Marge's steak and ale pies, washed down with a few pints of Theakston."

CHAPTER TWENTY THREE

Penelope Bright scrolled down the page to the last post she remembered reading. It was a rant from a woman who liked to complain about her husband at every possible opportunity. The name on the profile was *Angry Meg*, but Penelope didn't think her name was Meg, or Megan. Most of the people who posted on the page did so anonymously – that was the whole point of it. The page was set up so that men and women could express their deepest emotions without fear of repercussions.

Penelope prided herself on her ability to weed out the cranks and the trolls, but now and then some of these imposters did fall through the cracks, and it was her responsibility to ensure that they were removed before any real harm was done. She couldn't quite pinpoint what had roused her suspicions with *Angry Meg*, but there was something in her posts that gave her a sense of unease.

Angry Meg's comments always featured a philandering husband. She was aware of his deceit, and she'd tolerated it for years. Her posts always attracted a high number of comments afterwards. These opinions varied – some offered sympathy, a few voiced their opinions on suitable punishments for unfaithful husbands, and a small percentage of them wondered why she didn't just up and leave. Penelope got the feeling that *Angry Meg's* whole online persona was fake. She was simply someone who liked the buzz that the comments brought with them.

It was always a difficult decision to exclude someone from the group and Penelope had to be absolutely sure it was justified. There were people on here who were already surrounded by dark clouds – they were vulnerable, and it was possible that a small thing like getting deleted from a social media group they relied upon could push them over the edge.

Angry Meg had told everyone in the group about her husband's latest exploits. She'd suspected something for a while, and she'd listened in to some of his phone calls. Last week he told her he was meeting some friends for drinks and she'd followed him. There were no friends, and there were no drinks. *Angry Meg* had watched as the man she'd married flung his arms around a woman outside a hotel. They'd gone inside and *Angry Meg* had returned home, opened a bottle of wine and spent the evening crying into the wine glass.

Penelope made up her mind. *Angry Meg* had to go. Her posts read like stories she'd once read. They were cliched tales of affairs that she wasn't involved in. Meg was just someone who craved the attention that social media had to offer. Penelope wasn't even convinced that the posts had been written by a woman. It made no difference now. Two seconds was all it took to exclude *Angry Meg* from the group forever.

"You're a fake," Penelope said. "The tooth fairy is more real than you *Angry Meg*."

* * *

Megan Lambert looked at the screen of her laptop and wondered if there was a glitch on Facebook. It wouldn't be the first time. She minimised the page and opened up her Google. A quick check on there told her there had been no problems reported. The social media platform was running as it should, and Megan was advised to close it down and log back in again. If that didn't work, it was possible that clearing her cache would help.

Megan did this but it didn't make any difference. She still couldn't access the page she spent more time on than any other. She couldn't read the posts and none of her previous comments were available. She couldn't even contact the admin of the page. She'd been well and truly locked out. A quick *Control, Shift, N* took her into *Incognito* mode on the browser, and she opened up Facebook on there. She logged into her second profile and looked up the page she'd been excluded from. She keyed in a short message under the new profile and tapped send. She knew that she would have to wait for approval, but it was better than nothing. The group had become a huge part of her life, and she couldn't bear to think about how she would cope without it.

Zak was attending a conference in Manchester. That was what her husband had told her anyway, and she didn't believe a word of it. It had been a few months since his last indiscretions and Megan knew the pattern by now. He couldn't last much longer than that before he was out on the prowl again.

He hadn't even tried to disguise the fact that he was cheating on her with the last one and it had stung. When he was confronted, even his excuses seemed rehearsed. He was truly sorry – he was a terrible husband, but he would change. Blah, blah, blah. Megan had squeezed him for a new car from that one. It had been the biggest score yet, but she reckoned she deserved it. Roses and new clothes didn't quite cut it anymore.

A quick glance at the laptop told her that her comment was under review. It was a start, and Megan was confident that she would be back in the group in no time. She closed the page and logged out. Zak wasn't due back until Wednesday and Megan wondered if his latest mistress would be able to tolerate him for that long. The thought made her smile, and she decided that she would do something she hadn't done for a long time – she would get drunk. Perhaps she would open a bottle of wine from Zak's collection. She would find the most expensive one and slug it straight from the bottle. It was fantasy she'd shared with the people on the Facebook group, and she decided that she would make it a reality.

Megan went downstairs and grabbed the handle on the door to the small cellar Zak used to store his wine. The door was locked, but she knew where he kept the key. She'd seen him stick it under the mouse mat in his study.

Megan went in and switched on the light. The key was where it always was and she took it back to the cellar. She recalled Zak mentioning a bottle of wine that he was planning on keeping as an investment. It was a Chateau Latour Bordeaux that he'd paid five thousand pounds for. He'd bragged that it would be worth ten times that in a few years and Megan was looking forward to seeing his face when she told him what she'd done.

When she unlocked the door to the cellar and switched on the light, two things occurred to her concurrently. She wasn't going to have the satisfaction of glugging down Zak's priceless wine as though it were a bottle of cheap beer. The second thing that Megan Lambert realised when she saw the man staring into her eyes inside the cellar was a horrifying one. She knew that he had every intention of using the knife he was holding in his left hand. She stood frozen to the spot as his head tilted to the side as though she was something interesting to look at. Then he lowered his hood and nodded. Just before the knife was plunged into her chest, Megan looked into his eyes, and her final thought was a sombre one. Her killer's eyes were kind, but there was more sadness in them than Megan had ever seen.

CHAPTER TWENTY FOUR

The Hog's Head had a peculiar effect on Smith. It always had done – ever since he'd first set foot in the pub almost twenty years ago, he was filled with an instant sense of calm. He couldn't pinpoint exactly what it was about the traditional pub that caused his blood pressure to fall and his mind to relax, but that's what happened when he came in and this time was no different.

They ordered a couple of Theakstons from the bar and took them to the table by the fire. It wasn't cold, the fire wasn't lit, but this was where Smith preferred to sit. He was a creature of habit at heart, and that's why when the waiter asked them what they were going to have to eat, Smith replied by telling him he would have the only thing he'd ever eaten in the Hog's Head.

"Steak and ale pie," Whitton elaborated when she noted the bewildered expression on the young man's face. "Make that two, please."

Smith took a long drink of his beer. "That's better. They should prescribe this at stress clinics."

"Beer isn't the answer to all life's problems," Whitton said.

"Since when?"

"It just isn't. I'm worried about Robert Rogers."

"And I'm not," Smith said. "I'm not going to let a psychopath who can climb walls bother me either, and we won't mention my car woes."

"About that."

"Did you not just hear me?" Smith said. "All of that shit can wait. Robert fucking Rogers is just a dickhead who can't handle the fact that we can take care of Fran a million times better than he ever could. *The Spider* might be able to scale walls like nobody else, but he's just a killer like any other we've caught before. And now I understand his motivation, it's only a matter of time before I catch him. As for the old Sierra, everything will work out for the best."

"Are you thinking about getting a new car?"

"Fuck that," Smith said. "There will be a starter motor out there that will work. Those cars were popular in their day, and they made loads of them."

"You swear far too much."

"Nonsense," Smith said. "I swear as much as is necessary. What's taking the food so long?"

The pies arrived five minutes later. Smith ordered another two Theakstons and got to work on the masterpiece that was Marge's steak and ale pie. Whitton watched him and the expression on her face switched from disbelief to mild amusement as he went through the same motions he always did when he prepared himself for what was to come. The first bite was accompanied by a contented smile as he chewed and savoured the taste of his favourite pie. Then he got to work. The plate was clean in less than fifteen minutes. It was by no means a new record, but it was a decent effort, nevertheless.

Whitton finished hers shortly afterwards and smiled at him.

"Well?" Smith said.

"Well, what?"

"Admit it," Smith said. "That pie is like nothing else in the world."

"It's a pie, Jason. It's just a pie."

"I give up. I may have a plan to get Robert Rogers off our backs."

"I thought he wasn't on the agenda for tonight."

"Just hear me out. I still don't think he has a leg to stand on. Everything in Fran's adoption application was done in accordance with the guidelines, but if there is a miniscule chance of him throwing a spanner in the works, his criminal record isn't going to do him any favours."

"He doesn't have a criminal record," Whitton reminded him.

"Not yet, but that may change very soon."

"No," Whitton said.

"No what?"

"No. I am not even going to have this discussion with you. We'll speak to a lawyer, and we'll take it from there."

"I reckon I could…"

"No means no. End of story."

Smith admitted defeat. He excused himself to go to the Gents and when he returned, he was glad to see a fresh pint of Theakston on the table. He was enjoying himself and he didn't feel like going home just yet.

"It's bugging me how *The Spider* is choosing his victims," he said. "And I think we might be onto something with our suggestion that he could be finding them on social media. He knows too much about them."

"It's possible he's been watching them the old-fashioned way."

"I don't think he is. Even if he's been following his victims, how does he find out about the private aspects of their lives? All of his victims were victims, if that makes sense."

"It does," Whitton said. "And for what it's worth I believe your theory about punishing the ones left behind is a valid one. What does that tell us?"

"Why is he doing it?" Smith said.

"To make the people responsible for the misery suffer even more. Their loved ones are dead, but they have to live with the guilt."

"I didn't mean it like that. Why is he doing it? What makes him tick? He did not suddenly wake up one morning and decide to start killing people to punish those closest to them. Something caused him to do that."

Whitton took a sip of her beer and thought for a moment.

"This is personal, isn't it?"

"Murder usually is," Smith said. "He's punishing people because he was made to suffer by somebody just like them. It's simple psychology and I could be wrong, but I don't think I am. Murder tends to have its roots in something that happened long before the killing is even contemplated. I think *The Spider* has been severely abused in some way at some time in his life and he's making amends for it now, albeit in a rather twisted manner."

"Do you think he's going to keep going?" Whitton said.

"Absolutely," Smith said. "This is one of those killers who will not stop until someone puts them out of action."

CHAPTER TWENTY FIVE

Smith had barely set foot inside the station the next morning when he was met by a very irate looking DI Smyth.

"What's up, boss?" he asked.

"We've got a problem."

Four words that Smith had heard too many times before. He asked the DI to elaborate.

DI Smyth took out his phone and showed him the screen.

"This is the York Post's online thing," DI Smyth said. "This went out first thing this morning."

Smith looked at the screen. "Shit."

"Indeed."

The headline was brief - *The Spider*. There was a photograph below it, and it was a familiar one. It was a still shot of the man York CID were hunting. It showed him halfway up the wall outside Brian James's flat. Smith had to admit that it really was a striking shot, and the headline was appropriate. The figure scaling the walls of the apartment block did look like an arachnid.

"We don't have to ask where this photograph came from," DI Smyth said.

"The CCTV from the hotel opposite the block of flats," Smith said. "What are they saying about him?"

"Read it for yourself."

"I don't have my glasses."

"What's the point of getting glasses if you never wear them?" DI Smyth said.

"I still haven't got used to them. What does it say in the article?"

DI Smyth read it word for word.

"York CID are hunting a killer, the likes of which the city has never seen before. He climbs like a spider, and he kills like one. A witness from the scene of one of his three murders described him as possessing superhero-like powers. He can scale impossible heights, and he kills quickly. York Police are refusing to comment at this stage, but so far it appears that they have no idea who this creature is."

"You can stop there," Smith said. "Who comes up with this shit? And where did they get their info from?"

"Social media, no doubt," DI Smyth said. "This looks bad for us, Smith."

"We can expect a press conference, can't we?"

DI Smyth nodded. "No doubt about it."

"Please keep Uncle Jeremy away from it."

"I'll do my best," DI Smyth said. "And it's Superintendent Smyth to you. This is pressure we could do without right now. *The Spider* is a hot topic, and we're going to have every journo in the city watching our every move."

"I think I might have a theory we need to consider," Smith said. "But I want to get the advice of an expert before we pursue it further."

"A psychological profile?" DI Smyth guessed.

"Something like that."

"Who did you have in mind? Not Porter."

Porter Klaus was an accomplished psychologist and a talented hypnotist. Smith had used his skills before in murder investigations, and he had a lot of respect for him. DI Smyth and Porter were in a relationship, and things were serious between them.

"I was thinking more along the lines of someone like Dr Vennell," Smith said.

"Whitton is not going to like it," DI Smyth pointed out.

"There is nothing going on between me and Dr Vennell."

"Try telling her that. The woman is clearly in love with you – she doesn't even try to hide it."

"You let me deal with Whitton," Smith said. "I reckon it'll help to get an idea of what makes this bastard tick. I'm convinced that something turned him into what he is today, and Dr Vennell can assist us in getting inside his head."

"I suppose it can't hurt. As long as it's free."

"Me and Dr Vennell have an agreement," Smith said.

"That's what concerns me."

"I'll give her a call."

"What's the story with your car?" DI Smyth said.

"Same story as always, boss. It stops working – I get Darren's brother to fix what's not working, and it works again for another six months or so, until it doesn't, thus starting the cycle all over again."

"You really need to accept the fact that the car is a piece of junk."

"Don't be so dramatic," Smith said. "That Sierra just needs to be handled with care."

"Surely you can afford a new one."

"That's irrelevant."

"What's irrelevant?" Bridge said.

He'd just walked through the door.

"If it's irrelevant," Smith said. "Why do you want to know what it is?"

"Fair enough. Have we had any developments overnight?"

"The York Post have got hold of the CCTV footage of *The Spider* climbing up Brian James's wall," Smith told him.

"Bloody hell."

"They must have got it from the hotel across the road," Smith said. "And they've written some sensationalist piece about the bloke."

"Do they know any details?"

"Enough. I'm not fazed. Although it looks like a press conference is on the cards."

"What's the plan of action for today?" Bridge asked DI Smyth.

"We dig deeper into the lives of the victims," DI Smyth said. "The man you're all calling *The Spider* knows far too much about them and I want to know how he knows so much."

"I want to speak to Donna Baron first," Smith said. "Her reluctance to talk makes me suspicious."

"Don't forget your pretty shrink," DI Smyth said.

"She is not my shrink," Smith said. "And I haven't forgotten."

"Are we talking about Dr Vennell?" Bridge said.

"We are," Smith said.

"Whitton isn't going to like it."

"For fuck's sake," Smith said. "I'm going outside for a quick smoke. Is that fine with you, boss?"

"Don't let me stop you," DI Smyth said.

Smith left the station and lit a cigarette. He took out his phone and found Dr Vennell's number. She answered on the second ring.

"I was expecting you to call."

"I presume you've heard about *The Spider*?" Smith said.

"I read it on the York Post's thing. Who is this man, or should I say *what* is he?"

"He's a freak who happens to be able to run up walls," Smith said. "But he's also a serial killer and I'm going to catch him."

"What do you need from me?"

"I want you to try to get inside his head," Smith said. "There are certain aspects of his MO that I'm finding hard to get my own head around, and I was hoping you would help me."

"I'm always willing to help you, Jason," Dr Vennell said. "You know that. I have patients all morning, but I can get away for a few hours this afternoon. I think it's better if I come to you."

"You're probably right."

"How does two o'clock sound?"

"I'll let the boss know. Thanks, Dr Vennell."

"How many times?"

"Thanks, Fiona," Smith humoured her. "See you this afternoon."

The door to the station opened and Bridge came outside.

"A phone call has just come in," he said. "And the boss wants us to check it out."

"Another body?" Smith said.

"We're not sure yet. A bloke called because he's worried about his wife. He's away on business and he can't get hold of her."

"There could be any number of reasons for that," Smith said. "Her phone could have died. She could have lost it."

"He thought about that," Bridge said. "He called the neighbour and asked her to check on his wife. She's not answering the door."

"And the boss thinks it's worth us looking into? We've got a lot on right now."

"He's the boss."

"Is it a flat?" Smith said. "Do they live in a flat?"

"The husband didn't say. Come on – it's five-minute drive from here. We can be there and back in thirty minutes."

CHAPTER TWENTY SIX

The address they'd been given wasn't a flat. Megan and Zak Lambert had a three-bedroom house in Badger Hill.
"This is a waste of time," Smith said. "Why is the boss so adamant that Megan has come to harm?"
"It was something the husband said. He told Baldwin that he'd heard about *The Spider* and he was worried about his wife."
"Has he got something to hide?" Smith said.
"Who knows? Anyway, Baldwin got the sense that there was something more to the call and she alerted the DI."
"Baldwin's sixth sense is rarely wrong. Let's have a look, shall we?"
The PCs Griffin and Bowler were already outside the house. Smith walked over to them.
"Have you tried knocking on the door?"
"Of course, Sarge," PC Bowler said. "No answer."
Smith checked the door. It was locked.
"What do you reckon?" he said to Bridge. "Do we have reasonable grounds to break in?"
"It's a tricky one," Bridge said. "But I think the fact that the husband called us constitutes reasonable grounds."
"I agree," PC Griffin said.
"We didn't ask for your opinion," Smith said. "Stand back."
He gave the door a good kick.
"Fuck, that hurt."
"Break the window, you berk," Bridge said. "Kicking in a door only works in the movies."
Smith bent down and grabbed one of the bricks that had been put down to line the path to the door. Without warning, he flung it through the

windowpane next to the door. He knocked the remaining glass away and stuck his arm in. He located the door handle, and he was relieved to find the key in the lock. He turned it and opened the door.

"Mrs Lambert," he shouted. "Police."

Nothing.

"Megan. This is the police. Are you in there?"

"Perhaps she went out," PC Griffin suggested.

"With the door locked," Smith said. "And the key on the inside? Make yourself useful and make sure nobody comes near the house."

"We should call Webber," Bridge said.

"You know he won't come out based on a gut feeling," Smith said.

"What's your gut telling you?"

"It's telling me I overdid it with the Theakstons last night. I'm going in."

He called out Megan's name again with the same result. He made his way down the hallway, making sure not to touch anything. The living room was empty, as was the room that was being used as a dining room. The kitchen door was closed. Smith pushed it open and stopped dead.

The stains on the sheet covering what had to be the body of Megan Lambert told him that *The Spider* had taken another victim, but something felt terribly wrong. Smith left the kitchen and went back outside. Webber wouldn't thank him for lingering inside the house too long. Smith needed to air his concerns with Bridge.

"She's dead," he said.

"Is it Megan Lambert?" Bridge said.

"I'm working on the assumption that it is, but there's something wrong here."

"It's a bit convenient, isn't it?"

"That's exactly what I was thinking. I need to check something."

It didn't take long. After a two-minute conversation with PC Baldwin Smith was able to ascertain that the call that came in was from a man who claimed to be Zak Lambert. According to Baldwin, he sounded agitated and he was convinced that something had happened to his wife. He mentioned *The Spider*, and he made her promise to check out the house. Smith asked Baldwin to see if she could locate the husband – she did just that and Zak Lambert told her that it wasn't him who called the police.

"She was meant to be found," Smith said. "We now know that the husband was supposed to come home on Wednesday. He's at a conference in Manchester. The fucker knew this. *The Spider* was aware of the husband's schedule, and he called in and pretended to be the husband because he wanted Megan to be found before Wednesday."

"How does he know what he knows?" Bridge said. "As far as we're aware, the victims weren't acquainted, so where does *The Spider* get his information from?"

"He does a lot of homework," Smith said. "Not only does he know everything about the victims, but he also knows all about the people closest to them."

Webber's car pulled up, and the Head of Forensics got out. Billie Jones got out of the passenger side. Bridge gave her a smile, and it was reciprocated with a subtle nod of the head.

"She's in the kitchen," Smith told Webber. "I haven't touched anything."

"Anything else?" Webber said.

"The front door was locked, and the key was inside. It will have been impossible for him to exit the house via the front. This one is different to the others."

"I won't offer my opinion on that just yet."

"She's been covered with a sheet," Smith said. "Something is really bugging me about this murder."

"I'm sure it'll occur to you in time."

"Have you got a spare SOC suit?"

"Is that a rhetorical question?"

"I want to take another look," Smith said. "You don't mind, do you?"

Webber didn't reply and Smith took this as permission to re-enter the house.

CHAPTER TWENTY SEVEN

Smith's eyes were focused on the strange door in the kitchen. Megan Lambert was on the floor in front of it, and he wondered what was behind the door. There was an odd stain on the Lino and Smith pointed it out to Webber.

"It looks like she was moved," the Head of Forensics said.

This made sense to Smith. The body was a couple of feet from the mystery door and the smear of what he assumed was blood was between the door and her.

"He was standing in the doorway when he killed her," Smith speculated. "She fell to the floor, thus preventing the door from closing. He dragged her out of the way, didn't he?"

"You're sharp this morning," Webber said. "I believe that's exactly what happened. And what does that tell us?"

"He needed to close the door for some reason."

"Look at the shoeprints in the blood," Smith said.

Webber bent down. "If I were to hazard a guess, I'd say these are the same as the print we found on the downpipe at the scene of the first murder."

"Sherpa Ultra pro-grip," Smith said.

There was a key in the door and when he tried the handle the door opened.

"It looks like some kind of cellar," Smith said.

He felt for a light switch and located it on the wall just behind the door. He flicked the switch and the room lit up.

"Wine," he said. "It's a wine cellar."

He went inside and took in the wine racks. He guessed there had to be more than a hundred bottles in there. The racks covered most of the wall space. There was a device he didn't recognise on a table in the corner. He took a closer look and saw that it was some kind of humidity regulator. Whoever the wine collector was, they took it seriously.

Something caught his eye behind one of the wine racks. There was light coming in from somewhere and the wine rack was at a different angle to the rest. It had been moved. The light source was a small window, and the latch had been forced. Smith looked out and he could see some thick foliage blocking most of the view of what looked like a fence behind it.

"I think he got in through the window in there," Smith told Webber back in the kitchen. "I'm going to take a look outside."

"You'll do no such thing," Webber said. "Stay here – I'll go. If you're right, whatever is outside that window is part of a crime scene, and we might get lucky."

Smith didn't argue. Instead, he took out his phone and brought up a number. He dialled it and soon afterwards, Webber's phone started to ring. The Head of Forensics observed him as though he'd lost his mind.

"I don't know exactly where the window opens out," Smith explained. "There's some type of plant in the way and it'll probably be difficult to see from outside. I'll keep an eye out from inside the cellar and let you know when I see you."

Webber shook his head, but he didn't argue. He answered the call and left the kitchen.

"What can you see?" Smith asked him shortly afterwards.

"The front door," Webber replied. "I haven't even left the house yet."

"No worries."

"There's a gate that opens onto a path that goes around the side of the property. I'm opening it now."

"Can you see any foliage?" Smith asked.

"Ivy," Webber said. "It's covering most of the wall. I can't see what's behind it."

"I'm going to tap on the window to make it easier for you."
Smith looked around the room for something to use and decided on one of the bottles in the racks. He slid out the closest one and glanced at the label. It was a wine he'd never heard of – Chateau Latour, and Smith didn't think it looked too expensive. He tested its weight in his hand and tapped the neck against the window. It barely made a sound. He put a bit more force behind it and on the third tap there was a crunch as the neck of the bottle broke, together with the windowpane.
"Shit," Smith said.
Red wine splashed on his hands, and he dropped the bottle. He watched as it landed on the floor and shattered, releasing its contents all over the floor.

"What the hell is wrong with you?" Webber's voice was heard over the phone.
"I don't know my own strength sometimes," Smith said. "Did you find it? Did you find the window?"
"The ear-piercing smashing of the glass sort of gave it away."
"Sarcasm doesn't suit you," Smith said. "Well?"
"The ivy has definitely been disturbed," Webber said. "It's been pushed away from the window and pushed back."
"That's how he got in and out. My work here is done."
"Thank God for that."
"I might have made a bit of a mess in here," Smith said. "I just hope the shit that's all over the floor wasn't a special vintage."
"Get out of there," Webber said. "Get out before you do any more damage."

Smith left the cellar and headed outside, leaving a trail of wine-coloured footprints in his wake. Webber wasn't going to be impressed. He went outside and removed the suit and protective footwear. Billie Jones came out after him.

"There were no open windows upstairs," she said. "It doesn't look like he came in that way."

"He got in through the window in the cellar," Smith told her.

"You smell like wine."

"I had a bit of an altercation with a bottle of the stuff. Did you find anything upstairs?"

"I think I might have," Billie said. "There was a laptop in one of the bedrooms and when I woke it up, I got the home screen of a Facebook page."

"What kind of page?" Smith said.

"Some forum for victims to share their stories by the looks of things."

"Interesting. Mrs Lambert was another victim. This could be the breakthrough we've been waiting for."

CHAPTER TWENTY EIGHT

"Before we make a start," DI Smyth said. "There's something I need to bring to your attention."

The team had gathered in the small conference room for an afternoon briefing. The recent developments meant that Smith had no choice but to reschedule Dr Vennell's visit. The pretty psychologist told him she would always make time for him, and Smith didn't quite know how to interpret it. He informed her that he would be in touch.

"We've got a rat in our midst," DI Smyth added.

"A rat?" DC Moore said.

"A mole," DI Smyth said. "Informant, whatever you want to call them. Certain details of the murder of Megan Lambert have been leaked to the press – the York Post to be exact."

"News spreads quickly these days," Smith said.

"No," DI Smyth said. "This is not something that a nosy neighbour could have picked up and leaked to the press. The York Post reported on how the killer gained access to the house. The wine cellar was mentioned specifically."

"What are you implying?" Smith said.

"That information could only have come from someone who attended the scene of the murder."

"I was worried you were going to say that."

"Who was there?" DC Moore said.

"Me and Bridge," Smith said. "PC Griffin and PC Bowler were already there when we arrived, and Webber and Billie showed up soon afterwards."

"My money's on Griffin," DC Moore said. "I've always thought there was something shifty about him."

"Let's not start throwing accusations around without proof," DI Smyth said.

"How much do we know about PC Bowler?" Whitton said.

"She's only been here five minutes," Smith said. "And she seems like a decent person. I doubt she would risk everything by leaking info to the press."

"Well, somebody did, and that somebody had to be at the scene earlier."

"It's definitely not Webber," Smith said.

"Or Billie," Bridge said. "And it wasn't me or you, so it has to be one of the uniforms."

"There is one explanation we haven't considered," Smith said.

"*The Spider*?" DC King guessed.

"The very same. It wouldn't be the first time a serial killer has worked with the fourth estate."

"Why would he leak details to the press?" DC Moore said

"For the same reason he called the police, pretending to be Megan's husband," Smith said. "He's upping his game by dictating the narrative. And when they do that it makes me nervous."

"Now that I've made you aware of that," DI Smyth said. "Let's move on to the murder of Megan Lambert."

"She was killed in the kitchen," Smith said. "Next to the door to the wine cellar."

"I believe you demolished a bottle of expensive wine," Whitton said.

"I don't think it was that expensive."

"Let's hope not."

"*The Spider* got into the house through a small window in the cellar," Smith said. "And he killed Megan next to the cellar door. There were stains on the floor that suggested he moved her in order to be able to close the door again. He killed her and left the same way he came in."

"He changed his MO for this one," DC King said.

"Which suggests he's adaptable," Smith said. "Megan was covered with a sheet, just like the others."

"Has the husband been informed?" DC Moore said.

"Mr Lambert was contacted when we suspected the person who called the station earlier wasn't him. We were right – Zak Lambert was not the one who made the call claiming to be concerned about his wife. It wasn't the most ideal way to learn about a dead spouse, but it's done now and there's no point dwelling on it."

"Where was he when it happened?" DC King said.

"Manchester," Smith said. "Some work thing."

"Was there anything else at the scene we need to consider?" DI Smyth said.

"I think so," Smith said. "Billie found a laptop in the main bedroom. When she woke it up it was logged into a Facebook page. It was probably the last thing Megan Lambert was looking at before she was killed."

"What kind of Facebook page was it?" DC King said.

"*You're not Alone*," Smith said. "That was the title on the page. It's a support group where men and women can share common experiences. It looks like it's a group for victims."

"Do you believe it's significant?" DC Moore said.

"It's extremely significant, Harry. All of the victims of *The Spider* were victims before they became his victims, if that makes any sense."

"We need to look more closely at that Facebook page," DI Smyth said.

"Billie told me the members have to be admin approved," Bridge said. "So, I don't know how we'll be able to access it."

"We find out who the admin is," DC Moore said. "And force them to let us in."

"Unfortunately, we can't do that," DI Smyth said. "Not without a court order. And Facebook is notoriously difficult to reason with. That kind of process could take weeks, if not months."

"What if we were to appeal to the admin?" Whitton said. "Explain the situation and request access?"

"That won't work," Smith said. "The very nature of those kind of sites is their anonymity. And for all we know, *The Spider* could be involved with the page."

"It's worth thinking about," DC King said. "It's actually a genius way of selecting a victim."

"I reckon there's another way," Smith said.

"Are you going to give me more grey hairs?" DI Smyth said.

"I wouldn't dream of it, boss," Smith said. "We need to play the victim. We'll gain acceptance to that page by asking to join the support group."

CHAPTER TWENTY NINE

"You can't use this account."
It took Barry Stone less than a minute to come to this conclusion. Barry was a friend of Bridge's, and the team had used his IT expertise many times before. Smith didn't know anyone who was more clued up in all things computer-orientated than Barry.

"It's quite obvious that this is the Facebook account of a copper."
"I suppose you're right," Smith said.
"When was the last time you signed in?" Barry said.
"God knows. It's been quite a while."
"You have seven friends. Really?"
Smith shrugged his shoulders. "And more than half of them are no longer breathing."
This was true. His friends list consisted of his wife, his adopted daughter Lucy and Darren Lewis. They were the ones who were still alive. The other four friends were Paul *The Ghoul* Johnson, Nigel Brown, DC Yang Chu and David *Whitey* White. All of them had been dead for years, and Smith was still friends with them on Facebook.

"You really are a strange bloke," Barry said. "There is no way this is going to fool the admin of a page like *You're not Alone*. The very nature of a group like that is its attention to detail when it comes to accepting new members. We're going to have to create a more appealing account."
"How do we do that?" Smith said.
"I've got a few dormant ones on the go. We can modify one of them to make it look like a profile that fits the bill. Leave it with me."
"How long are we talking about?" Smith said.
"An hour, tops."
"And will we be able to find the admin of the page that way?"

"Leave that with me too," Barry said.

"I won't ask how you're planning on doing it."

"You wouldn't understand anyway."

"That's why I'm not going to ask," Smith said. "The killer the city is calling *The Spider* is selecting his victims from that page – I'm sure of it."

He left Barry to it and headed outside to smoke a cigarette. PC Griffin came out after him.

"Have you got a minute?" the piggy-eyed PC said.

"What is it?" Smith said.

He lit a cigarette and exhaled a cloud of smoke.

PC Griffin coughed. "I saw the stuff the York Post put out this morning."

"And?"

Smith wondered if he was here to confess. He was going to be sorely disappointed.

"I think Angie was responsible for the info they broadcast."

"That's a pretty heavy accusation to make," Smith said. "I presume you have some kind of proof."

"No, Sarge," PC Griffin said. "Not exactly."

"Then you need to keep your opinions to yourself. You start throwing accusations about your colleagues around and your time in this job is going to be very short."

"That's why I came to you, Sarge," PC Griffin said. "I don't have concrete proof, but I do know that Angie's brother works for the York Post."

"Are you sure?" Smith said.

"Positive, Sarge. She's mentioned it a few times. I'm not telling you this out of spite – I like PC Bowler, but something like this could be detrimental to the investigation."

"OK," Smith said. "Thanks for bringing it to my attention. But PC Griffin."

"Sarge."

"Nobody likes a rat, especially in this job. I'm sure you have work to do."
He walked away from PC Griffin to indicate that the conversation was over.

He debated what to do with the information the ugly PC had just handed him. If PC Bowler was the one who leaked the information about Megan Lambert's murder to the York Post, he didn't think she did it maliciously. There had to be another explanation for it. He hadn't known the young PC for long, but he sensed that she was an honest person, and this seemed somewhat out of character. He decided he would have a quiet word with her. No real harm had been done, and Smith didn't think it was necessary to take matters any further.

He finished his cigarette, and he was about to go back to work when DCI Chalmers appeared. Smith thought it would be rude to leave now so he lit another cigarette and walked over to the DCI.

"How are things, boss?"

"The Super is doing my nut in," Chalmers said.

"What's new?"

"He's reached a new level of irritation I didn't think it was possible to achieve."

"What has he done now?" Smith said.

Chalmers lit a cigarette. "The public-school tosser is throwing around an idea about a new initiative he believes will improve the wellbeing of the workforce."

"God help us all."

"Super foods," Chalmers said. "He's convinced that the men and women tasked with sorting out the scumbags of this city will be more efficient on a healthy diet."

"Nothing will come of it."

"He's going for it," Chalmers said. "He brings the shite to work with him. If I'm asked to try another plant I can't even pronounce, I may not retire with my pension intact. We can expect a special meeting in the not-so-distant future."

"I'll look forward to it," Smith said.

"What's the latest on your Spider?" Chalmers said.

"I think I've figured out his motive," Smith said.

"That's half the battle won then."

"But I'm not sure how we're going to catch him. He moves like nobody I've ever seen before. If it comes down to a chase, we've got no chance."

"There are many ways to skin a cat. You'll figure it out."

"I suppose I'd better get back in and do what I'm paid to do." Smith said.

A white car pulled up and a woman who looked to be in her late twenties walked towards the entrance of the station. Smith thought she looked nervous. She glanced in his direction then she did a double take. It was clear that she'd recognised him, but Smith had never seen her before. She approached and Smith asked her if he could help her.

"You are DS Smith, aren't you?" she said.

"That'll be me. Do I know you?"

"We've never met. My name is Penelope Bright and I'm the admin on a Facebook group."

"Facebook?" Smith said.

"It's a support group for people to talk about problems in their lives – *You're not Alone.*"

Smith was suddenly wide awake.

"Go on," he said.

"I think I've made a terrible mistake. I deleted someone from the group and now I think she's dead."

CHAPTER THIRTY

"I thought she was a fake."

Penelope was sitting opposite Smith in his office. He'd got them both a strong coffee from the canteen and he was waiting to hear what she had to tell him. He'd informed Barry Stone that his assistance was no longer needed – the admin from the Facebook group they were looking for had given herself to him on a plate.

"Who are we talking about?" he said.

"Megan Lambert. She went by the name *Angry Meg* on the group."

"Angry Meg?" Smith repeated.

"The majority of our members don't use their real names, but Megan all but did."

"Why did you think she was a fake?" Smith asked.

"We get a lot of them," Penelope explained. "Unfortunately. I set up the page so people could talk about their experiences anonymously, without the risk of repercussions. Members on the *You're not Alone* page can open up without anyone passing judgement. I don't know how often you use social media."

"Very rarely."

"There are a lot of trolls out there," Penelope said. "Malicious people who get off on spouting venom. I didn't want that on my group and that's why there's a vetting process for potential members. I can usually spot a troll a mile away, but I got it so wrong with Megan."

She stopped there and Smith waited for her to speak. This was important – he was sure of it, and he decided to let Penelope Bright continue without interruption.

"I read about her murder in the York Post," she said. "And I knew it was *Angry Meg*. The article mentioned the wine cellar and that was when it came to me. *Angry Meg* posted something a while ago about what she wanted to do with her husband's wine. He had some expensive bottles, and she wondered what he would do if she drank some of them while he was out chasing women around. She received a lot of words of encouragement with that one. Dozens of people told her to go for it."

"Plenty of people have wine cellars," Smith said.

"Not all of them are called Megan."

Smith couldn't argue with that, and he thought it was too much of a coincidence to ignore.

"She mentioned one particular wine," Penelope said. "A Chateau Latour Bordeaux. It's worth thousands of pounds. You can check, can't you? You can see if there's a bottle of that wine in the cellar?"

Smith didn't have to. He was sure he could still smell it on his hands. He didn't mention this.

"What else did you find out about Megan?" he asked instead.

"Her husband was a philanderer," Penelope said. "He had a high-powered job, and he was away a lot, but Megan knew he wasn't always working. She caught him at it more than once."

"Tell me why you excluded her from the group."

"I made a mistake. Her posts felt too rehearsed somehow. It was as though she was fabricating everything to make her life more interesting. I'm so sorry."

"It's not your fault," Smith said. "I need your help."

"I'll help in any way I can."

"I need access to that page,"

"Absolutely not," Penelope said.

"This is important," Smith said. "And you have my word that none of the information on the page will go any further."

"I have an obligation to the men and women on that page. You have to understand that these people are extremely vulnerable. The group offers them a safe place to talk with like-minded people. They trust me, and I cannot break that trust."

Smith decided to tell her the truth.

"We have reason to believe that your page has been infiltrated. We're also reasonably confident that the killer everyone is calling *The Spider* is selecting his victims on there."

"You can't be serious?"

"I never joke about murder. This is as serious as it gets. More people are going to die. Please, help me."

Penelope looked him in the eyes. Smith kept her gaze.

"Please," he said once more.

"You promise that the details of the members won't be disclosed?"

"I promise," Smith said. "Firstly, I want to ascertain that *The Spider's* victims did in fact come from that page. Does the name Christine Snow mean anything to you?"

Penelope shook her head. "It's not familiar."

"OK," Smith said. "Christine's husband is an accountant."

"It still doesn't ring any bells."

"He spends all of his free time playing football."

The spark of recognition in Penelope's eyes was obvious.

"Is she dead?"

"I'm afraid so," Smith confirmed. "What about Brian James? His fiancé was using him as a punchbag. The abuse had been going on for some time, but he wasn't able to leave her."

"There is a man on the group who sounds like it could be him. Women abusing men isn't too common."

"Brian is also dead," Smith said. "George Baron. His wife is always away and theirs is a cold marriage."

"*Barren Fields*."

"Excuse me?" Smith said.

"That's the name he uses on the page. It has to be him. Is he..."

"He was *The Spider's* third victim."

"Oh my God," Penelope said. "What have I done? This is all my fault."

"None of this is your fault," Smith said. "Somehow *The Spider* latched onto your page and decided it was an easy way to choose his victims."

"What do you want from me?" Penelope said.

"We have a team of IT specialists," Smith said. "But I'm not going to bring this to their attention just yet. Things could get extremely unpleasant for you and your group members if I go that route."

"I don't understand."

"There's a bloke we use once in a while who is not only better than all of the IT team put together, but he'll also be discreet. I gave you my word that none of the info on your members will go any further and I'm going to keep that promise."

Penelope nodded.

"What happens now?" she said. "What will happen to the page?"

"Business as usual," Smith said. "In the meantime, Barry will get to work – he's the IT bloke, and he'll talk you through what he needs from you. Rather you than me. Half of the time, he may as well be speaking Albanian. You're doing the right thing."

"Do you know why I set up the page?"

"You don't have to tell me," Smith said.

"I want to. I started it in the aftermath of a string of toxic relationships. I couldn't seem to break the cycle, and I was at my wits end. Then I woke up one day and I had some kind of revelation. Victims are often victims because there are people out there who prey on those kinds of people. People who get their kicks from manipulating vulnerable men and women. But that can only happen if a victim allows them to do it. The group was set up as a place for people to grow in strength, surrounded by people just like them. It was a positive place, and I like to think that it helps."

"It does," Smith said.

"And when I encounter men like you," Penelope said. "It just reinforces my belief that there are still good men in the world."

"Would you mind telling my wife that?" Smith said.

Penelope smiled for the first time. "I think she already knows."

CHAPTER THIRTY ONE

Peter Snow passed the ball to the man on his left and raced up the pitch. He'd spotted an opening, and he hoped his winger had seen it too. He was in luck – the ball slid beautifully between two of the opponent's defenders and landed at Peter's feet. He took aim and slotted the ball into the back of the net. 4:0.

Peter was looking forward to a few drinks after the match. It had been a stressful couple of days, and he needed something to take the edge off. On Saturday, he'd come home from playing football to find his wife dead in their bedroom. After what felt like a three-day interrogation from the police officers at the scene he'd been forced to face the humiliation of a formal police interview, lawyer and all. Luckily, he'd been able to use one of the accounting firm's legal representatives, free of charge. The interview had left him feeling drained. It wasn't an ideal way to spend a wedding anniversary.

It was late at night when he'd been allowed access to his house, and he'd slept on the couch in the room he used as a study. He slept badly, but he did manage a few hours, and he'd spent the whole of Sunday parading as a football manager online. He'd spent the night in the study again, and when he woke up this morning, he felt wide awake. He'd called in sick – they couldn't deny him a few days off after what had happened, and he'd managed to find the details of a company that specialised in industrial cleaning. He'd paid double to get them to scrub the bloodied carpet in the bedroom as soon as they could, and a new bed was delivered before midday. By two that afternoon, all traces of the murder had been wiped out, together with the memory of his wife.

None of this had gone unseen. Peter wasn't aware that the activity at the house was being observed. There was someone there taking a keen interest in the proceedings.

Peter had spent the rest of the afternoon logged into one of his *Football Manager* accounts and with a rare flash of brilliance, his Wigan Athletic had destroyed Real Madrid, three-nil. He'd changed into his football kit before walking the half-a-mile to the indoor sports centre. His stalker had been twenty feet behind him the whole way there.

"Nice one, mate."
Peter Snow didn't normally appreciate physical contact, but the pat on the back felt good now.
"That fourth goal was genius," Andy Bullock added. "Drinks on you in the bar then."
Peter smiled. "With pleasure. God knows I need a few."
"I heard about your missus. Sorry, mate."
"Shit happens. I'm not going to let it get to me."
"I was surprised to see you," Andy said.
"I couldn't let the lads down," Peter said. "I'm going to have a shower, and I'll see you out front."

He headed for the changing rooms. He pushed the door open and stopped dead.
"Bastards."
Someone had taped an *Out of Order* notice on the door of the shower cubicle.
"Yeh, right."
It had happened before, and Peter knew it was one of the lads having a joke. He tore the notice down and went inside the shower room. There was a mirror on one of the walls and Peter took a moment to admire his reflection in it. He removed his shirt and sucked in his stomach.
"Not bad. What the fuck."

In the mirror he could see that someone was standing behind him. The figure in black wasn't moving and Peter wondered if he was imagining it. He blinked a few times and closed his eyes for a couple of seconds. When he opened them again, the figure was gone.

"Shit."

Peter really needed a drink. The last two days hadn't been easy. He bent down to take off his football shorts; there was a sharp pain in his lower back and he froze. He wasn't stiff with fear – he really was frozen to the spot for a moment. His spinal column had been severed at the base. He was aware that he was falling sideways, but he had no sensation of it happening. He landed on his back and gasped. His bowels and bladder emptied but he only knew this because of the thick, putrid stench that crept into his nostrils.

The figure in black was standing over his paralysed body. Peter knew he was about to die. The knife he could see in front of his face left little doubt about that. But the blade didn't come down again. The man who had left him numb didn't move.

"I'm not going to kill you."

Peter didn't understand, but the questions he wanted to ask refused to come out. He managed a groan.

"You shouldn't have played football."

Peter had no idea what he was talking about. The man bent down and whispered something into his ear.

Peter looked on as the figure in the black hood turned and leapt onto the top of one of the shower cubicles with absolute ease. He watched as he slid through the window above the shower and was gone. Peter Snow's heart started to beat faster, and his breathing became rapid. He placed a hand on his lower back and felt the warm blood pumping out. He could feel the blood on his hand, but he had no sensation of the hand on his back.

CHAPTER THIRTY TWO

"Barry Stone has managed to link all of the victims to the *You're not Alone* Facebook page," Smith said.
It was late, but he felt that a final briefing was in order.
"Christine Snow, Brian James, George Baron and Megan Lambert all logged on to the group in the past few weeks."
"What's the next plan of action?" DI Smyth said.
"We now know how he chooses them," Smith said. "And we need to ask ourselves how he got wind of the page in the first place."
"Is it possible he trawled social media for suitable forums for his hunting?" DC King said.
"Very possible."
"Do we know how many similar pages are out there?" Whitton said.
"I imagine there are quite a few," Smith said. "But we'll focus on *You're not Alone*. According to Penelope Bright, there are fifty-eight people in that group. The majority of those are women, but sixteen are men."
"That's not an awful lot really," DC Moore said.

"The way I see it," Smith said. "There are two possible scenarios we need to consider. Either *The Spider* somehow managed to gain access to the group by hacking into it, or he's a member. I'm inclined to believe that the latter is more likely. He poses as a victim and is accepted into the group. Once he's in he has full access to the posts, and he can select a victim as he sees fit. It's a lot of work but we need to scrutinise all fifty-four members."
"I thought you said there were fifty-eight," DC Moore said.
"Four of them are now dead, Harry," Bridge reminded him.
"Oh, right. Don't mind me – I'm a bit thick sometimes."

"Unfortunately," Smith said. "Very few of the people in the group post using their real names."

"And if *The Spider* is one of them," Whitton said. "There's no way he'd use his real name."

Smith nodded. "But we have a secret weapon in the form of Barry Stone. Barry will be working closely with Penelope Bright and I'm confident that between the two of them we'll get something to look at very soon."

"Do you think he's finished?" Bridge said.

"No," Smith said. "And that's why we need to work quickly. Everyone in that Facebook group is at risk. We know that he doesn't discriminate between men and women, and any one of those people could be his next victim."

"We need to warn them," DC King said.

"Already set in motion," Smith said. "Penelope has put a warning out on the page."

"If *The Spider* is in the group, he's going to be aware of it," Whitton said.

"It can't be helped," Smith said. "Penelope did consider private messaging, but it wouldn't have changed anything. *The Spider* would have been alerted via Messenger if he's in the group."

"I hate social media," Bridge said.

"You're not the only one, mate. Does anyone have anything to bring up before we call it a day?"

Smith waited. He knew that one of them would have something to say. He wasn't wrong, and it was DC King as usual who spoke first.

"What about trying to flush him out?" she said.

"That might work," DC Moore said.

"What did you have in mind, Kerry?" Smith said.

"Stick something on the group," DC King said. "Tell him that we're onto him, and it's only a matter of time before we find him."

"But we're not onto him," Bridge pointed out. "Do you know how difficult it is to find someone hidden in the depths of the Internet."

"It's worth a try," Smith said. "If only to rattle him a bit. We use the *You're not Alone* page against him for once. It's a hell of a lot more subtle than what we did with *The Optician*."

"I'll run it past Barry," Bridge said.

"We're getting closer," Smith said. "We know how he's choosing them, and we know what's motivating him. That's half the battle won. What's the word with the press conference?"

This question was addressed to DI Smyth.

"Tomorrow afternoon," the DI confirmed. "And Superintendent Smyth has not been invited.

"Thank God for that," Smith said.

"I want you to head it up," DI Smyth said. "And before you voice your objections, it's not up for debate."

"Fair enough."

"You have an appointment with the press liaison officer at ten tomorrow morning."

"I'll look forward to it," Smith said.

"I suggest we wrap things up there," DI Smyth said.

"He's slowing down," Smith said.

"Where did that come from?" Bridge said.

"I have no idea. It just occurred to me. Christine Snow and Brian James were both killed on Saturday. George Baron and Megan Lambert were murdered yesterday, but we've had no reports of anything today. Why is he slowing down?"

"Statistically speaking," Bridge said.

"Here we go," DC Moore said.

Bridge was undeterred. "Serial killers start off slowly. Often weeks, or even months can go by between the killing. But when they get the taste for it, the cooling off period becomes shorter. If we look at the timescale of *The Spider,* we see that his cooling off period is getting longer."

"Not all serial killers follow this pattern," Whitton said.

"True," Bridge said. "It's very possible that his first four victims were taken quickly because they were the easiest. The other people on his list could be trickier to take out."

"We don't even know if he has a list," DC Moore said.

"Oh, he definitely has a list, Harry," Smith said. "I reckon that'll do for today."

He got to his feet before anyone else could bring up anything else.

"Can I get a lift with you?" he asked Whitton.

"You don't have much choice, do you?" she said.

"I just need to run a quick errand. Give me fifteen minutes."

"I won't ask."

"I'll see you out front in fifteen," Smith said.

He was in luck. PC Angie Bowler was in the canteen, and she was alone in there. Smith sat down opposite her without being invited.

"Can I have a word?" he said.

"Of course, Sarge."

"Did the information the York Post printed come from you?" He came straight to the point.

"What?" PC Bowler said.

"There were certain details in that article that they couldn't possibly know about. Did you pass on information to the York Post?"

Her silence told him everything he needed to know.

She rubbed her temples and closed her eyes.

"Well?" Smith said.

"I think it was my fault," PC Bowler said.

"You *think*? Either it came from you, or it didn't."

"It's not how it seems."

"Tell me how it is then."

"My brother is the sub-editor for the Post."

"And?"

"Me and my brother are close," PC Bowler said. "I was round there yesterday evening, and I might have spoken about the wine cellar without realising it. Everyone heard about you and that bottle of expensive wine and I didn't think. I thought I was just telling a funny story about my day. I'm sorry. I didn't mean for it to get published. Am I going to get into trouble for this?"

"I don't think it needs to go any further."

"I really didn't mean it."

"I know you didn't," Smith said. "No harm was done. In fact, it was that article that gave us our biggest lead. We would have never made the connection between the victims and the *You're not Alone* page if the admin for the page hadn't seen the York Post thing."

"I'll be more careful in future," PC Bowler said. "I really am sorry."

"Just be more mindful about what you say in front of your brother."

"Thank you. Can I ask you something?"

"As long as it's not going to end up in the papers."

PC Bowler smiled. "I deserved that."

"Ask away," Smith said.

"I can't figure you out," PC Bowler said. "You're a police officer sworn to uphold the law, but I've seen you disregard plenty of infringements when your eyes are on the bigger picture."

Smith thought about this. PC Bowler was absolutely right.

"I'm paid to catch killers," he said. "It's the only thing I was destined to do, and I happen to be very good at it. If I come across someone who's fiddling the taxman or driving without insurance along the way, I figure it's not important in the greater scheme of things."

"I wish I could afford to think like that."

"You'll get there one day," Smith said.

"How did you find out about my brother?" PC Bowler said.

"That's not important," Smith said. "What's done is done, and it's not going to happen again, is it?"

"Definitely not, Sarge. I won't let you down."

Smith didn't comment on this. He got up and left the canteen.

Whitton was waiting for him by the front desk. Bridge and the DCs King and Moore were also standing there.

"*The Spider* has struck again," Whitton said.

"Fuck it," Smith said. "Just when I thought he was slowing down. What do we know?"

"It's Peter Snow, Sarge," DC King said. "He was found in the changing rooms of the sports centre in Bootham."

"Peter Snow?"

"A witness saw a man matching the description of *The Spider* fleeing the scene," Whitton said. "And he left this one alive."

CHAPTER THIRTY THREE

Smith drove with DC King. DI Smyth had made a quick decision. They didn't all need to attend the scene of Peter Snow's attack, so he'd asked them to decide amongst themselves. Smith was the first to put up his hand, and DC King had been next. Whitton, Bridge and DC Moore were sent out to the spouses and the fiancé of *The Spider's* other victims. They didn't yet know if they were definitely in danger, but in light of what had been done to Peter Snow, DI Smyth couldn't afford to take any chances. It was very possible that he was working to an agenda, and this was the next stage in his plan.

"Do you really believe the others are at risk?" DC King said.
They'd just passed Foss Islands and were heading north towards Bootham.
"We have to work on the assumption that they are," Smith said. "Christine Snow was the first victim. And now her husband has been attacked. Perhaps this is what he planned all along. He kills the victims and then he goes for the reason for them being victims in the first place."
"I fail to see the logic behind that."
"Me too," Smith admitted. "What the hell was Peter Snow doing playing football? His wife isn't yet cold, and he's out kicking a ball around as though nothing has changed."
"People handle grief in different ways," DC King said.
"I don't buy that bullshit. People may grieve differently, but there is usually a common denominator in the form of shock or sadness or anger, but Peter Snow was acting like nothing had happened. He was married to Christine for seven years. That is not normal behaviour."

They arrived at the sports centre five minutes later. Even though it was Monday evening the car park was half full. DC King parked close to the entrance, and they got out of the car. Smith couldn't see any evidence that this was a crime scene, and he wondered why that was. There was no police tape, and he watched no fewer than four people go inside the centre while he was standing there.

"Have we come to the right place?" he asked DC King.

"This is it, Sarge," she said.

"Why hasn't it been closed for business? A man was brutally attacked in there, and people are still going in and out. Do we know who was first on the scene?"

"PC Miller and PC Griffin."

"Very strange," Smith said. "PC Miller is an experienced officer. Let's go and see what's going on."

Things were made a bit clearer when they went inside and spoke to the man behind the reception desk.

"You're looking for the indoor football pitch," he said. "It's on the other side of the complex."

"How do we get there?" Smith asked.

"Exit the car park and follow the signs all the way round. What's going on?"

"I felt the sudden urge to kick a ball around with a whole bunch of other grown men," Smith told him. "Apparently it's *so* much fun."

"You're terrible, Sarge," DC King said back in the car park.

"I just can't see the attraction of football," Smith said.

"You came to the wrong place then. Football is like religion in this country, and people don't appreciate it when you badmouth it."

"Tell someone who cares."

They got back in the car and DC King followed the road round.

"That's more like it," Smith said when he glanced at the outside of the building that housed the indoor football pitch.

Two police cars were parked next to the entrance with their lights flashing. Police tape had been stuck to the bollards in front of the building and uniformed officers were milling around.

"Webber's here," DC King said.

"I'm going to beat him to a crime scene one day, Kerry. If it kills me, I'm going to get there first."

"Good luck with that. How does he do it?"

"I think he has an inbuilt murder detector. It's like a barometer. The man isn't human."

PC Simon Miller greeted them outside the entrance. He informed Smith that nobody had been allowed in or out since the assault, and Smith wasn't surprised. PC Miller was an exceptional police officer.

"The bloke who found him has been told to stick around," he added.

"Good work," Smith said. "Does this place have CCTV?"

PC Miller nodded. "Front and back. PC Griffin is liaising with the security company as we speak. All the cars that come in and out are captured by the cameras too."

"For what it's worth," Smith said. "This guy travels on foot. Is there anything else we need to know?"

"It's not my job – you're the detective, but what I managed to get out of the blokes he was playing football with suggests he was being watched. He told them he was going to grab a quick shower before hitting the pub. It could be that he always does this and the killer was aware of it."

"Do we know how *The Spider* gained access to the showers?" DC King said.

"*The Spider*? You're not telling me..."

"How did he get in?" Smith said. "I believe there was a witness who saw him fleeing the scene."

"There are windows above all the showers," PC Miller said. "We're not sure if he got in that way, but he definitely exited the building through one of them. The witness saw the whole thing."

"Where is this witness now?" Smith said.

"Still here, Sarge. Everyone was asked to remain in the building until they're told otherwise."

"Where's Webber?"

"In the changing rooms," PC Miller said.

Smith's phone started to ring. The ringtone told him it was Whitton. He stepped away to answer it.

"Donna Baron and Zak Lambert have been located," she told him. "But we haven't been able to find Georgia Francis. Brian James's fiancé isn't at home and she's not answering her phone."

"Shit," Smith said. "Brian was the second victim and it's possible *The Spider* has already got to her. Are you sure she's not at home?"

"According to a neighbour, she went out shortly before we arrived, and she hasn't returned."

"Did the neighbour know where she was going?"

"No," Whitton said. "But apparently, Georgia shares the house with another woman, and the neighbour said the housemate always gets home from work around seven-thirty. We're going to wait here for her. Any news on Peter Snow's condition?"

"He's been taken to hospital," Smith said. "And hopefully we'll be able to talk to him soon. I'll keep you updated."

He ended the call and walked back over to DC King. He told her what Whitton had told him.

"If he's watching them," she said. "It means Georgia Francis is in danger, doesn't it?"

"It does," Smith said. "Come on – I'm not leaving here without some answers."

CHAPTER THIRTY FOUR

He wasn't going to get many from Grant Webber. The Head of Forensics found nothing inside the changing rooms that told them any more than what the witness had given them. Peter Snow had been found opposite one of the shower cubicles. He was dressed in just a pair of football shorts, and he was lying breathless and unable to move. Peter had no obvious injuries, and it was only when the paramedics arrived and turned him onto his side that they noticed the deep wound in his lower back. Peter had been uncommunicative, and he hadn't been able to inform them that he no longer had any feeling in his legs. He'd soiled himself and the initial conclusion the paramedics came to was that his spine had been damaged. He was carefully lifted onto a stretcher and taken to the City Hospital.

Forensics didn't find much from the showers, but Billie Jones did spot something that told them the person who had maimed Peter James was definitely the same person who had killed his wife two days earlier. The imprint from the climbing shoe was very familiar to them now. This was the work of *The Spider*.

Smith decided to turn his attention to the witnesses. He wanted to speak to the man who'd seen *The Spider* leave the indoor football centre. Doug Ingram was outside indulging in what he described as a *sneaky smoke* when he spotted the man dropping from one of the windows.

"I know it sort of defeats the object of the exercise," he said. "I mean, why bother to put yourself through a workout if you're only going to undo everything by poisoning your lungs afterwards, but once you're hooked, you're hooked. You probably wouldn't understand."

Smith did understand but he didn't particularly care. He wasn't interested in this.

"Tell us what you saw," he said instead.

"*The Spider*," Doug said without hesitation. "If I'd known he would be here, I would have made sure to have my phone camera ready. Probably could have got a few bob for the picture."

"Describe exactly what you saw?" DC King said.

She sensed that Smith was becoming irritated, and she knew he could be unpredictable with witnesses when that happened.

"I was over by the fire exit next to the indoor pitch. It's usually left open when it's not too cold out. I'd just lit a smoke when I spotted something out of the corner of my eye. I got a closer look, and I saw it was a bloke."

"He escaped out of one of the windows in the changing rooms," Smith said.

"Aye, I figured that much."

"Did you try to stop him?" DC King said.

"What for?" Doug said.

"Perhaps because he was leaving through a window eight feet up in the air," Smith said. "Or is that a regular occurrence here?"

"It wouldn't have made any difference. By the time I knew what was going on he was on the ground and legging it across the grass towards the wall surrounding the centre. He got over it like it wasn't even there. No way I was going to catch someone like that. It was *The Spider*, wasn't it?"

"We can't comment on that," DC King said.

"That's good enough for me. Wait until I tell the lads down the Black Swan."

Smith didn't think Doug Ingram was going to give them anything useful. He told him to stick around until someone had taken a statement from him and went to find some of the people Peter Swan had been playing football with.

The men had been told to stay on the indoor pitch and when Smith and DC King went in there it was clear they weren't happy about it. Most of them were sitting on the benches set out for spectators. Two of the men were kicking a ball around by the net.

"How long do we have to stay here?" one of them asked.

It was a short man with an unfortunate Mullet hairdo.

"I apologise for the inconvenience," Smith lied. "But a serious assault has occurred, and it can't be helped."

"Is Peter going to be alright?" Mullet asked.

"I don't know," Smith said.

"He didn't look too clever when I found him."

This was a tall man with a big beard.

"You were the one who found him?" DC King said.

"We were supposed to be going out for a few pints, and he was taking forever – eating into our drinking time. The name's Colin."

Smith asked Colin to follow them outside. He wanted to talk to him away from his friends.

"How long are we going to be stuck here?" Mullet shouted after them.

Smith didn't give him an answer. He'd taken an instant dislike to the man, and he would make him wait as long as possible.

"What time did you go and check on Peter in the changing rooms?" he asked Colin outside.

"Must have been about quarter to seven."

"Are you sure?"

"Thereabouts," Colin said. "We book the pitch from half-five to half-six every Monday. Peter has a quick shower, and he's usually done in five minutes."

"What did you do while you were waiting for him?' DC King said.

"Not much. Chatted to the lads about football. Nothing memorable."

"How long have you been playing here on a Monday?" Smith said.

"Just over a year now," Colin said.

"So, it's a regular thing?'

"I suppose."

"Would you say you know most of the people who use the centre?"

Colin replied with another, *I suppose*.

"Can you think of anyone who's been hanging around recently?" Smith said. "Someone you hadn't seen before?"

"I don't think so. Has what happened to Peter got something to do with his wife?"

"We think it has," Smith said. "Did you know Mrs Snow?"

"Never met her," Colin said.

"Did Peter ever mention her?" DC King said.

"We don't play football to talk about our wives."

"You're married then?" Smith said.

"Have been for fifteen years. She's a good woman – she doesn't mind me playing football most nights of the week."

"She probably does," Smith said.

"What?"

"I think that's all for now. Just one more question. When you found Peter, did you touch anything in the changing rooms? Did you touch Mr Snow?"

"Are you saying I'm some kind of deviant? Of course I didn't touch him."

"That's all for now," Smith said. "Someone will be along to take a statement shortly."

CHAPTER THIRTY FIVE

Smith's phone started to ring as they were walking back to DC King's car. It was DI Smyth.

"We've just finished at the football centre," Smith told him. "There was a witness who saw *The Spider* getting away, but apart from that we got nothing useful. Is there any news on Peter Snow's condition?"

"The hospital has promised to keep us up to date. Are you still at the sports centre?"

"We were just about to head off."

"Whitton spoke to Georgia Francis's housemate," DI Smyth said. "And she mentioned something about a club Georgia often goes to on a Monday."

"I didn't think any nightclubs were open on Mondays," Smith said.

"This one is. It's a place off Malton Road that appeals to a certain type of clientele."

"Malton Road?" Smith said. "That's not far from where we are now."

"That's why I called."

"What's the name of this club?"

DI Smyth gave it to him. He also told him not to go inside the nightclub until backup was in place. It was possible that *The Spider* was aware of Georgia Francis's Monday routine and he would be waiting for her there.

"I'll bear that in mind, boss," Smith said.

"I'm serious, Smith. You are not to go in until we have the place surrounded. And there's one more thing."

"That's my line," Smith said.

"It's actually Columbo's line. I should probably tell you what kind of nightclub it is."

The first thing that Smith registered was the name. He'd been inside plenty of nightclubs in his time, but the name on the signboard outside the club had to be the most original one he'd ever come across.

"*Release the Bats*," he read.

"It's a Darkwave club, Sarge," DC King said. "I Googled it."

"What's Darkwave when it's at home?" Smith said.

"It's a combination of Industrial, Emo and Goth."

"Creatures of the night?" Smith guessed.

"Something like that. Some of the music is quite good. Places like these have absinthe bars and likeminded folk can get trashed to dark music."

"Sounds lovely. Are these people dangerous?"

DC King laughed. "Not at all. They might look like they're going to drain your blood, but they're generally harmless. It's big business in Europe."

"We've got a photograph of Georgia," Smith said. "But if she's dressed like those two, we've got a problem."

They were opposite the nightclub and two people, Smith wasn't sure if they were men or women were waiting by the entrance to be let in. Both of them were dressed all in black, and their hair was also raven black. One of them turned around to reveal a pale face plastered in black makeup. Smith wondered if these people wore suits to work during the day. He had no idea where the thought came from.

"We might have another problem," he said. "We're not exactly dressed for a place like this, are we?"

He was wearing a pair of blue jeans, and his Led Zeppelin T-shirt was hardly going to go down well in a place like *Release the Bats*. DC King wasn't doing much better. Her jeans and green shirt were hardly Emo attire.

"We'll wing it," she said.

The pounding bass hit Smith as soon as he opened the door. It was a rhythmic thrum and there was something hypnotic about it. The music was repetitive, but it wasn't entirely unpleasant. A man was lamenting about death in a deep baritone. There was nobody behind the door and Smith wondered where they had to pay. The club was almost pitch black and it took him a while for his eyes to adjust to it. The door opened behind them and a man on his own walked past and continued down a short flight of stairs. He paid Smith and DC King no attention.

Smith followed him down with DC King close behind. At the bottom of the staircase was a desk lit up by a dim orange glow. A woman was screaming something to the man in front of them, but the volume of the music meant Smith couldn't hear what she was telling him. He watched as the man lay his hand flat on the desk and let the woman stamp something on it. Then he disappeared into the smoky darkness of the club.

The woman behind the desk looked Smith and DC King up and down and yelled something unintelligible. Smith looked at DC King. She leaned in and shouted in his ear.

"It's ten pounds each."

"Do you have any money?" he screamed back.

Smith rarely carried any cash on him. Whitton was always complaining about it.

DC King took a twenty pound note out of her pocket and handed it to the woman. She allowed her to grab her hand and place it on the table. Smith placed his hand down too. The stamp resembled those used to indicate that bills had been paid and it tickled. Smith looked to see what had been stamped there and saw that it was a bat with its wings outstretched. The woman behind the counter screamed at them once more and once again, Smith had no idea what she was telling them.

A different song was playing when they emerged into the main body of the nightclub. It was a melodic tune, and it wasn't as loud as the first one.

"What did she say before we came in here?" Smith asked.

"I think she knew we hadn't been in here before," DC King said. "She was telling us that we can get one free drink behind the bar if we show the bat on our hands."

"Sounds like a plan. I didn't think it would be this busy so early in the evening."

It wasn't yet eight and Smith estimated there to be at least fifty people there already. Most of them were seated at the tables dotted around the room. A few stood at the bar at the back and some of them were dancing to the strange music.

They walked over to the bar and Smith showed his hand to the barman. He was given a once over in return. The skinny man looked at his T-shirt and made eye contact.

"What can I get you, Led Zeppelin?"

"Beer, I suppose."

Smith had no idea what beer he would find in a place like this, but he doubted there was Theakston on offer.

There wasn't. Two glasses of flat, brown liquid were placed in front of them and Smith dared to take a sip. It tasted like water that had been flavoured with beer, and it had a chemical aftertaste. Smith decided he would stay sober in *Release the Bats*. He suggested they find a table and simply observe for a while.

They found a table far enough away from the speakers to enable them to have a conversation.

"You left your beer at the bar," DC King said.

"I tasted it," Smith said. "I'd rather drink the slobber Theakston leaves behind in his water bowl. Do you think she's here?"

"Her housemate seems to think she will be."

"I don't like this. From an operational perspective, it's hardly ideal. It's dark, the music is blaring, and when you look at what most of these people are wearing, it would be easy to disguise yourself and still blend in."
"What's the plan if we do see her?" DC King said.
"It's possible *The Spider* is here too," Smith said. "He could be any of the people here. He could be doing whatever dance they're doing on the dance floor. I reckon if we do spot Georgia Francis we make as much of a scene as we can. We cause a bit of chaos and get her out of here as soon as possible."

"Speak of the devil," DC King said. "I think that's her."
She nodded in the direction of a figure walking past their table. The woman was wearing purple leggings and a white sleeveless T-shirt. She wasn't wearing any makeup, and she stuck out like a sore thumb in a nightclub full of black clad Goths.
"Something doesn't feel right," Smith said.
"You're talking about her clothes?"
"Follow her," Smith said. "It won't look so suspicious if you follow her."

DC King stood up and started walking towards the woman they believed to be Georgia Francis. She stopped when Georgia stood in front of a door to the side of the bar. The door opened, there was a brief exchange of words and Georgia was allowed inside.
"Shit," DC King cursed, and made her way back to the table.

"I think she works here," she told Smith.
"The housemate didn't mention anything about that," he said.
"She went through a door at the side of the bar, and she was definitely not dressed for a club like this."
"We need to find out where she went," Smith said. "She could be in danger."
"How are we supposed to do that?"
"Knock on the door and ask to see her."

The man who opened the door was not someone you would want to piss off. DC King wasn't short, but this giant had to be at least a foot taller than her, and he was broad with it.

"What?" he said.

"I'm looking for someone," DC King said.

"Good for you," the ape told her.

"I can pay."

"Not here. You want to watch, speak to Janet behind the bar."

With this, the door was slammed in her face.

DC King had no idea what was happening. She walked over to the bar and looked for someone who might be Janet. Three men were busy pouring drinks but there was definitely no Janet.

The same barman as before came over. "What can I get you?"

"I'm looking for Janet," DC King said.

"You're looking at him."

"Oh. I was told to speak to you if I wanted to watch."

"Who told you that?"

"The big bloke behind the door at the side."

"Are you police?"

"Yes," DC King said and grinned.

The barman smiled too.

"How much are you hoping to see?"

DC King had no idea what he meant. "All of it."

"Twenty quid."

DC King paid him and was issued a receipt of sorts. She followed his directions to another part of the club, showed the receipt to another giant of a man and she was allowed inside a room that was completely dark apart from two gaps in a curtain at the back of the room. Slivers of lights were coming in from somewhere behind them. A bench had been placed below the gaps in the curtains and DC King's gut instinct was telling her to get out of there now.

She ignored it. She sat on the bench, and, with her fingers, she opened the gap in the curtain wider.

"Fucking hell."

She got to her feet and raced out of the room.

CHAPTER THIRTY SIX

DC King gave Smith twenty pounds and told him to pay at the bar with the man who'd served their drinks. He met her by the room with the slits in the curtains and he asked her what was going on.

"You have to see it to believe it, Sarge," she said.

They went inside and DC King opened the curtains wide.

"What the fuck," Smith said.

"That's what I thought."

In front of them was a makeshift boxing ring. A man and a woman were squaring up to one another and Smith flinched when the woman landed a blow on the man's chin. He fell to his knees and looked up at her. The expression on his face was confusing. She hit him again and his smile grew. Punch after punch was thrown and soon the man's face was a mess of blood and snot. The woman moved off and turned around. It was Georgia Francis. A song was playing, and it seemed vaguely familiar to Smith. A man was screaming.

Release the bats.

Smith really couldn't remember where he'd heard it before.

"That explains her clothes," he said. "What the fuck is going on out there?"

"I think it's some kind of BDSM," DC King said.

"Which is?"

"In extreme cases, some people pay to suffer physical assault."

"You cannot be serious?"

"That's what I think it is," DC King said. "That bloke looks like he's enjoying it."

"What do you suggest we do?"

"Nothing, Sarge. In terms of the law, it's a grey area and that's not why we're here, is it?"

"We need to stop it," Smith said. "She's going in for another go."

The voice over the speaker was louder now. The man was yelling over screeching guitars.

Horror.

Georgie Francis landed a blow on her opponent's nose. The blood gushed out but the man managed to keep smiling.

Vampire.

Georgia aimed a kick at the man's stomach.

Bat.

The song was reaching its crescendo. The bats had been released, and the singer let the guitars bring the track to its conclusion.

"I have to stop this." Smith said.

He left the room and felt two strong arms on his shoulders.

"Where do you think you're going?"

It was the gorilla who'd let them in.

"The woman out there is in danger," Smith told him.

"From where I'm standing, it looks like she can handle herself pretty well."

"I need to get her out of here," Smith said.

"No fucking likely, pal. She's fully booked for most of the night. We've got a party of ten booked to watch her at nine."

Smith couldn't believe his ears. This was all wrong.

He persuaded the giant ape to release him and went back to rejoin DC King.

"The heavy outside is having none of it," he said. "I'm calling it in."

"She's got another victim," DC King said.

Smith looked at the tatty boxing ring. The man from earlier had been replaced with someone else. The figure had its back to them, and something stirred in the pit of Smith's stomach. Something terrible was about to happen. He watched as Georgia Francis approached her opponent with a malicious grin on her face. She was clearly enjoying this.

She landed a blow on the man's face, but he didn't react. Smith watched as he dodged the next punch and with astonishing agility somehow managed to get behind her. Georgia's smile vanished instantly. She wasn't expecting him to do that. Then her expression changed completely. Her mouth opened wide and the look in her eyes was one of absolute terror. She fell to her knees and, as if in slow motion, she toppled forwards. The man leaned over and pulled the knife out of her lower back. Then he moved closer to her and spoke into her right ear.

"Call in it," Smith yelled.

He looked back out to the boxing ring and gasped. Georgia Francis was alone – the man who Smith knew instinctively was *The Spider* had gone.

Smith felt numb when he stepped outside *Release the Bats* into the fresh air. His hands were shaking as he struggled to light a cigarette. An alert had gone out, and every available police officer in the city was on the lookout for the man who'd stabbed Georgia Francis, but Smith didn't hold out much hope. He knew for a fact that *The Spider* was long gone. Nobody had seen him leave the nightclub, and Smith wondered if they were ever going to catch him.

"What the hell happened in there?" It was DI Smyth.

Smith didn't know what to tell him. The entire operation was a balls-up of biblical proportions. He and DC King had stood by and watched the most proficient serial killer they'd ever come across attack a woman they were there to protect.

"We fucked up, boss," Smith said.

"That's the understatement of the year," DI Smyth said.

"I had no idea what was happening. I didn't know that this sort of thing went on in this day and age. People actually pay to get the shit kicked out of them, and other people pay to watch it. Georgia Francis was there to fulfil the desires of the sick bastards who get off on violence. Why didn't you tell me what sort of hellhole you were sending us into?"

"I had no idea," DI Smyth said. "I thought *Release the Bats* was simply an alternative nightclub – I didn't know it was a front for the other thing."

"*The other thing*?" Smith said. "What kind of sick world do we live in when people get aroused by someone punching them in the face? It's a world I really don't want to live in anymore."

"You need to calm down."

"I'm done," Smith said. "I'm done with this shit. Someone else can clean up the filth on the streets of this cesspool of a city from now on."

"Grow up."

Smith's cigarette flew out of his mouth. DI Smyth's words had stung.

"Go home," DI Smyth said.

"Where are the other two?" Smith asked. "Where are Zak Lambert and Donna Baron?"

"They're safe," DI Smyth told him. "We've got them both at the station."

"I want to speak to them."

"You'll do no such thing. You've had a shitty night, and you need to go home."

"I need to do something," Smith said.

"You need to go home. We'll talk about this tomorrow."

"We fucked up," Smith said. "I fucked up. I really had no idea."

"We'll deal with it in the morning," DI Smyth said. "We'll fix it."

Smith picked up his cigarette and took a drag. It had gone out, and he didn't bother relighting it.

CHAPTER THIRTY SEVEN

Smith woke from a dream about bats. Inky wings were covering his mouth and nose, suffocating him. The dream had a smell to it – a putrid stench that Smith could still detect when he opened his eyes. It was the reek of decay and death.

Whitton wasn't in the bed next to him and Smith wondered what the time was. He got out of bed, dressed and did what he needed to do in the bathroom. He went downstairs to find a hot cup of coffee on the table for him. He took a sip.

"I needed that."

"How are you doing?" Whitton said.

"Confused," Smith said. "What me and Kerry witnessed in that club last night didn't seem real. I thought I'd seen depravity on every level, but that shit was totally new to me. People pay to get the crap kicked out of them."

"We live in a sick world."

"Where are the girls?"

"Still in bed. Darren has offered to walk them to school. Oh, and this arrived yesterday afternoon."

She handed him an A4 envelope. The first thing Smith noticed was the large *Registered Mail* sticker on the top.

"We weren't home," Whitton said. "But Lucy signed for it."

"Let me guess," Smith said. "Robert Rogers?"

"Got it in one. It's an official letter from his lawyer."

"Throw it in the bin where it belongs."

"This isn't going to go away, Jason. The contents of that envelope mean that a process has been set in motion."

"What does it say?" Smith said.

"You need to read it."

"I can't remember where I left my glasses."

"We're obliged to respond," Whitton said. "Robert Rogers has lodged a formal request to re-open the adoption order application."

"He's bluffing," Smith said. "That order cannot be undone."

"His lawyer seems to believe it can."

"It's part of his bluff. Anyone can pay fifty quid to get a lawyer to draft a letter. We've got bigger things to worry about."

"Bigger than losing Fran?"

"It's not going to happen," Smith said.

"What do you suggest we do?"

"A bluff only works if your opponent falls for it. We'll call his bluff and take it from there."

"What's a bluff?" Laura had come into the kitchen.

"It's when someone lies to get what they want," Smith said.

"Timothy Green did that."

"The Australian kid?" Smith said.

Laura nodded. "On cupcake day, he lied and said he hadn't had one yet, but he had."

"The sneaky little bastard," Smith said.

"Jason," Whitton warned.

"That's not exactly a bluff," Smith said. "That's what's known as a little white lie. Did he get his hands on another cupcake?"

"No," Laura said. "Brian Finch saw him eat the first one and told Mrs King he was talking shit."

Smith started to laugh.

"Laura," Whitton said. "Language. Go up and get yourself ready for school."

"That's my girl," Smith said when she'd gone.

"How many times have I told you about your language in front of the girls?" Whitton said.

Smith smiled.

"It's not funny," Whitton said.

"It is a bit funny," Smith said. "Go on – admit it."

"Alright," Whitton said. "It's slightly amusing. Are we going to catch this creature?"

"We're going to catch him."

"What time is the press conference?" Whitton said.

"Shit," Smith said. "I'd forgotten all about that. No doubt the vultures will have got wind of the debacle at *Release the Bats* last night. We dropped the ball there."

"You weren't to know what was going to happen."

"We knew exactly what was going to happen," Smith said. "We were there to stop him, but we failed miserably. We should have grabbed Georgia as soon as we spotted her. Heads are going to roll because of this. I'll be lucky to come away with my job intact."

"It won't come to that."

"It could. I'm going to have a quick shower," Smith said. "I smell like bats."

Whitton was accustomed to the weird things that came out of her husband's mouth, and she paid his latest one no heed. Instead, she turned her attention to the letter that had arrived by registered post. Robert Rogers' lawyer was informing them that a petition to the courts to reopen the adoption order application had been set in motion. They were being given the opportunity to oppose the petition, and mediation had been suggested as a first resort.

Whitton thought about this. She knew that Smith would never consider what the lawyer was suggesting. Smith would sooner fight Fran's biological father in court than sit down with the man to discuss a possible compromise, and Whitton couldn't see any way around it. There was no way that Smith was going to allow Robert Rogers back into Fran's life, no matter how convincing his arguments were. Smith simply wouldn't allow it to happen.

Whitton's thoughts were interrupted by the sound of the front door. Darren Lewis came in and asked if the girls were ready. Right on cue, Laura and Fran came in. Both girls were dressed in their school uniforms and Laura had her jumper on back to front and inside out. Whitton didn't ask her to put it on properly.

CHAPTER THIRTY EIGHT

"We've got good news and bad news from the hospital," DI Smyth began the morning briefing. "Peter Snow's condition is serious, but he's stable. We can confirm that his spinal column was severed at the base and the damage is irreversible. Mr Snow will spend the rest of his life in a wheelchair."

"Is he totally paralysed?" Smith said.

"He has no feeling from the waist down."

"Bloody hell," Bridge said.

"Mr Snow suffered a single knife wound to his lower back," DI Smyth said. "But one stab was enough."

"*The Spider* knew exactly what he was doing," Smith said.

"It appears that he did, especially in light of Georgia Francis's injuries. Her attack was a carbon copy of Peter Snow's – a single laceration to the base of the spine. Miss Francis will never walk again."

"Have either of them said anything?" Smith said.

"We haven't been allowed anywhere near them," DI Smyth said. "As soon as that changes, we'll be informed but it's not going to be any time soon."

"If we follow the logical sequence," Smith said. "Donna Baron will be next."

"Correct," DI Smyth said. "Donna's husband was the third victim, and *The Spider* is working to a strict agenda. Unfortunately for him, Donna is safely tucked away here at the station."

"Don't underestimate this bastard, boss," Smith said. "He's not going to let a building full of police officers stop him."

"Security measures at the station have been ramped up," DI Smyth said. "Nobody will be allowed inside without being thoroughly vetted."

"With respect," Smith said. "He's not likely to come in through the front door. That's not how he operates. The man can climb walls like a fucking spider. If breaking and entering was an Olympic sport he would win gold without breaking into a sweat. We need to move them somewhere else – somewhere he won't think to look in a million years."

"Have you seen what the York Post put out this morning?" DC Moore said out of the blue.

"Who cares?" Smith said.

"You need to read it, Sarge," DC Moore said. "The general consensus is that public opinion is swinging in *The Spider's* favour. The Post has latched onto his motive and he's actually garnering a lot of public sympathy."

"You know how I feel about public opinion, Harry," Smith said. "The average man in the street is an idiot, and I will not let the press dictate how I conduct an investigation."

"You haven't forgotten about your meeting with the press liaison officer, have you?" DI Smyth said.

"It's in my diary, boss."

"Good, because when I hear you make statements like that one, it's clear that you need a hell of a lot of coaching before you stand in front of the men and women of the fourth estate."

"Do we have any idea who the rat is?" Bridge said.

"My money is still on PC Griffin," DC Moore said. "I've never liked that bloke."

"He is an acquired taste," Smith said. "But it wasn't him."

"How can you be so sure?" DC Moore said.

"I just know. I also know that there will be no more surprises where the York Post is concerned."

"Is there something you're not telling us?" DI Smyth said.

"Yes," Smith replied. "But what's done is done, and it's not going to happen again."

DI Smyth eyed him suspiciously, but he didn't press the matter.

Smith's appointment with PC Walker was at ten, and that was in an hour. He wanted to speak to Donna Baron before then. He told DI Smyth as much. "Mrs Baron disappeared to her brother's before we arrived at the scene of her husband's murder," he said. "And she's been reluctant to talk to us since then. I want to know why that is."

"Her reaction was a perfectly normal one," DI Smyth said. "She was probably in shock, and she sought comfort at her brother's house."

"When someone refuses to talk, it makes me suspicious, boss. She's right here at the station, and I want to ask her a few questions, that's all. It'll just be a quick chat."

"OK," DI Smyth said. "Do it off the record, and if you think there's something she's not telling us, we'll get her in an interview room."

Smith smoked a quick cigarette outside in the car park first. He wondered what extra security measures had been put in place when he went back inside. Baldwin was speaking to someone on the phone behind the desk. PC Miller and PC Griffin were deep in conversation off to the side and Smith walked past them all without them giving him a second glance. He walked down the corridor and stopped. He turned around and headed back to the front desk.

"Did any of you see me?"

Baldwin looked at him. "Sarge?"

"What about you two?" Smith said to the PCs Miller and Griffin.

"You went outside," PC Griffin said. "And you came back in five minutes later, stinking of smoke."

"You stopped, halfway down the corridor," PC Millier said. "And you came back. Is something up?"

"No," Smith said. "Nothing at all. As you were."

He didn't need to see their facial expressions. He could guess what they were thinking. He wondered if he was being overly paranoid. He decided that he was, but it was necessary.

Donna Baron was sitting on the bed in one of the holding cells, and it was clear that she wasn't happy about it. The door wasn't locked, but the cells were not designed with creature comforts in mind. The bed was hard and uncomfortable, and the cell had a smell to it that was impossible to ignore. Smith went in and asked her if she needed anything.

"You can't keep me locked up like this."

Smith thought she looked to be in her late thirties. Her face was pale, and her black hair only accentuated it. Her eyes were dark blue, and they were rimmed with red. It was clear that she hadn't slept much recently.

"I apologise for the inconvenience," Smith said. "But, until we're able to make further arrangements for you, this is for your own protection."

"I don't need protecting," Donna said.

Smith detected a trace of an accent. Donna wasn't from York.

"Where's that accent from?" he asked her.

"Birmingham. When will I be allowed to go home?"

"I'm going to be honest with you, Donna," Smith said. "Is it alright if I call you Donna?"

"Call me what you like. I just want to go home."

"Your husband was the third victim of the most gifted serial killer I've ever seen," Smith said. "And I've seen a few. This man is extremely dangerous and he's fiercely driven. I've never come across determination like it. He absolutely must finish what he's started, without exception."

"If you're trying to scare me, I can save you the bother. I'm not someone who scares easily."

"You need to be afraid of this man," Smith said. "Because he will attack you if he gets the chance. He won't kill you, but he'll leave you so severely maimed that you'll wish he had. Are you listening to me?"

Donna didn't reply. She rubbed her eyes and sighed.

"Why is he doing this?" she asked.

"We don't know all the details," Smith admitted. "But we do know that you are next on his list."

"How do you know that?"

"Because he's already carried out the attacks on the people closest to the first two victims. Neither of them will ever walk again. This is serious."

"What do you want from me?"

"I want you to appreciate the gravity of the threat to you. I'm not trying to scare you – I'm telling you how it is. We tried to contact you on numerous occasions, but you went to great lengths to avoid us. Why did you do that?"

"I needed some time to process what had happened."

"I don't believe you," Smith said.

"It's the truth."

"OK," Smith said. "You found George when you returned from a business trip, is that right?"

"I was in Shanghai," Donna said.

"What were you doing there?"

"We have an office there. We export goods from China."

"Are you often out of the country?" Smith said.

"Probably half of the year."

"How did George feel about that?"

"He was fine with it," Donna said. "He knew what he was getting himself into when he married me. Why are you asking me about my job."

"Did George ever voice concerns about your extended absences?"

"Never. And if he had done, I would have done something about it. We had a happy marriage."

"Hmm," Smith said.

"What's that supposed to mean?"

"Did you know that your husband was a member on a Facebook support group?" Smith asked.

"*You're not Alone*," Donna said without hesitation.

"You knew about it?"

"Of course. George and I don't have secrets."

"That group was set up so victims could talk about their experiences," Smith said. "It's for people who have suffered in their lives. If George was so happy, why would he be in a group like that?"

"He's in a few of them," Donna said. "And I fully support him. I've seen that they help. It took me years to fully understand what he went through."

"I don't understand what you're saying."

"George had a terrible childhood," Donna said. "From the age of three, George was sexually abused by his father on a daily basis. It carried on until he left home when he was sixteen."

For once, Smith was unable to find any words. This was not what he was expecting to hear.

He managed eventually.

"The bastard is still out there," Donna said. "That monster should be locked away for good, but he's still free. George had nobody to tell. He was stuck in a permanent hell and sometimes I wonder if he's still there."

"I'm so sorry about that," Smith said.

"We were good together," Donna said. "George told me I was the only person he's ever been able to talk about it with. We loved each other."

Smith was beginning to understand that now. He also knew that Donna Baron was not the next intended victim of *The Spider*, but he needed it confirmed.

"Do you know if George talked about the abuse on the *You're not Alone* group?"

"That's why he was on there," Donna said. "He wasn't the only one it had happened to. That's what the group is all about, isn't it – you're not alone?"

"I need the name of George's father."

"You think he's in danger, don't you?"

"I do," Smith confirmed.

"Good," Donna said. "In that case, you can go to hell. That bastard deserves everything he's got coming to him."

CHAPTER THIRTY NINE

It wasn't difficult to track down George Baron's father, even without Donna's help. Norman Baron owned a house in Heworth. He'd lived there for thirty-five years, and a car had been dispatched to his address as soon as his identity became known. Smith didn't think it was going to help. George's sixty-year-old father had already met *The Spider*.

He cursed himself for not looking into the details of George Baron's reason for joining the Facebook group. It was a mistake they shouldn't have made, and it was just another error in a long line of them. The *Spider* investigation had been riddled with mistakes, and Smith wondered if he was going to add to the list during the press conference that was due to take place shortly. He voiced his concerns with Neil Walker.

"You can't afford to think like that," the press liaison officer told him.
"*The Spider* is running rings around us," Smith said. "He's making us look like fools."
"From what I've gathered," PC Walker said. "What we've seen with *The Spider* is unprecedented."
"It certainly is. I don't know how we're going to beat someone like this."
"The press conference can help."
"How?"
"Firstly," PC Walker said. "You need to stop looking at press conferences as though they're the enemy. They're really not, and they can be extremely useful in cases like this."
"I'm not a big fan of the press."
"This isn't about the press. It's more about how the public can help."
"I'm not too keen on the general public either," Smith said.
PC Walker sighed and shook his head.

"What I'm suggesting is unorthodox," he said. "In the past, we've tended to err on the side of caution where information is concerned, but I suggest we don't do that today."

"Are you suggesting we give the public more than we usually do?"

"We give them everything," PC Walker said. "Absolute transparency, if you like."

"You're the expert."

"I'm by no means an expert, but I do have an understanding about how the general public think en masse. We're dealing with a killer who's driven by something more than we usually see. Is that correct?"

"We don't know what's driving him yet," Smith said. "But it's something big enough to make him think his actions are justified."

"He murders the victims and then he punishes the people responsible for their misery. In doing that, he's gaining a certain amount of sympathy from the public."

"That makes no sense whatsoever," Smith said. "He's murdering people whose only crime is to end up as a victim. How can anyone sympathise with someone like that?"

"The murders are forgotten about when the subsequent attacks on the people close to the victims come to light. That's the fickle nature of journalism. In general, the public are easily manipulated, and opinions can swing in an instant. That's what we need to do today."

"I'm not the right bloke for the job," Smith said.

"You're the only bloke for the job," PC Walker said. "And I can only work with what I've been given. It's not ideal, but I'm stuck with you."

"Thanks," Smith said. "How are we going to play this?"

PC Walker spent the next thirty minutes explaining it and by the time they were finished, Smith almost believed that it would help. Almost – he wasn't absolutely sure, but beggars couldn't be choosers and right now, he was willing to grab at any scraps that came his way.

Smith's gut feeling was confirmed soon after he left PC Walker's office. Bridge informed him that Norman Baron had indeed become another victim of *The Spider*. George's abusive father had been in the garden when he was attacked. His spine had been severed at the base, and he was never going to be able to use his legs again. A neighbour had witnessed the attack, but the details were still unclear.

"So, that leaves one," Bridge said.
"Zak Lambert," Smith said. "Regardless of what kind of scumbag he is, he needs round the clock protection. We've messed up throughout this investigation, and we have a chance to get this one right. We need Mr Lambert guarded twenty-four seven."
"It can be arranged. What's the plan for the press conference?"
Smith told him.

"It's risky," Bridge said. "Especially if we're to stand any chance of drawing *The Spider* out into the open."
"PC Walker seems to think it'll work," Smith said. "And he's the expert on press conferences."
"He's going to come for Zak Lambert, isn't he?"
"Of that, there is little doubt," Smith said. "But we can make it extremely difficult for him. Unless…"
"I hate it when you say that."
"Something just came to me."
"No shit, Sherlock," Bridge said. "You've got that disturbing psycho look on your ugly mug again."
"I might have a plan, and you're the one who gave it to me."
"I have no idea what you're going on about."

"You mentioned drawing him out into the open," Smith said. "We have the ideal carrot right here."

"Are you thinking what I think you're thinking?"

"Zak Lambert," Smith said. "We're going to use the philandering bastard as bait."

CHAPTER FORTY

Smith had always despised press conferences. In his opinion, the only purpose they served was to blindside the general public into believing an investigation was progressing faster than it actually was. He had no time for the fourth estate, and his sentiment where the general public were concerned rarely changed. He was deadly serious when he said the average man in the street was an idiot. That was just the way of the world and Smith didn't think it was going to change any time soon.

He was surprised when he was informed that this was going to be a press conference with a difference. The press liaison officer had hand picked a select number of guests, and the attendance was expected to be a lot smaller than usual. Smith wasn't sure if this was a good or a bad thing.

He had five minutes before it was due to start and PC Walker wanted to have a quick run through what they'd discussed earlier. Smith still had his doubts.

"You do realise that if we do this," he said. "We're going to have every nutjob and timewaster in the city hounding us?"

"It can't be helped," PC Walker said. "We have specially trained officers who will be able to sift through the irrelevant info. Somebody must know who this man is – his actions thus far have hardly been subtle."

Smith agreed. "He's trained extensively to reach the level of fitness he's achieved. And from what I've seen so far, the parkour community is a small one. We could get lucky there."

"Just follow the script we discussed earlier and you'll be fine."

Smith counted roughly a dozen people in the large conference room, and it felt somewhat deserted. He'd debated whether to move the press conference to the smaller room, but there was a big difference between transparency and *transparency*, and there were details on the whiteboard in the room where they held their briefings that he definitely didn't want the press to see. That would be taking things a bit too far.

"Good morning," Smith said into the microphone.

A man in the front row laughed rather loudly.

"That doesn't exactly fill us with confidence," he said. "He can't even tell the time."

Smith didn't rise to the bait. He made eye contact with the man and held it for a few seconds.

"I have more important things on my mind than the time," he said. "As you can probably understand.

The man opened his mouth, but no words came out.

There were a number of cameras pointed in his direction, but Smith pretended they weren't there.

"The Spider," he said. "Is like no killer we've ever seen before. In fact, I don't believe there has been a serial killer like him anywhere on earth. He moves with incredible agility and he kills quickly. He's murdered four people in the space of a few days, and he's also succeeded in maiming three more victims. How do we catch a man like this?"

"Are you asking us?" It was a woman sitting in the second row.

"I'm thinking out loud," Smith said. "I do that a lot. Someone must know who this man is. You do not achieve the level of fitness he's achieved overnight – it will have taken years of training. He can scale heights, very few people would even consider tackling. Where did he learn to do that?'

The silence inside the room was unsettling but Smith had the full attention of everyone inside the room.

"We've moved into a new era of murder," Smith said.

This part was all PC Walker's brainwave and Smith had been reluctant to go along with it.

"We've moved past the days where a killer would select a victim by watching them on the streets. Those days are long gone. We've reached an age where the hunt is no longer carried out in a physical manner. A predator can do all of his stalking in the safety of his home. Social media has become the perfect hunting ground, and very few of us are aware of the dangers it poses."

"That's a bit dramatic, isn't it?" It was the loudmouth who'd pointed out Smith's inability to tell the time.

"It's fact," Smith told him. "This is how *The Spider* operates. All of his victims were members of one particular Facebook group."

A few hands were raised. A man with huge ears spoke up.

"Do you have the details of this Facebook group?"

"I can't go into the details," Smith said.

"Why not?"

"Because it's a crucial part of an ongoing investigation."

"Why did you even mention it then?"

"I can't comment on that."

"Is he going to kill again?" big ears asked.

"It's very possible that he will," Smith confirmed. "And that's why I'm asking for your help. Somebody must know who this man is. His athletic ability aside, we believe that he is IT savvy and he is fiercely driven."

"What would you say to him if he's out there, watching this?" A woman at the back asked.

Smith knew she wasn't a journalist. He'd spoken to her briefly before the press conference. This had been PC Walker's idea too. Her name was Jemma Pratt, and her sole purpose was to steer the narrative in the direction that PC Walker wanted it to go in.

"If he's watching this," Smith said. "I would urge him to stop. Whatever it is that's motivating him to commit these horrendous crimes, his victims are blameless. We believe he was a victim himself at one stage. Something happened to him that changed him and turned him into what he is today."

"Are you suddenly a shrink?" Big ears said.

"I don't claim to be a qualified psychologist," Smith said. "But I have learned a bit about the psyche of serial killer over the years."

"Whatever. Could you stick to the detective work and leave the head shrinking to the experts."

"I'll do that," Smith said. "I'd like to introduce you to an expert in the field. Dr Vennell."

CHAPTER FORTY ONE

Smith had been reluctant to agree to this too. PC Walker had suggested that Dr Vennel be a part of the press conference and Smith had no problem with that. What he was unsure about was the dramatic entrance. He reckoned it was a bit over the top, but PC Walker had insisted that it would carry more weight if the press weren't expecting it.

Dr Vennell looked every bit the professional in a smart black jacket and trousers. The makeup she was wearing was subtle, but even without it Smith knew she would still be strikingly attractive. She offered him a smile and sat down next to him.
"Are you OK?" she whispered.
"I will be when this circus is over," Smith told her.
He shifted the microphone, so it was in front of her.

"Good afternoon," she said. "My name is Dr Fiona Vennell and I'm a psychologist. If you have any questions, I'll try to answer them when I'm finished. Before I begin, I want to say that my findings are by no means conclusive. My purpose here is simply to give you an insight into how I believe the man York Police are looking for thinks. Psychological profiles are, in general rarely accurate and I can only work with the information at my disposal, but I can tell you a number of things straight away."
Smith's phone started to ring. He'd forgotten to turn it off for the duration of the press conference. A glance at the screen told him it was Bridge. He rejected the call and switched the phone to silent. He mouthed a silent *sorry* to Dr Vennell.

"The man the city has dubbed *The Spider* is between twenty and thirty," she said. "His level of physical fitness suggests this. The dedication necessary to reach such a high level suggests a fiercely determined individual. He is driven and he's not distracted easily. From a social perspective, he'll be somewhat of a loner."

This earned her a few sniggers from the people in front of her. Dr Vennell knew why – the loner serial killer cliché was an old one, but she remained undeterred.

"The method he uses to select his victims is interesting," she continued. "And somewhat paradoxical. He chooses them from a social media support group. His victims are all victims themselves and therein lies the paradox. If I were to delve deeper into his psyche, I would probably reach the conclusion that he suffers from some form of PTSD. He has been hurt and the emotions he's suffered as a result of this trauma have manifested into something deeper and more sinister. Simply put, I believe he's carrying out these murders in an attempt to alleviate his own pain. I've barely scratched the surface, and there is simply no quick diagnosis in psychology. Any questions?"

"How do we catch him?" Smith spoke the words before his brain could stop him.

"You're more qualified to answer that question than I am," Dr Vennell said. A subtle shake of her head told Smith he should shut up.

"What turned him into what he is today?" the man with the elephant ears asked.

"It's difficult to say with absolute certainty," Dr Vennell said. "It could be something that happened to him when he was a child, or it could be a recent event that triggered a change in him."

"It's usually childhood stuff, isn't it?" big ears said.

"Very often, yes. Very few serial killers are born that way. Something almost always happens to them that causes them to kill."

"The people he's killed have all been victims in one way or another," a woman who'd remained silent up until now said. "And once he's killed them, he goes after the people responsible for that. Why does he leave these people alive?"

"He severely maims them," Smith said. "He's made sure that three people will never be able to walk again."

"OK. Why does he do that? Dr Vennell?"

"By leaving them alive," Dr Vennell said. "It's possible he believes he's punishing them in the worst possible way. He's leaving them to live with the guilt and that could be considered a fate worse than death. As for the mutilation, it could be he simply wants to add to their suffering. Perhaps he believes that by leaving them paralysed, he's ensuring that their pain is concentrated elsewhere. He's damning them to a life of misery, and one cannot imagine what kind of hell these people will have to live with."

"Can we go back to the ones he kills?" big ears said. "The details from the crime scenes were vague, but he covered his victims up after he killed them, didn't he?"

"I can't comment on that," Dr Vennell said.

"I can," Smith said. "And you're correct. All four victims were covered with a sheet afterwards."

"Why do you think he did that?"

"I believe he wanted to demonstrate remorse, and he wanted to give them some respect. Their murders were necessary – nothing more, nothing less. He took no pleasure in killing them."

Big ears nodded thoughtfully. "Going back to a previous question – how do you plan on catching him?"

"The same way we've caught all the others," Smith said. "By never giving up. York CID has the finest team of detectives in the country, and we will not stop until we've caught this man. He will kill again. Of that there is little doubt, but we will catch him."

"I believe you."

This took Smith by surprise.

"Are there any more questions?" he said. "A press pack has been prepared, and we're giving you a lot more than we usually do. In there, you'll find times and dates and information that York CID would like you to make the public aware of. Once again, I'm asking for your help. Someone must know who this man is. The number to call with any information will be distributed shortly. This is your city, and if we work together, we can make it safe again."

He got up and headed for the door. The closing statement had made him cringe as soon as the words had left his mouth, and he wished he could go back in time and delete it. He ignored the questions that were fired at him as he walked and left the large conference room.

Bridge was outside waiting for him. He looked extremely annoyed.
"What's wrong with you?" Smith said.
"Why didn't you answer your phone?" Bridge said.
"Why do you think? I was in the middle of a press conference. What's wrong?"
"What's wrong," Bridge said. "Is the next victim of *The Spider* has done a runner."
"You have got to be kidding?"
"I wish I was. Zak Lambert has gone, and nobody knows where he went."

CHAPTER FORTY TWO

"I had no grounds to hold him."
Jack Finch was used to Smith's temper, and he wasn't going to be bullied now. The seasoned duty sergeant had grown a thick skin over the years, and it took more than an irate Australian to rattle him.
"You were told to keep him here," Smith said. "You've all but sent him out to the slaughter."
"I'm not scared of you, Smith," Sergeant Finch said. "I've done nothing wrong."
"You've led a man straight into the hands of the worst serial killer this city has ever seen. Where have you been for the past week?"
"He was not under arrest. Do you want me to write this down for you?"
"I left my glasses at home," Smith said.
"Then I'll say it slowly. Mr Lambert was not under arrest. We had no grounds to hold him, and I didn't have the authorisation to keep him if he didn't want to be here."
"Alright," Bridge said. "Did he say where he was going?"
"He didn't and he was under no obligation to tell me."
Sergeant Finch folded his arms and held up his chin.
"You're a fucking idiot," Smith informed him.
"And you're lucky I'm in a good mood," Sergeant Finch said. "Otherwise, I could end your career with one carefully written complaint. I've done nothing wrong. Mr Lambert chose to leave, and there wasn't a thing I could do about it."
Bridge took hold of Smith's shoulder. "Come on. We'll find him – he can't have gone far."
"You need to work on your anger management issues," Sergeant Finch said.

"I wouldn't have to," Smith said. "If the people I worked with weren't such incompetent dickheads."

"Don't push me now."

"It's not worth it," Bridge said to Smith. "We'll find him."

"What an arsehole," Smith said outside in the car park.

"He was right," Bridge said. "We had no legal grounds to keep Zak Lambert. Sergeant Finch's hands were tied."

"He should have informed us. He was aware of the risks of letting Zak leave."

"Leave it," Bridge said. "Our focus needs to be on locating Mr Lambert. But even if we do find him, we can't do much unless he wants us too."

"What about an Osman Warning?" Smith said.

"You need to keep up to date with the terminology," Bridge told him. "It's called a TTL now – *Threat to Life*. And it still doesn't help if the individual in question refuses to acknowledge it. All we can do is offer advice. A TTL does not give us extra powers."

"Fuck it. Zak Lambert knew he was in grave danger. He can't ignore the facts. Why did he run off like that?"

"We know what car he drives," Bridge said. "And we'll check to see if he's at home, but I reckon he'll be hiding out somewhere else. Somewhere he believes *The Spider* won't find him."

"*The Spider* will find him," Smith said. "That fucker has some kind of sixth sense."

"Spidey sense," Bridge said.

"That is not funny."

The grin spread across Smith's face and then he started to laugh. It was raucous laughter, and it felt good. It lasted for quite some time and stopped just as abruptly as it had started.

"Have you quite finished?" Bridge said.

"I should apologise to Sergeant Finch, shouldn't I?"

"He'll have forgotten about it already. You know what he's like."

"We've just lost our best hope of catching *The Spider*," Smith said.

"Perhaps it's for the best."

"How do you figure that out?" Smith said.

"If we did go ahead with your hairbrained scheme to use Zak Lambert as bait and it went tits-up, the consequences don't bear thinking about."

"It would have worked. It can still work. We can track him via his phone."

"Not without reasonable grounds," Bridge pointed out.

"What the fuck is wrong with the legal system in this country? A man is in grave danger, and we're not allowed to do anything about it because it goes against his rights as a citizen. I'm going to speak to Baldwin."

"Don't do anything stupid."

"Baldwin knows people," Smith said.

"That's what I'm worried about."

Smith found Baldwin behind the front desk. She didn't appear to be busy, so he asked her to come outside with him.

"Someone has to keep an eye on the desk," she said.

It took Smith less than a minute to find that someone. PC Angie Bowler was more than happy to oblige. Smith reckoned she owed him after the thing with the York Post.

"What is it?" Baldwin asked.

Smith took out his cigarettes and lit one.

"I suppose you heard about Zak Lambert doing a runner."

"I did."

"I need to find him," Smith said. "I need to find him before *The Spider* finds him. We can track his phone. I know you know someone who can help us."

Baldwin nodded. "Leave it with me."

"Do you know his number."

Another nod. "We got his details when he was brought it. You're sure about this, aren't you?"

"A hundred percent," Smith said. "Thanks Baldwin. And I won't ask where you get your info from."

"If I told you, I'd have to kill you."

"How long are we talking about?"

"If the phone's switched on I can have a rough area pretty soon," Baldwin said. "If he answers the phone when I call it, I'll be able to narrow it down to a more accurate location."

Smith took a long drag of his cigarette and watched her walk away. He really didn't know how she'd managed to acquire such useful contacts and he'd never asked. It was better for everyone not to know. His phone started to ring, and the screen told him it wasn't someone stored in his list of contacts.

He answered it. "Smith."

"I don't know if you remember me." It was a woman. "My name is Sharon Billing. We met at the climbing wall in Murton."

"I remember you."

"You asked me to call you if I saw that bloke again," Sharon said. "The one you think is *The Spider*."

"Go on."

"I'm looking at him now."

"Where are you?" Smith said.

"Badger Hill."

Smith could feel his face heating up.

"Hold on a second," he said.

He raced inside the station.

He covered the phone with his hand.

"I want as many bodies as possible over to this address in Badger Hill," he said to PC Bowler.
He gave her the address.
"Do it now," he added and went back outside.
"What can you see?" he asked Sharon Billing.
"It's definitely the same man I saw by Water End."
"What's he doing?"
"He's just lingering by the house," Sharon said. "No, he's opening the gate."
"Help is on the way," Smith said. "I need you to get away from the house. Is there a car in the driveway?"
"A black Mercedes."
"Okay," Smith said. "Move away from the house and try to be as casual as possible."
"Hold on," Sharon said.
"What is it?"
"Shit, I think he's seen me."
"Get away from there."
"He's definitely seen me," Sharon said. "He's walking over to me."
The drone on the other end of the line told him that she'd hung up.

CHAPTER FORTY THREE

"There was nobody at the house," DI Smyth said.

It had been the most stressful ten minutes of Smith's life. Two cars had gone to Zak Lambert's house in Badger Hill – the car Sharon Billing had described was indeed parked in the driveway, but Zak was nowhere to be seen. He wasn't inside the house and there was no sign of him outside. Sharon had also disappeared. Smith had tried calling her but each time he was informed that the person he was trying to contact was not available at present.

"I was positive we were close to catching him," Smith said. "Do you mind if I smoke?"

"Since when have I allowed smoking in my office?" DI Smyth said.

"Fair enough. He was there, boss. *The Spider* went to Zak Lambert's house."

"Are you sure this young woman can be trusted?"

"Why would she lie to me?" Smith said. "And when you think about it, where is the most logical place for *The Spider* to look for Zak first? His house, of course. I think *The Spider* was there and he got spooked when he realised that Sharon was acting strange. This bloke is not stupid."

"We need to bring her in," DI Smyth said.

"I'm aware of that, but it's easier said than done. All I have for her is a phone number and she's not answering. Damn it – we were so fucking close."

"If Zak Lambert isn't at home," DI Smyth said. "Where else would he go?"

"One of his floozies, perhaps," Smith said. "Something is bugging me about that phone call from Sharon Billing."

"What was she doing in Badger Hill?"

"Something like that. I didn't get the chance to ask her. It's quite a coincidence, don't you think?"

"And I know how much you love coincidences. What are you thinking?"

"It's a bit convenient for me," Smith said. "Not long after Zak Lambert decides to leave, I get a call from another parkour junkie claiming to have seen *The Spider*. Shit like that just doesn't happen. What if *The Spider* isn't working alone?"

"You're clutching at straws again."

"Are you sure I can't smoke in here?"

"Absolutely not," DI Smyth said. "If you want to pollute your lungs, you can do it away from me."

"I'll do that then," Smith said. "I need to think."

This was an understatement. It had been a hell of a day, and it was about to get even stranger. A figure approached at speed from the direction of the main road and when she got closer Smith recognised her. It was the young woman he'd spoken to at the climbing wall. Sharon Billing was running like her life depended on it. She stopped when she spotted Smith and he waited for her to get her breath back.

It didn't take long. She let out a long sigh and looked at him.

"Are you alright?" Smith asked.

"I ran all the way here."

"From Badger Hill?"

Sharon nodded. "I thought he was going to kill me."

"What happened?"

"When he started to walk over, I legged it. He chased after me and that's when I lost my phone. I managed to hop over the Travelodge and make it onto Hull Road."

"Hop over the Travelodge?" Smith repeated.

"It's not difficult. It has overhangs on the first-floor windows and balconies on the second floor. I got onto the roof, but he was still behind me. I really thought I was going to die. I ran across the roof and jumped down. That's when I lost him. He didn't follow me down, but I still ran. I ran the entire length of Hull Road. Probably set some kind of record."

Smith couldn't believe what she was telling him. It really was an incredible story.

"OK," he said. "I need you to put everything you've just told me on record. Can you do that?"

"Of course."

"I presume you're over the age of eighteen."

"I'm twenty-one."

"That makes like easier. Are you OK? Do you require medical assistance?"

Sharon looked like he'd asked her if she required Botox and Smith took that as a no. He asked her if she wanted a drink. She informed him that she didn't touch coffee, but a bottle of water would be much appreciated. He asked her to wait in the canteen while he went to have a quick chat with DI Smyth.

"Mystery cleared up then," the DI said when Smith had told him what had happened.

"Is it though?" Smith said. "Something still doesn't feel right."

"Nothing ever feels right with you. The poor woman was chased by a psychopathic serial killer – she ran all the way from Badger Hill, and she came straight here. What's the problem?"

"Firstly," Smith said. "He's not a psychopath. Nothing *The Spider* has done so far suggests he has any psychopathic traits."

"I'm running out of patience, Smith," DI Smyth said.

"I was just stating a fact. Secondly, I still think it's a bit suspect that Sharon happened to be exactly where Zak Lambert lives."

"Bring it up in the interview."

"I intend to."

"What's the problem then?" DI Smyth said.

"There's no problem at all," Smith said.

"Fuck off."

"Excuse me?" Smith said.

"You heard. Grey hairs are sprouting from my scalp as we speak – I can actually hear them growing. Go away."

CHAPTER FORTY FOUR

The response to the public appeal was unlike anything anyone in the team had ever seen. It was three hours after the press conference had gone live, and they hadn't received a single phone call. It was suspected that the phone number that had been given out was incorrect – it had happened before, but it was confirmed that the number was indeed the right one. It was unprecedented for an appeal to garner such a reaction from the general public and the officers given the job of answering the phones were somewhat disappointed. What they wouldn't give right now for a regular busybody to call in, but even the usual timewasters seemed to be otherwise engaged.

DI Smyth brought up the dearth of public interest in the afternoon briefing.

"There are only two possible explanations for it," he said. "Either the general public are genuinely losing interest in *The Spider*, or nobody knows anything about him."

"I'm inclined to go for the second one," Smith said.

"The latter," DC Moore corrected.

"What?"

"It's better grammar," DC Moore said. "When you're referring to the second of two possibilities, it's the latter."

"The second one is also grammatically correct," DC King pointed out. "It's just not so formal."

"Please," DI Smyth said. "I don't know what this investigation is doing to your brains, but whatever is going on in your heads is rather disturbing. Can we please continue."

"There's not much we can do about the lack of information," Smith said. "We should have expected as much. The way this man moves isn't human and I don't think he'll have found it difficult to stay under the radar for so long. I've just come from an interview with a witness, but it didn't give me what I'd hoped for. Sharon Billing remembered seeing a man who had to be *The Spider* earlier in the week and she saw him again outside Zak Lambert's house in Badger Hill today. She phoned me immediately, but she was seen. *The Spider* gave chase and Sharon managed to get away from him."

"How did she do that?" DC Moore said.

"Sharon is also an accomplished parkour athlete," Smith said. "She ran from Badger Hill, jumped onto the roof of the Travelodge by Hull Road and that's where she lost him. This gives us a glimmer of hope."

"How do you work that out?" DC Moore said.

"Sharon escaped from him, Harry," Smith said. "Which means he is human after all. He can be beaten."

"By another freak who can climb up walls and jump off buildings," Bridge joined in. "Not a normal person."

"He's not invincible," Smith said.

"What was Sharon doing there?" Whitton said.

"I thought it was a bit suspicious that one of the first people to notice this man in the city happens to call me from outside the house of one of the victims, but it appears that it was simply a coincidence. Sharon's parents own a house in Badger Hill and Sharon still lives at home."

"We almost had him, didn't we?" Bridge said.

"I believe we did," Smith said.

"Zak Lambert wasn't at home," DI Smyth said. "And he is still proving to be elusive."

"I'm working on that," Smith said.

"I don't want to know."

"You're dead right there, boss."

"Where do we go from here?" DC King said.

"Facebook," Smith said. "I'm still convinced that he's a member of that Facebook group. *You're not Alone*. We've drawn a blank with the public appeal, and until we find Zak Lambert we have nothing to lure him out into the open with, so I suggest we occupy our time with that Facebook page."

"What exactly did you mean when you mentioned luring Mr Lambert out into the open?" DI Smyth asked.

"Until he's been located, there's no point in even discussing it."

"No," DI Smyth said. "What have you been planning behind my back?"

"It's just a hypothetical plan at this stage, boss. Nothing definite."

"Glad to hear it."

"*You're not Alone*," Smith said. "Of the original fifty-eight members, there are fifty-four left – fourteen men and forty women. The odds are in our favour."

"Not necessarily, Sarge," DC King said. "The admin on the page told us that most of the people on that page post using aliases and that could apply to their sexes too. He could be posing as a woman on the page."

"I considered that," Smith said. "But I think Penelope Bright would see through it – the vetting process is a strict one, and Penelope is very astute when it comes to spotting the trolls and the phonies."

"She got it wrong with Megan Lambert," Bridge said.

"Can you all stop pointing out faults in my theories," Smith said.

"It's our job to do that," DI Smyth said. "We need to go through that list with a fine-toothed comb, and we will disregard gender in the process. We've seen what *The Spider* is capable of, and we cannot discount him posing as a woman on that Facebook group."

"Barry has agreed to work on it flat out," Bridge said. "If anyone can throw a few potential suspects our way it's Barry."

"I hope the budget can stretch to it," DI Smyth said.

"Don't worry about that, sir," Bridge said. "There won't be any fees – Barry owes me a few favours."

"I appreciate it."

Smith's phone beeped to tell him a message had arrived. It was from Baldwin and the message consisted of a few words and a ping location. Smith smiled. Baldwin never let him down.

"I know where Zak Lambert is," he said. "Or at least I know where his phone is."

CHAPTER FORTY FIVE

"How does that ping location thing work again?" Smith asked DC Moore for the third time.
They were heading east in the direction of Holtby. The A66 was busy today and the Londoner's Subaru BRZ had been stuck behind the same truck for five minutes. Zak Lambert's phone had been traced to a location between Dunnington and Holtby.

"When a phone is switched on," DC Moore said. "And connected to Wi-Fi or GPS, it emits a number of signals and with the right software it's possible to track those signals to within a distance of a few metres."
"What if the phone isn't switched on?" Smith said.
"Then there are certain hacks around it. You send a message to the phone in question and as soon as it's switched on again the message is received. With the correct program and the know-how, you can force a GPS activation, thus enabling you to pick up the satellite signal."
"Is that legal?" Smith wondered.
"Hardly, but it's almost impossible to prove. Baldwin knows some useful people, doesn't she? What a prick."
He was referring to the lorry that had pulled out to overtake a car towing a caravan just up ahead. He waited for it to pull back into the slow lane, engaged a lower gear and gunned the accelerator. Smith closed his eyes as the engine revved, and the car shot forwards. When he opened them again, they'd passed two trucks and the caravan.

"Not bad eh, Sarge?"
"I think something in my spinal column just popped," Smith said.
"Nonsense. You've been spending too much time with DS Bridge. There is nothing wrong with this car. At least she starts in the morning."

Smith's facial expression told him it was time to change the topic of conversation. The only reason Smith had agreed to get into DC Moore's backache inducing vehicle was because it was the fastest car in the car park, and in hindsight it hadn't made much difference anyway with the volume of traffic on the roads.

Smith's phone beeped again.

"Zak Lambert's phone is on the move," he said after glancing at the screen. "And the speed he's travelling at suggests he's on foot. He's on Holtby Lane heading in the direction of the glamping ground. What the hell is a glamping ground?"

"Camping without the hassle, Sarge," DC Moore said. "You really need to get out more."

Smith wasn't listening. His eyes were still glued on the screen of his phone. "He's definitely heading for the hassle-free camping ground."

A sign for the campsite appeared on the side of the road five minutes later. DC Moore slowed down, indicated and turned left.

"It's nice weather for it, anyway."

"What?" Smith said.

"Glamping," DC Moore said. "Spring is definitely here. Is he still on the move?"

"He's stopped. Put your foot down."

"These cars are not designed for dirt roads, Sarge."

"This is a ridiculous vehicle."

The camping ground was quiet. Smith expected it to be on a Tuesday in early March. DC Moore parked in the car park by the reception building and they got out. Smith couldn't resist stretching his arms wide very dramatically.

"Oh, come on," DC Moore said. "The seats in the BRZ are ergonomically designed for maximum comfort."

"If you're one of the seven dwarves," Smith said.

The reception area consisted of a small room with a desk at the back. A man was tapping on a laptop keyboard. He stood up when he saw the two detectives.

"Can I help you?"

"How many people are staying here at the moment?" Smith asked.

"Just the one unit is taken. Are you boys looking for something special?"

Smith was sure that he winked at him after he'd spoken.

"What?" he said. "No. God no."

He took out his ID as quickly as possible.

"We're looking for a man. Zak Lambert. Has he booked to stay here?"

The receptionist shook his head. "The person staying in unit 1 is a woman."

"Where is this unit?" Smith said.

"First one on the right. Turn left out of reception and follow the road round. All the units are numbered."

Smith thanked him and they left him to his laptop.

"Did you see that wink?" he said to DC Moore outside.

"I certainly did, Sarge. He thought we were a couple, didn't he?"

"What a horrible thought. Perhaps he saw your car and simply assumed."

DC Moore didn't comment but the pout on his lips resembled that of a sulky child's.

A small white car was parked outside unit 1. Smith stopped to take in the surroundings. The glamping ground was set in a few hectares of reclaimed farmer's fields. Surrounding the campsite were fields as far as the eye could see. The unit was basically a canvas tent covered with a green tarpaulin. Smith wondered what was glamorous about it.

"How are we going to play it?" DC Moore said.

"See if Zak is in there." Smith pointed to the large tent.

"What does his phone location say?"

Smith looked at the screen of his phone. "He's here."
He approached the tent and saw that it was nothing like an ordinary tent. There were no zips on the front – this one actually had a proper door. He pushed it open and took a step back.

"What the hell."

The voice was that of a woman. Shortly afterwards she appeared in the door of the tent. A man was standing behind her and their state of undress told Smith everything he needed to know.

"Mr Lambert?" Smith said.

"What do you want now?" Zak said.

"I want you to put some clothes on and come with us."

He realised that they had a slight problem. DC Moore's car was nippy, but it was a sports car and there were only two seats.

"Call it in," he said to the man from London. "We need a car here as soon as possible."

"You can't make me come with you," Zak said.

"No," Smith said. "But I suggest you do as we say. Unless you fancy spending the rest of your life unable to use your legs. This man will come for you, and he will maim you. Get dressed."

The door was closed, and Smith took out his cigarettes. He lit one and inhaled deeply.

"A car will be here in ten minutes," DC Moore informed him. "What sort of bloke shacks up with a woman so soon after his wife has been murdered?"

"The kind of man *The Spider* likes to hunt," Smith said. "Keep your eyes and ears open."

"What?"

"I don't know," Smith said. "I've got a bad feeling about this. It feels like we're being watched."

DC Moore looked around. "There's nowhere to hide around here."

"There are a dozen unoccupied units, Harry. Something doesn't feel right."

The door to the tent opened and Zak Lambert emerged.

"What now?" he said.

"A car is coming to pick you up," Smith said.

"This isn't what it looks like."

"I don't give a fuck what it looks like. I'm here to do a job. I don't like you – you make me sick, to be honest, but my job is to protect the people of this city, no matter what kind of disgusting human beings they are."

A noise behind him caused him to turn around. A figure in a black hooded top was walking calmly towards them. He was holding a hunting knife in his left hand.

"Put down the knife," Smith said.

The man kept coming.

"It's over," Smith said. "Put down the knife and get on the ground."

He realised how ridiculous this sounded. Here was a man with superhuman powers. Smith had no chance if things turned violent.

The Spider's eyes were focused on his target. He was concentrating only on Zak Lambert, and that's why he didn't see DC Moore behind him. The man from Wimbledon was approaching him slowly. Smith wanted to tell him to stop, but he didn't want to alert *The Spider* to his presence. The knife was raised and DC Moore lunged for it. Smith watched as DC Moore's fingers gripped *The Spider's* wrist and using a manoeuvre he'd never seen before, managed to loosen it from the man's grip. The hunting knife fell to the ground and DC Moore kicked it out of reach.

Smith moved in to help, but *The Spider* was already on the roof of the tent. He landed behind it and ran. Smith knew he stood no chance of catching a man like this. He watched as *The Spider* raced towards the reception building and leapt up onto DC Moore's prized car.

"My car." DC Moore had seen it too.

Smith was already on the phone to DI Smyth. He told him that *The Spider* was there, but they'd lost him.

"He's heading east in the direction of the memorial. We need to block off Stamford Bridge Road, Common Lane and Holtby Lane. We've got him, boss – I know we've got him."

CHAPTER FORTY SIX

"He got away," Smith said. "We blocked off the roads in every direction, but the bastard still got away."

"At least we got the knife," Whitton said.

Smith was sitting in her car on the way to the garage where Darren Lewis's brother worked.

"He can easily go out and get another knife," he said. "I really thought we had him."

"Zak Lambert is taking this seriously now," Whitton said. "That's something at least."

Zak was back at the station, waiting to hear what was going to happen to him. Protective custody was warranted, but it took time to arrange so for now he was enjoying the best hospitality York Police had to offer.

Whitton parked outside the garage.

"Gary's Auto Repair," she read the sign over the entrance. "He's gone up in the world."

"He's good at what he does," Smith said. "I don't trust anyone else with my car. I don't have any money."

"What's new?" Whitton said. "I'm sure he'll accept an EFT."

Gary had called Smith earlier to tell him he'd found another starter motor and the car was starting as it should again. He hadn't told Smith how much it was going to cost.

"Do you want me to wait here?" Whitton said. "Just in case."

"Oh, ye of little faith," Smith said. "The old Sierra is back to her former glory. I'll see you at home."

"All we need to do now is catch *The Spider* and come up with a solution to the Robert Rogers problem and we'll be home free."

"I think I might have the perfect solution to getting rid of Robert Rogers," Smith said. "In fact, it just occurred to me."

"I won't ask," Whitton said.

"It's better if you don't."

He waited for her to drive away and walked over to where Gary Lewis was chatting to a man Smith knew well.

"Gary," he said. "I can't thank you enough."

The other man realised who Gary's customer was and made a sharp exit. He wasn't even subtle about it.

"How much do I owe you?" Smith said.

"The starter was forty quid, so make it fifty."

"That's far too cheap," Smith said.

"Family rates," Gary said. "It took me twenty minutes. Anything for family."

He handed Smith the car keys and a slip of paper.

"That's the invoice from the tow company. You can pay them separately. They'll accept an EFT."

"How do you know Wayne Kemp?" Smith said.

"We were at school together," Gary said.

"What was he doing here?"

"Business," Gary said. "Business I told him to take elsewhere. I don't do that stuff anymore."

"Glad to hear it," Smith said. "Is he still up to his old tricks?"

"Wayne will never change."

"But you still keep in touch?"

"We meet up for a few pints now and then."

"I need to ask you a favour," Smith said. "And your relationship with Wayne Kemp might help me."

"How can Wayne help you?" Gary asked.

Smith told him. It took a lot of persuading, but Gary finally agreed.

"Pop round in about an hour," he said. "And I'm going to need cash. Wayne does not accept bank transfers."

"I appreciate that," Smith said. "And I appreciate your help."

When he turned the key in the ignition it felt like he'd been reacquainted with an old friend. The Sierra was back, and Smith was determined to keep it that way. As he drove, he thought about what he'd asked of Gary Lewis. He knew he'd put him in an awkward position, and he also understood that it could have grave repercussions for himself, but he decided it was worth it. It would obliterate one of his problems in one fell swoop.

He parked the car outside his house and got out. He patted the roof and smiled when he recalled the dent *The Spider* had left in the roof of DC Moore's treasured Subaru. He'd landed hard and it was going to take a lot of panel beating to repair the roof. Smith had thought DC Moore was going to cry and he wished he'd recorded the expression on his face.

He went inside and headed for the kitchen. Whitton was looking at something on her phone. Laura and Fran were sitting at the table engrossed in something in their schoolbooks. Smith took a beer out of the fridge and bent down to kiss Theakston on the nose. The porky Bull Terrier turned his head to the side at the last minute.

"Do you want me to feed you this evening?" Smith said.

The dog walked off, and Smith was sure he expressed his indifference by breaking wind as he went.

"Theakston just farted at me," he told Whitton.

Laura started to laugh. "You said *fart*."

"Did you hear it?" Smith said. "That dog needs to learn some manners."

"My mum wants to know if we want to go round there for a meal at the weekend," Whitton said.

"I don't know if we'll be able to get the time off," Smith said.

"I explained that to her," Whitton said. "But I said we'd try. She's feeling lonely."

"Tell her we'll be there then. We'll have caught *The Spider* by then."

"That's more like it. I thought you were about to lapse into another one of your maudlin moods earlier."

"Me?" Smith said. "I don't do maudlin."

"Of course you don't."

"Do we have a bank card?" Smith said. "I need to draw some cash for Gary Lewis."

"In my purse where it always is."

"What's the pin?" Smith said.

"Really?"

"Really," Smith said.

Whitton told him. "How much was it?"

"One fifty," Smith lied. "But I'm going to give him two hundred. He can't afford to give us family rates. I'll go to the ATM now and get it out of the way."

"Why are you acting strange?" Whitton said.

"I'm not acting strange. I'll see you in a bit."

CHAPTER FORTY SEVEN

Smith's first port of call the next day when he arrived at work was the locker room. He was hoping to find PC Angie Bowler there and he was in luck. She was talking to PC Griffin next to the row of lockers.

"Can I have a word?" Smith asked her.

"Of course, Sarge," she said.

"In private," Smith said for the benefit of PC Griffin.

The piggy-eyed PC got the hint and made a sharp exit.

"What is it, Sarge?" PC Bowler said.

"I need to ask a favour," Smith said.

"Anything."

"You haven't heard what it is yet."

"I'm all ears."

Smith told her. He also explained that he understood if she didn't want to go through with it. It was a huge favour to ask, and it could end badly for both of them if it ever came to light.

"OK," she said after thinking about it for precisely five seconds.

"This could have serious consequences for both of us," Smith reminded her.

"I'll do it. I owe you big time after you kept quiet about me leaking info to my brother."

"After this, we're quits," Smith said.

"Deal."

She held out her hand, but Smith didn't shake it straight away. Instead, he reached inside his pocket and took out the small packet he'd picked up from Gary Lewis yesterday evening. Then he shook the hand and placed the packet in it. She didn't look at it. Smith watched as she put it inside her jacket pocket.

"He'll be at this place at this time." Smith gave her the details.

"Sounds like a simple arrest, Sarge," PC Bowler said. "I'll keep you updated."
"Thank you," Smith said. "You really are doing me a massive favour here."

He left the locker room and made his way outside for a cigarette. He took out the phone he'd got from Gary Lewis yesterday and dialled a number he'd stored in it earlier. Robert Rogers answered immediately.
"Yes."
"Robert," Smith said. "It's Jason Smith. We need to talk."
"If you're going to try to scare me," Robert said. "I'll save you the bother. I don't scare easily. You'll have received the correspondence from my lawyer, I assume."
"That's what I need to talk to you about. I've given it a lot of thought, and I don't think dragging this out through the courts is going to do any of us any good. We have to think of Fran first – she has to be the main priority."
"What are you saying?"
"I think we should meet up," Smith said. "To discuss this like adults."
"I'm not backing down."
"Neither am I," Smith said. "But I may be open to discussing a compromise. A compromise that doesn't involve lawyers and legal expenses. We can come up with something that suits all of us. We can't ignore the fact that you're Fran's biological father."
"I'm listening," Robert said.
"We need to do this face to face. There's a pub on the Tang Hall Estate – The Green Man."
"I know it. It's a dive."
"I'm aware of that," Smith said. "But it's somewhere neutral, and we won't be disturbed there. Let's say in about an hour."
"I'll be there. I knew you'd see sense in the end."

Smith ended the call and opened the phone. It was a cheap one – it had cost him fifteen pounds. He removed the sim card and snapped it in two. He dumped it in the rubbish bin outside the entrance to the station. He debated whether to do the same with the phone but decided not to. It might come in useful later. He lit a cigarette and smiled. Robert Rogers's day was about to get a whole lot worse.

Smith was halfway through his cigarette when DC King came out.

"I thought I'd find you out here, Sarge. The DI wants us to head over to the hospital. Peter Snow is up to talking to us."

"Do we know if he has anything to tell us?" Smith said.

"It looks like it. The doctor the DI spoke to told him that Mr Snow wants to talk."

"Sounds promising. We'll go in my car."

"Is it fixed?"

"Nothing can kill that Sierra, Kerry," Smith said.

"Is everything OK?" DC King asked on the way.

"Everything's great," Smith said. "Why do you ask?"

"You seem a bit preoccupied. You're miles away."

"I often get like that when I'm driving," Smith said. "And I have a lot on my mind."

"He's going to slip up. He's going to make a mistake – they all do eventually."

"I'm not going to sit around and wait for him to fuck up," Smith said. "I'm going to catch him before he does that. His sole focus right now is Zak Lambert, and we've made it almost impossible for him to get anywhere near him, and I still think the best way forward is to allow him access to Mr Lambert. With the requisite security in place, of course."

"The DI won't go for it."

"I'll have a word with him. This sort of thing has worked in the past. He tried to attack Zak with me and Harry standing in his way, and he didn't care. He's got blinkers on, and we saw today that we can use that against him."

"I heard that Harry disarmed him," DC King said.

"It was an impressive move."

"Not to mention a risky one. It goes against everything we were ever taught in self-defence classes. Disarming an assailant with a knife is virtually impossible using pressure points."

"Harry must have got lucky," Smith said. "Anyway, *The Spider* got his revenge by putting a great big dent in Harry's precious Subaru. The expression on his face was priceless."

CHAPTER FORTY EIGHT

The expression on DC Moore's face told Bridge that he'd found something he thought was significant.

"Out with it then," he said.

"Out with what?" DC Moore said.

"You've had a face like a smacked arse ever since *The Spider* damaged your car and now you look like you've just been crowned village idiot of the year at the annual Village Idiot Convention."

"I was looking through the people on that Facebook group when something occurred to me."

"Is this going to take long?"

"Just bear with me," DC Moore said. "What do we believe is driving *The Spider*?"

"He's been badly treated somewhere down the line."

"And he's targeting victims and the people he thinks are responsible for their miserable existence. All of the people on that group fit the bill, and so does the person who set up the page in the first place."

"Penelope Bright happens to be a woman, Harry," Bridge reminded him.

"I know that," DC Moore said. "But it doesn't rule her out. She could be directing the action from the sidelines."

"I think you're way off the mark there."

DC Moore sighed loudly. "I want this bastard. When he damaged my car, he made it personal."

"It's just a bloody car," Bridge said. "A panel beater will sort it out in no time."

"It's not an ordinary car. Do you know how much it's going to cost to fix?"

"That's why you pay insurance. Stop whining and keep going with that Facebook group."

"I still think Penelope Bright is worth checking out."

"She really isn't," Bridge said. "She was the one who came to us. She's been obliging and she clearly wants to help. The woman has nothing to do with *The Spider*."

"Why is it that when Smith comes up with a seemingly hairbrained theory, everybody takes him seriously?"

"Because nine times out of ten those theories lead somewhere. Keep looking at the members in that Facebook group."

DC Moore sighed again and turned back to his laptop. Barry Stone had given them a list of seven members who he thought needed to be checked out more thoroughly. Six men and one woman had sounded some warning bells with their online activity. One of them in particular deserved careful scrutiny in Barry's opinion. The ID they'd used on the *You're not Alone* page was innocuous enough – MaggiePie13, but Barry knew that meant nothing. The first thing that struck him as odd about MaggiePie13 was the lack of online presence anywhere else apart from the Facebook support page. That in itself was suspicious. It was rare for someone who posted on a social media forum to be so quiet elsewhere online. Barry had somehow traced the IP address of MaggiePie13 and with some software that wasn't strictly legal he'd tracked the device he or she was using to a house in Bootham.

"According to the council," DC Moore said. "The owner of that property is a man by the name of Martin Porter."

"What else do we know about him?" Bridge said.

"I looked for Martin Porters on Facebook, and I couldn't find anyone fitting the bill. There are plenty of people with the same names but only one in York, and he happens to be seventy-six."

"It still could be him."

"I'm not doubting that," DC Moore said. "But *The Spider* is definitely not an old codger."

"How old is the Martin Porter in Bootham?"

"I have no idea."

"Let's go and find out then," Bridge said. "I need a change of scenery. It's not healthy to stare at a computer screen for too long – it's been proven."

* * *

The Spider closed his eyes but the image he'd been staring at on the screen was still clear. He'd had the dream again, but the face of the girl disappeared when he throttled the life out of her. He couldn't understand why that had happened – it had never happened before, and it had shaken him.

You're not really alone, she'd told him and he wondered why she kept telling him that. He opened his eyes again and reached for the glass of water that he always kept by his bed. He took a drink and wiped his mouth. The water was warm and slightly stale. He turned his attention back to the screen. He didn't have many photographs of his sister, and this had always been his favourite. So many summers had passed since the photo was taken, and *The Spider* knew that there would never be another summer like the one reflected in his sister's eyes.

Zak Lambert was going to be difficult to get close to. It was a mistake trying to get to him at the campsite and it was going to cost him. His actions were not going to go unpunished.

A noise outside caused him to stand up. He pulled the curtain aside and looked down. Two men were getting out of a black car. *The Spider* recognised one of them. He watched as they approached the house next door and rang the doorbell. They were going to be disappointed. Martin Porter was not going to answer the door. The retired schoolteacher wasn't going to answer the door ever again. *The Spider* had made sure of that when he'd taken his life.

That wasn't the only thing he'd taken from his elderly next-door neighbour – shortly after he'd stolen the last breath of air from the old man, he'd stolen his entire identity.

CHAPTER FORTY NINE

Peter Snow wasn't so cocksure of himself today. The arrogance he'd displayed when Smith first met him was gone, and he looked like a broken man. His face was grey, and his lifeless eyes were focused on nothing in particular. He'd been placed on his side, facing the window of the room and a sheet was covering his useless legs.

The doctor Smith had spoken to explained that Peter had been administered sedatives, but he was lucid. He asked them to keep the visit brief, and he also insisted that they do not cause him any distress. Smith promised to make it as painless as he could and he explained that it was possible that Peter could give them something that might help them track down the killer everybody in the city was talking about.

"Peter," he said. "Are you up to answering a few questions?"
He received a subtle nod of the head by way of a reply.
"I won't ask how you're feeling."
"How I'm feeling," Peter said in a croaky voice. "I'm not feeling – that's the problem. He's ruined my life."
"We're going to catch him," Smith said. "And that's why we need to talk to you."
"He should have finished the job. Look at me. Look at what he's turned me into. I shit myself and I don't even feel it. I smell it, but I don't know I'm doing it. I will never play football again. I'll never have sex. I might as well be dead."
Smith wasn't here to listen to the self-pity of a man he had very little sympathy for. He did think the punishment he'd received was unjust, but he was here for answers.

"What can you remember about the attack?" he asked.

"All of it," Peter said. "I always have a shower after a game, and I was looking forward to a few pints afterwards. I played a blinder, and I was in the mood to celebrate."

"Some people might think it's strange that you chose to play football so soon after your wife's murder," DC King said.

"Life goes on. What was I supposed to do – spend the rest of my days moping? It's my life and how I choose to live it is nobody's business but mine."

"Talk us through the events that led up to the attack," Smith said.

"I went to the changing room," Peter said. "Someone had put up an *out of order* sign on the door of the shower rooms."

"Are they often out of order?" DC King said.

"Never. The lads sometimes do it to wind me up."

"Why?" Smith said.

"Because they know how OCD I am about taking a shower after a game. It's just a bit of fun."

"You ignored the sign and went into the shower rooms," Smith said. "What happened next?"

"I started to get undressed," Peter said. "I looked at myself in the mirror and he was standing right behind me."

"What did this man look like?" Smith said.

"That part's all a bit blurry. I thought I was seeing things at first. It had been a hell of a few days, and I thought my brain was playing tricks on me. I closed my eyes and when I opened them, he was gone."

"What then?" Smith said.

"The bastard stabbed me. I remember the pain in my back and then there was nothing. He helped me to the floor, and I shat myself for the first time without realising it."

"He helped you to the floor?" DC King said.

"My legs weren't working and he grabbed my shoulders and put me on the floor. Then he just stood there and looked at me. He told me I shouldn't have played football."

"Why do you think he said that?" Smith said.

"How should I know? The psycho had just paralysed me and he's telling me I shouldn't have played football. He's a proper psychopath."

Smith didn't think it would help to explain that *The Spider* had shown no traits that could lead them to label him a psychopath.

"I need you to describe him," he said instead. "What was he wearing?"

"Black tracksuit pants," Peter said. "And a black hooded top."

"How old would you say he is?" DC King said.

"Probably mid-twenties. He had some kind of scarf over his face."

"What about his eyes?" Smith said.

"He was wearing sunglasses."

"When he spoke to you," Smith said. "Did he sound local?"

"I think so. And he had a strange voice."

"What do you mean?"

"He told me I shouldn't have played football, but he said it with real regret in his voice. It was like he was implying he wouldn't have done what he did if I hadn't played football. I can't explain it. What's the point in trying to justify the actions of a psycho?"

"Did he say anything else?" Smith said.

"He did. He bent down and whispered in my ear."

"What did he say?"

"He asked me if I recalled that day on the beach."

"What do you think he meant by that?"

"God knows. The man's a proper psychopath."

Smith decided to change tack.

"Were you aware that your wife was a member of a Facebook support group?"

"What?"

"Christine was on a Facebook group," Smith said. "*You're not Alone*. It's a place where victims can talk freely with likeminded people."

"Victims?" Peter said. "Christine was hardly a victim."

"Were you aware of this Facebook group?" DC King said.

"Never heard of it. What's a social media page got to do with what happened to us?"

"All of the victims were chosen from that Facebook group," Smith said.

"I wasn't. I don't even have a Facebook account."

"You were chosen by proxy," Smith said. "We won't take up anymore of your time."

"That's right," Peter said. "Because as you can see, I'm a busy man. I might pop out and have a few pints with the lads later. Oh, no I can't can I? Because that psychopath made sure I'll never walk again. He should have finished the job – he should have just fucking killed me."

CHAPTER FIFTY

Something was happening when Smith and DC King got back to the station. Smith could hear the raised voice before he even went inside. The voice was familiar, and Smith suddenly remembered the favour he'd asked PC Bowler for.

"Someone isn't happy," DC King said.

"You can say that again," Smith said.

Robert Rogers was being restrained by PC Miller and PC Griffin. He spotted Smith and tried to break free.

"You bastard. You set me up."

"Do you know this man, Sarge?" PC Miller said.

"I don't think so," Smith said. "What's going on?"

"Drugs bust," PC Griffin said. "Angie and I were sent out to the Green Man on the Tang Hall estate when we got a tipoff about a possible deal going down."

"It's a set-up," Robert said. "He set me up."

"I really have no idea what he's talking about," Smith said. "Who tipped us off?"

"Anonymous caller, Sarge," PC Bowler said. "A man matching Mr Rogers' description was seen dealing in The Green Man."

"What did he have on him?"

"Two ounces of weed. Skunk by the smell of it."

"She planted it," Robert said. "You're not going to get away with this."

Smith moved closer to him. "That's a serious allegation to make. And to be honest, you're not the first dealer to try it on like this."

"Dealer? You're not going to get away with this."

"No," Smith said. "You're not going to get away with it. Two ounces will probably get you a suspended sentence and a fine. Of course, you'll get a record, and certain privileges will fall away. You weren't planning any trips to the US, were you?'

"You're going to pay for this."

"I don't have time for this," Smith said.

"I've got proof."

"Tell it to the judge."

"I've got proof that you called me this morning and asked me to meet you at that pub."

Smith wondered if he'd made a huge mistake. Had Robert Rogers recorded the phone call he'd made earlier?

He hadn't.

"My phone is in my jacket pocket," he said. "I'll prove to you that he phoned me earlier."

Smith reached inside the jacket and took out the phone.

"Show us this proof then."

He handed the phone to Robert. A smile appeared on the face of Fran's biological father as he unlocked it and brought up his call history.

"There," he said and showed the screen to Smith. "Deny that."

"That's not my number," Smith said. "It wasn't me who called you."

"Let's see you talk your way out of this one."

Robert tapped the call option and looked Smith in the eye. He put the call on speakerphone. It didn't even ring. A monotone voice informed him that the number he'd dialled was no longer in service.

Smith took out his own phone and asked PC Bowler to phone it. Shortly afterwards the iconic guitars of *Shine on you Crazy Diamond* could be heard.

"My phone is well and truly still in service," he said. "I haven't got time for this nonsense."

"You won't get away with this," Robert Rogers said.

"I really have no idea what you're talking about. You'll be booked in, and you'll have the opportunity to speak to a lawyer. I presume you have a lawyer?"

He didn't wait for an answer. He walked past Robert Rogers and headed for his office.

He didn't even make it halfway. He was stopped by DI Smyth.

"Can I have a quick word?"

Smith followed him to his office. DI Smyth closed the door and asked him to take a seat.

"What's up, boss?" Smith asked, even though he had a good idea what it was about.

He didn't think Robert Rogers would go down without a fight, and he was expecting some questions to be asked.

That wasn't why DI Smyth had called him into his office.

"Is there something you want to tell me?"

"Boss?" Smith said.

"This investigation," DI Smyth said. "Your heart isn't in it, and I was hoping you could shed some light on why that is."

"My heart is in it," Smith said.

"You're making mistakes. We all are, but it's rare for you to drop the ball like this. What's going on, Smith?"

"Nothing is going on. *The Spider* is the best we've ever seen, that's all. It's going to take something special to beat him."

"The mistakes you've made are rookie errors," DI Smyth said. "And it's not like you. You've been somewhat preoccupied for a while now, and your focus isn't where it should be. I'm not an idiot."

"I know you're not," Smith said. "And you're right – I have had a lot on my mind, but my head is in this investigation. This one isn't going to be easy to

catch, but we will catch him. We just have to think differently. Where exactly has this come from?"
"I've worked with you long enough to know when something isn't right with you. And I expect you to trust me enough to be able to tell me anything. Well?"
"OK," Smith said. "I admit, the thing with Fran's biological father has stressed me out a bit, but that's all about to go away."
"Glad to hear it."
"I'll try not to lose sight of the prize in future," Smith said.
"I have no idea what that means, but good. Now, how did it go with Peter Snow?"

Smith told him. He didn't think anything that Peter Snow had told them was going to move them forwards.
"Why did he tell him he shouldn't have played football?" DI Smyth said. "And what did he mean about the beach?"
"God knows. Perhaps that wasn't the reaction he was hoping for from killing Christine. Maybe he wanted him to show a bit of grief over the death of his wife. And the way Peter explained he said it, makes me wonder if Peter would still have the use of his legs if he had acted like a normal grieving husband. Look at the others. Georgia Francis carried on like nothing had happened after her fiancé was murdered. She went to that godawful nightclub and got off on beating the crap out of men. We messed up with George Baron. We should have taken a closer look at his posts on the support group, and we would have known about the abuse by his father. Norman Baron didn't stand a chance. And then we have Zak Lambert. His wife was barely cold, and he was shacked up with another woman. You have to admit, there's a certain justice being doled out here."
"We can't afford to think like that."

"We need to think like him if we're to stand a chance of stopping him. Hold on."

"What's on your mind?"

"Why has he stopped?" Smith said. "From the little I've seen on that Facebook group there are plenty of people he could go after next, but he hasn't."

"Do you think he's finished?"

"It's just strange that he's suddenly stopped."

"Perhaps none of the others ticked all the boxes."

"Perhaps," Smith said. "I want to speak to the other people he left paralysed. I want to see if he said anything to them during the attacks."

"What for?"

"Peace of mind I suppose. And I'm running out of ideas."

"Something will come to you."

"It will," Smith agreed. "It usually does."

CHAPTER FIFTY ONE

"He told Georgia Francis that she shouldn't have gone to *Release the Bats*," Smith said. "And he also asked if she remembered that day on the beach." He was determined that this briefing was going to be a productive one. He was feeling more positive than he had done in days. His car was running as it should – Robert Rogers wasn't going to give them any more problems and now he could focus solely on the killer they'd dubbed *The Spider*.

"According to the man who witnessed the attack on Norman Baron," he said. "*The Spider* also spoke to George Baron's father after he'd maimed him. He told him he was finally being punished for what he'd done to his own son. There was no mention of a beach."

"Now you've got that cleared up," DI Smyth said. "How is it going to help us?"

"I have no idea," Smith said.

"He's judging them," DC King said.

"He's doing more than that, Kerry," Smith said. "He's acting as judge, jury and executioner."

"Another crusader," Bridge said. "I bloody hate crusaders."

"Can I say something?" It was DC Moore.

"You're not in Kindergarten, Harry," DI Smyth said.

"Sorry, sir. I think it's worth looking more closely at Penelope Bright."

"I thought I told you to leave it," Bridge said.

"Let's hear it," Smith said.

"As the admin on that Facebook group," DC Moore said. "She's in an ideal place to orchestrate the murders."

"And she also happens to be a woman," Bridge said. "*The Spider* is definitely a man. You met the bloke, remember."

"I still think it's worth a shot. None of the profiles we've checked out seem suspicious. The only one that Barry found odd turns out to be an old bloke called Martin Porter."

"We checked out his house," Bridge said. "But he wasn't home. According to a neighbour, he hadn't seen Martin for over a week, but that's not unusual. He often visits his daughter in Manchester for weeks on end."

"What's he doing on a page like *You're not Alone*?" Smith said.

"Who knows?" Bridge said. "But he is most definitely not *The Spider*. The fact that he doesn't use social media much is not unusual. He's seventy-six, for Pete's sake."

Smith walked up to the whiteboard. Next to Georgia Francis's name he wrote the word, *beach*. He did the same next to Peter Snow.

"Two victims," he said. "Two beaches. It has to mean something."

"How?" Bridge said. "According to the witness who was there when Norman Baron was attacked there was no mention of a beach."

Smith nodded thoughtfully and his eyes found a section of wall at the back. The plaster had cracked into the shape of the map of Italy.

"He whispered it."

"The witness won't have heard it," DC King said. "We saw him whisper something in Georgia Francis's ear at *Release the Bats*. Peter Snow told us he whispered it after he told him he shouldn't have played football."

"Get hold of that witness," Smith said to nobody in particular. "The one who was there when George Baron's father was attacked. Find out if *The Spider* whispered anything in his ear after he paralysed him."

Nobody made any effort to move.

"Harry," Smith said. "Could you do it now please."

DC Moore obliged. He left the room and closed the door behind him.

"Are you suggesting that we've missed something important?" DI Smyth said.

"You were right, boss," Smith said. "My head has been otherwise engaged for the duration of the investigation, but now it's back. I'm back and I'm seeing things I was blind to before. I think there's a reason why these murders and subsequent attacks haven't made much sense, and it's because we've missed the real motive."

"I think I preferred it when your brain was fogged up," Bridge said. "What are you thinking? And if you tell me you'll let me know when you've figured it out, we're going to have a falling out."

"Asked and answered," Smith said.

DC Moore returned. He sat down and told them that the witness to Norman Baron's attack did see *The Spider* whisper something in his ear.

"We need to ask Mr Baron what he said," Smith said. "If it was something about a beach, we're on the right track."

"Are you suggesting we've been on the wrong track thus far?" DI Smyth said.

"Not really," Smith said. "We've just been guided by a faulty GPS. The Satnav is working properly now, and it's going to tell us we've reached our destination very soon. We're onto something here."

"It's good to have you back," DI Smyth said.

"The jury's still out on that one," Bridge said.

"Where is Norman Baron?" Whitton said.

"City Hospital," Smith said.

"His condition is serious," DI Smyth said. "And that's why we haven't been able to talk to him. Mr Baron has an underlying heart problem, and according to his doctors the attack put even more pressure on his heart, and it's touch and go whether he'll pull through."

"No great loss there," DC Moore said. "I doubt anyone will shed many tears over the death of a paedo."

"There's a beach somewhere that holds the key to this investigation," Smith said.

"Sarge?" DC King said.

"Are you on drugs?" Bridge asked.

"Moving on," DI Smyth said. "This is a fresh lead, and God knows we need one. Look into this beach. See if anything connects Georgia Francis and Peter Snow."

"And Norman Baron," Smith said. "My gut is telling me *The Spider* mentioned a beach to him too."

"You're definitely on drugs," Bridge said.

"Get onto it," DI Smyth said. "Not you, Smith. I want to talk to you about drugs."

CHAPTER FIFTY TWO

"What's up, boss?" Smith said.

"Don't *what's up boss* me," DI Smyth said. "What have you done?"

"You're talking about Robert Rogers?"

"The fact that you know exactly what I'm talking about concerns me."

"The man has no right to show up now and make claims on a child who he abandoned years ago. Fran doesn't even remember the bloke."

"That's not the point," DI Smyth said. "The stunt you pulled could end your career. You could face criminal charges for it."

"That's not going to happen," Smith said. "He's got no proof that any of it was my doing. Everything was done by the book."

"How exactly did you do it?"

"It's probably best if you don't know. It's a couple of ounces of weed. His lawyer will probably advise him to admit to possession. It's his first offence and it's a class B narcotic, so he'll get away with a suspended and a fine."

"What if he takes it further?"

"He doesn't have a leg to stand on," Smith said. "The Green Man is a notorious haunt for dealers, and we've always had a presence there. When a tip-off comes in about a possible drugs offence we're authorised to stop and search. He has no proof that it was me who arranged to meet him there, and he can't prove that the weed was planted during the search. End of story."

"Come on," DI Smyth said. "How did you do it?"

"Do you really want to know?"

"I need to know if anything is going to come back to bite you on the arse."

Smith told him what he'd done. He didn't mention where the marijuana came from and he didn't tell him where he'd got hold of the burner phone, but apart from that he left nothing out.

"I want you to give me your word that nothing like this will ever happen again," DI Smyth said when he'd finished.

"I can't do that, boss. When it comes to my girls, there is nothing I won't do to keep them safe."

DI Smyth let out a loud sigh. "Right. We're going to put this behind us and we're not going to speak of it again. Does Whitton know what you did?"

"Are you kidding? Do I look like I have a death wish?"

"How sure are you about this beach thing?" DI Smyth said.

"Are sure as I can be," Smith said. "*The Spider* whispered the same thing to two of his victims, and we can't ignore it. Norman Baron is a lost cause, but we can still speak to the other two again. Georgia Francis and Peter Snow know more than they're letting on. I need a smoke."

"You really should cut down."

"This job doesn't make it easy to do that, boss. And the nicotine helps me to think."

He got up and left the small conference room. The first thing he noticed when he went outside was someone standing next to his car. It was PC Angie Bowler, and she was looking right at him. Smith walked over to her, lighting a cigarette as he went.

"What are you doing by my car?" he asked her.

"I didn't want anyone to overhear us," PC Bowler said.

"Thanks again for the arrest of Robert Rogers. It worked out perfectly."

"That's what I want to talk to you about, Sarge."

"Go on."

"After the arrest I got thinking," PC Bowler said.

"And?"

"I appreciate you keeping quiet about me accidently leaking info to the York Post. I could have got into trouble for that."

"It's in the past," Smith said. "No harm done."

"That's what I was thinking about. No harm was done. If anyone found out that the Post had got their information from me, I probably would have been called into a disciplinary and asked to provide my version of events. I didn't do it on purpose, and it was all very innocent. I would have got away with a slap on the wrists."

"Where are you going with this, PC Bowler?" Smith said, even though he sensed exactly what direction the conversation was heading in.

"Planting evidence is a sackable offence."

"Spit it out, Angie," Smith said. "I haven't got time for this."

"I suggest you make time, Sarge. I put my career on the line for you today. I risked everything."

"And I appreciate it."

"I don't think you do. Before, you said we would be quits if I did this for you - I didn't think much of it, but I've had time to consider things more clearly."

"What are you saying?" Smith said.

"We're not quits, Sarge," PC Bowler said. "In fact, the way I see it, it is you who owes me now."

"Are you threatening me?" Smith said. "Because I can tell you now that threats do not work with me."

"I'm bringing something to your attention. You owe me, Sarge. I just wanted you to be aware of that."

The smile that formed on her lips caught Smith off guard. It was a cold smile that didn't reach her eyes. It really was emotionless and it chilled Smith to the bone.

"I'll let you enjoy your cigarette in peace, Sarge," she said.

"What is it you want, PC Bowler?" Smith said.

"I like you. I really like you, and I would never do anything to hurt you."

"Why all the veiled threats then?"

"I just needed to clear the air. I had to tell you what was on my mind. I transferred here specifically so I could work close to you. We could be good together."

"This conversation is over, PC Bowler," Smith said.

"We're very much alike, you and me. I think we'd make a good team."

"Get back to work," Smith said.

PC Bowler smiled her shark smile again. "See you soon."

Smith watched her go. He wondered if he'd just made the worst mistake of his life. The headache of Robert Rogers was gone, but Smith wasn't sure if it was about to be replaced with a much bigger headache. PC Bowler's parting expression left little room for interpretation. She wasn't going to let Smith forget about this.

CHAPTER FIFTY THREE

Smith wanted to re-examine the series of events. The conversation with PC Bowler was still on his mind but he pushed it to the side. He would figure out a plan to remove her from the equation later. Her threats were implied but there was little doubt about her intentions and after careful consideration, Smith came to the conclusion that should she take things further it would boil down to a case of her word against his and she would lose that battle. All that really mattered was Robert Rogers' claim on his biological child was now null and void. Fran would never know how much Smith was willing to risk for the little girl.

Christine Snow was murdered on Saturday morning, sometime between eight and noon. Her husband Peter had found her after returning from playing football. Peter was attacked and left paralysed two days later. This pattern was repeated with Brian James and his fiancé Georgia. Brian drew his last breath on Saturday evening and the woman he planned to marry had her spine severed on Monday, a few hours after Peter Snow had suffered the same fate. Smith wondered if this was important. He couldn't think how it could be.

George Baron was taken out on Sunday, and his father was attacked two days later. There was a pattern there and it probably would have carried on if Zak Lambert hadn't escaped from *The Spider*. Zak's wife was also murdered on Sunday.

"He gave them two days to grieve before he paid them a visit," Smith said out loud. "He kills the people closest to them and attacks them forty-eight hours later. He leaves them paralysed and he whispers something about a beach. I'm an idiot."

He got up from the desk and left his office. He made his way to the custody suite and hoped that Sergeant Finch wasn't on duty today. He was in luck – it was Sergeant Bill Plant who greeted him and Smith was glad. He liked Sergeant Plant.

"Is Zak Lambert still here?" He got straight down to business.

"Not for much longer," Sergeant Plant said. "We've got a place for him."

Smith was relieved that he'd got there in time. The Protected Person's Service was the remit of the NCA and once a witness was placed, the National Crime Agency took over. The details of the placement would be top secret and the process for gaining access to a protected person was a complicated and lengthy one.

"I just need to ask him a few questions," Smith said, and added. "Off the record."

"Thank God for that," Sergeant Plant said. "The bloke makes me nervous and the sooner he's someone else's problem, the better."

"Has he said anything to you?"

"Nothing worth writing home about."

"What time is he being collected?" Smith said.

"You know better than to ask questions like that. He'll be picked up and taken somewhere, and us low-life officers are not privy to that level of clearance. Good riddance to the man, that's all I can say. He's in suite number 9 – right at the end."

Smith thanked him and Sergeant Plant unlocked the security door. "I'm going to have to lock it behind you," he said.

"No worries," Smith said.

He walked past the other eight holding cells and stopped outside number 9. All of the cells were empty, and Smith wondered if that was intentional.

Zak Lambert didn't look happy, and Smith didn't blame him. He was in the crosshairs of the serial killer the whole city was talking about, and he was facing an uncertain future. Soon, he would be taken to an undisclosed location, and he would stay there until the people who made the hard decisions deemed the threat to him to have been eliminated. Smith knew that he was partly responsible for eliminating this threat, and the thought caused a shiver of excitement to rush through him. Zak Lambert's fate was partly in his hands.

"We don't have long," he told him.

"Where am I being taken?" Zak asked.

"I'm not privy to that information," Smith said. "It's for the best that the fewer people that know, the better."

"What do you want? Are you here to gloat?"

"No," Smith said. "I'm here to make sure your time in the wilderness is as short as possible, but I need your help with that."

"What's going to happen to my house?" Zak said. "My wine. I have some valuable bottles in my cellar."

"I'm sure your house will be fine."

"You don't get it," Zak said. "I picked up a special vintage Chateau Latour Bordeaux on eBay, and I haven't had it insured yet. You probably don't know much about wine."

"That one rings a bell," Smith said.

"That Chateau Latour is going to be worth more than you earn in a year. Do you get the picture now?"

"Clear as day," Smith said.

The picture of the neck of the bottle breaking on the window was very clear, as was the subsequent shattering of the rest of the bottle. Zak really should have got it insured.

"You need to help me here," Smith said.

"I'll do anything I can."

"I need you to be honest with me," Smith said. "Some new information has come to light, and we believe it's information that will get us closer to the man who killed your wife. What do you know about a beach?"

"A beach?"

"A beach," Smith said. "Does that mean anything to you?"

"I don't think so. What beach?"

"That's what we're trying to find out. Do you know a man by the name of Peter Snow?"

Smith looked for a sign that Zak had recognised the name but there was nothing there.

"What about Georgia Francis?" he said.

He got the same reaction.

"Norman Baron," he tried.

Nothing.

"I don't know any of those people," Zak said.

"Are you sure?" Smith said.

"I handle the accounts for multi-million-pound companies," Zak said. "A good memory is a prerequisite."

"I need you to think very carefully," Smith said. "Time is running out. The longer *The Spider* remains at large, the longer you're going to be out of circulation. You won't be allowed contact with anyone – life as you know it will cease to exist, and until we find this man, you will be stuck in limbo. Tell me what you remember about the beach."

Zak ran his hands through his hair and looked at Smith with watery eyes. "I don't know who Norman Baron is."

"Go on," Smith said.

"But I know Peter and Georgia," Zak said. "And I remember what happened on that beach like it was yesterday."

"Talk to me," Smith said.

Zak Lambert took a couple of deep breaths and then he told Smith everything.

CHAPTER FIFTY FOUR

"The recent murders have their roots in something that happened more than ten years ago," Smith began.
He'd raced from the custody suite as soon as Zak Lambert had finished offloading. Everyone was gathered in the small conference room five minutes later.

"Zak Lambert, Peter Snow and Georgia Francis were acquainted," he said. "They were all students at the university here in 2011."
"Why didn't we make the connection before this?" DC Moore wondered.
"Why would we?" Smith said. "There was nothing to suggest that they were friends and according to Zak, they drifted apart after the summer of 2011. It happened on the beach in Bridlington. South Sands to be more exact."
"I know it well," Bridge said. "We used to go there all the time when I was a kid. What happened there?"
"Zak, Peter and Georgia were there for the day," Smith said. "Apparently, it's about forty miles from York. It was summer, the university term was over, and they went there with one purpose in mind – to have as much fun as possible. They were in their early twenties, and they didn't have a care in the world."
DI Smyth's phone beeped to tell him he'd received a message. He read it and put his phone back on the table.
"Zak Lambert is no longer our problem. That's as much as I was told."
"Good riddance to him," DC Moore said.
"The day started off well," Smith said. "It was the end of June and Bridlington was enjoying one of its rare days of sunshine. The beach was packed with holidaymakers, and the three friends hit the pubs early. Zak told me that they were buzzing by lunchtime, and they didn't stop. After a few more drinks Peter suggested a walk on the beach and that's what

brought them to South Sands. I don't know the geography but he spoke of some kind of esplanade."

"It's a raised walkway that runs the whole length of the beach," Bridge said. "I don't know what it's like now, but when I was a kid it was full of tourist shops and places selling fish and chips."

"The esplanade was busy," Smith carried on. "And the three friends were already half-cut. Zak said they found another pub on the esplanade and stopped for a few more. It was late afternoon when they decided to head back. By then, they could hardly walk, and they started playing around. Pushing each other and generally causing a disturbance. Most of the people gave them a wide berth, but one woman wasn't so lucky. Zak can still remember her face. They somehow ended up close to the edge of the walkway and the pushing and shoving carried on. This is where Zak's account is hazy. He's not absolutely sure who pushed who, but somehow a fourth party joined their party unwillingly. The woman was just in the wrong place at the wrong time. One of the friends was shoved in her direction and the force was enough to knock her over the edge of the esplanade. She fell hard. Zak can remember the ice creams she was carrying."

"Was she alright?" DC King said.

"No, Kerry," Smith said. "She was not alright. She landed on her back on one of the bolts that had been used to affix the old railing below the esplanade."

"What did they do?" Whitton said. "Did they help her?"

"I believe if they'd helped her that day, we would never have had to deal with *The Spider*. Zak told me that all three friends sobered up in an instant. And they got out of there as quickly as they could. Zak still sees the ice creams in his nightmares."

"Poor Zak," Bridge scoffed.

"How does this tie in with *The Spider*?" DI Smyth said.

"Zak later learned the fate of the woman they'd sent over the edge. Her name wasn't released, but the extent of her injuries was. The bolt she landed on was rusty and sharp and her spine was severed in an instant."

"Bloody hell," Bridge said. "We need to find out who that woman is."

"Who were the ice creams for?" DC King said.

"What does that matter?" DC Moore said.

"It matters a great deal, Harry," Smith said. "I think *The Spider* is someone who didn't get an ice cream that day."

* * *

The Spider had scratched the skin on his back until it was raw. He'd attached a strip of 40 grit sandpaper to the wall in his room, and he'd rubbed the itch on his lower back for too long. The irritation of the itch was gone, but the burn that had taken its place was worse. He shouldn't have got the tattoo – it had given him nothing but pain.

Zak Lambert was gone, and nobody knew where he was. All of the people he'd spoken to at York Police had told him the same story – they couldn't give out any information at this stage. Zak hadn't gone back to his house in Badger Hill – *The Spider* had checked, and he couldn't find any recent evidence of him online either. He'd disappeared off the face of the earth and there could only be one explanation for that.

The Spider's thoughts turned once again to that day on the beach. He'd nagged and nagged until his mother had given in and promised to buy ice cream for him and his sister. He'd seen a shop on the esplanade, and he'd specifically asked for strawberry. His sister wanted pistachio, and *The Spider* knew that would entail a longer wait. The specialist shop was located right at the end of the esplanade, but his mother gave in – she always gave in to his sister.

It wouldn't have happened if his sister hadn't insisted on her pistachio ice cream. It wasn't her fault. *The Spider* knew this – all blame was on the three drunken students, but it didn't change anything. That's why the face of the little girl in his dream was always that of his sister. He'd strangled the life out of his twin sister every night for over a decade, and until he was able to get close to Zak Lambert again, he needed something to relieve the pressure in his head. It was building and he needed to find a way to release it.

He would invite his sister over. He would buy her some ice cream.

CHAPTER FIFTY FIVE

"The woman's name was Corine Perry," DC Moore informed Smith. "It was easy enough to find."

"What do we know about her?" Smith said.

"The accident occurred on June 27th, 2011," DC Moore said. "Mrs Perry sustained serious injuries from a fall from the esplanade in Bridlington."

"Why wasn't the walkway fenced off?"

"It's only a three foot drop to the beach below, Sarge," DC Moore said. "If it wasn't for the exposed bolt she probably would have walked away from it with no more than a few scratches. But she was unlucky. She fell backwards and the bolt went straight through her lower back, severing the spine in the process."

"Was there an inquiry?" Smith said.

"There was, but nothing came of it."

"The woman was pushed," Smith said. "Why weren't the police involved?"

"Nobody knew what had actually happened. Witness reports were vague, and nobody ever came forward with any information."

"Zak Lambert said the beach was busy that day. They were inebriated – surely someone would remember them."

"I'm just going by what I've seen in the reports. Mrs Perry was taken to hospital, and she lost the use of her legs, but nobody was ever held accountable."

"What about her version of events?" Smith said.

"Nothing. I can keep on looking."

"No," Smith said. "It's not important. Zak Lambert has already admitted to playing a part. What we need to do now is track down the kids. She did have kids, didn't she? She was taking those ice creams somewhere."

"Kerry is looking into that."

Smith was convinced they were on the right track. Zak Lambert's revelation had given them the most important lead in the investigation so far, but things were still moving far too slowly for his liking. Someone was avenging Corine Perry and Smith wondered why it had taken so long. She'd become paralysed more than ten years ago, so why was all of this happening now?

"Do we know where Corine Perry is now?" he asked.

"Come on, Sarge," DC Moore said. "We've only just found out about what happened to her. Give us a chance. It should be easy to find out. We know who she is now."

"Patience never has been one of my strong points. And you're right – it should be easy enough to find out all we need to know now we've got a name."

"Why did he kill all those people?" Smith said.

"Sarge?"

"Just thinking out loud again. If he's avenging Corine Perry why not just go after the people responsible? This one is a fucking living contradiction in terms."

Smith left his office, leaving DC Moore wondering what on earth he was talking about.

He found Bridge in the canteen with DC King. They were looking at something on the screen of a laptop.

"Is Barry still working with Penelope Bright?" Smith said.

"He's given us all he can find from the *You're not Alone* page," Bridge said. "We've checked out all the members and none of them fit the bill for *The Spider*."

"Do you have an address for Penelope?"

"Do you still think she's involved somehow?" DC King said.

"I'm still wondering about that Facebook group," Smith said. "In light of what Zak Lambert told us, our original motive sort of flies out the window, and it's bugging me why all those people had to die. None of the people responsible for what happened to Corine Parker are in that group, so how does it relate to the investigation?"

"Perhaps it was meant to throw us off the scent," DC King suggested. "We assumed that his motive was something related to his own suffering at the hands of someone close to him, and maybe that was his intention all along. We focused all our attention on that and disregarded anything else."

"Possible," Smith said. "But we can't ignore the fact that all of the people who were killed were connected to someone who was there on that beach that day, with the exception of George Baron. Where does he come into this?"

"You're trying to solve too many problems at once," Bridge said. "Our focus needs to be on Corine Perry. You can go off on your weird tangents when we have more information about her life."

"Weird tangents?" Smith said.

"You know what I mean."

"No," Smith said. "Weird tangents – I like it. Have you got that address?"

"I give up," Bridge said. "You've got Barry's number. He's been to Penelope's place a few times. More times than necessary, if you ask me."

"I thought Barry had settled down with someone."

"Barry isn't the settling down type," Bridge said. "Although he seems to have fallen hard for Penelope. Give him a call."

"I'll do that. What are you looking at?"

Smith nodded to the laptop.

"Old newspaper reports," DC King said. "None of them mention anything about children. If Corine Perry was taking the ice creams to her kids, there's nothing about it in the press."

"And it's not something they would leave out," Bridge added. "A woman paralysed on a beach is a good story but throw a couple of kids into the mix and you've got a much more appealing one."

"I hate the press," Smith said. "I'll give Barry a call."

CHAPTER FIFTY SIX

Two hours later, DC Moore thought he'd found something important. He was still convinced that Penelope Bright was involved in the murders somehow, and this conviction had morphed into obsession. He couldn't leave it alone. He was familiar with the posts on the *You're not Alone* page and he'd noticed that Penelope rarely posted anything on there. DC Moore wondered if she no longer needed the comfort the group offered its members.

He'd decided to focus his attention elsewhere and that's when he came across an article that made him stop in his tracks. It was a report on a school sports day and what had caught DC Moore's attention was the photograph that accompanied the article. The photo had been taken a few years ago but Penelope looked exactly the same. At the top of the piece the headline read:
Twins clean up in school athletics meeting.
Penelope was flanked by a man and a woman. DC Moore guessed their ages to be somewhere in the mid-forties and when he read the names below the photograph he saw they were Neil and Hillary Billing. A boy and a girl were standing next to them. The twins were called Lucas and Sharon, and they were thirteen at the time. According to the article they'd won eleven athletic events between them, and it was a new school record.

A quick phone call confirmed that Penelope Bright was born Penelope Billing. She was married in 2012, and she was still married according to the records. DC Moore also learned that the twins in the photograph were her adopted siblings. Penelope was much older than them. The man from London knew there was something here, but he wanted a second opinion.

He found Bridge and DC King in the canteen. Bridge was gazing out of the window and DC King was looking at something on the screen of her laptop.

"Penelope Bright had two adopted siblings," DC Moore said. "A brother and a sister."

"And?" Bridge said.

"According to what I got from the records," DC Moore said. "Lucas and Sharon were adopted by Neil and Hillary Billing in 2012."

"How does this tie in with *The Spider*?" Bridge said.

"What if one of those twins is *The Spider*? I knew Penelope Bright was involved in this."

"Hold your horses," Bridge said. "How exactly did you get from a woman with an adopted set of twins to a prolific serial killer?"

"I think I know how," DC King said. "Look at this."

She moved her laptop so they could see the screen.

"Corine Perry was a single parent," she said. "After the accident that left her paralysed she was unable to look after her two children, and they were put up for adoption. And there's more. She died very soon after the accident. Blood poisoning."

"The timing fits," DC Moore said. "Lucas and Sharon were adopted by the Billing's in 2012."

"They were taken into foster care after the accident," DC King said. "And the Billings took them in six months later. They were lucky – it's rare that a family will take twins, but the Billings did."

"And Penelope Bright is the big sister," DC Moore said. "I knew it – I knew she was involved in this."

"Bloody hell," Bridge said. "I think you're right. All the victims are linked to her Facebook group, and she's directly linked to the kids who were left without a mother because of what happened on that beach. Shit – Smith has gone to see her. He's with her now."

* * *

The first thing Smith noticed when he went inside Penelope Bright's house in Holgate was the modifications that had been carried out. All of the doors were wider than normal, and the light switches were lower than they usually were. That together with the ramp that sloped from the front door told him that somebody in a wheelchair lived there.

"My son," Penelope said when Smith asked her about it.
"What happened to him?" he said.
"Car accident. He was seven. He wasn't wearing his seatbelt, and he was thrown through the windscreen when the car hit a lamp post."
"I'm sorry," Smith said. "Who was driving?"
"His father. My ex-husband. I was visiting my parents, and I made the mistake of thinking he could take care of Robert. Worst mistake of my life. My ex was a drunk. He'd run out of booze, so he went out to get some more and took Robert with him."
"Where is he now?" Smith asked. "Your ex-husband, I mean?"
"God knows. When help arrived at the scene of the accident, he'd gone. He hasn't been seen since."
Smith didn't know why, but everything about this story sounded wrong. How could a father abandon a child that is seriously injured? And why is it that he was able to disappear without a trace? It just didn't ring true. He decided that now wasn't the time to bring it up.

He asked about the Facebook page instead.
"When we spoke before," he said. "You said you set up the *You're not Alone* page after a string of toxic relationships."
"I should have known better after what happened with David. He was my ex, but I let it happen. I haven't offered you anything to drink."
"I'm fine," Smith said. "Where is your son now?"
"He goes to a school just round the corner. It's one of the reasons I moved here."

"How old is he?"

"Thirteen. Why are you asking about Robert?"

"I've got a curious nature," Smith said. "Some new information has come to our attention, and I'd like to talk to you about it."

"OK."

A phone started to ring somewhere in the house. The sound of it caused Penelope to shoot up in her seat.

"I have to get that. It's Robert's ringtone."

"No worries," Smith said.

Penelope was barely out of the room when Smith's phone sounded with the Oliver's Army ringtone.

"Boss," he answered it.

"Where are you?" DI Smyth said.

"I'm still busy with Penelope Bright."

"Get out of there."

"Boss?"

"We have reason to believe that Penelope is involved with *The Spider*. The woman who was left paralysed on the beach in 2011 died shortly afterwards and she had two children. Twins. They were taken in by Penelope's parents in 2012."

"Fuck," Smith said.

"There's more," DI Smyth said. "Penelope's maiden name was Billing. The twins took their adoptive parents' name. Lucas and Sharon Billing."

"Sharon Billing," Smith repeated. "Her name has come up more than once in the course of the investigation."

"Get out of there," DI Smyth said. "Make up an excuse and leave."

"Somebody's here," Smith said. "I heard the sound of the front door. I have to go."

"Smith," DI Smyth said.

He was talking to himself. Smith had hung up.

Penelope Bright came back into the room, and she wasn't alone.

CHAPTER FIFTY SEVEN

"Lucas and Sharon Billing are not in the system anywhere," DI Smyth said. After the phone call to Smith, a car had been sent out to Penelope Bright's address, and they were waiting to hear from the officers who were dispatched.

"According to the records," DI Smyth said. "Neither Lucas nor Sharon have ever paid tax. There are no properties in their name, and no National Insurance numbers."

"I couldn't find any online presence either," DC Moore said.

"How old were they when their mother died?" Whitton said.

"Ten," DI Smyth said. "Which makes them twenty-one now. We know that they were taken in by Neil and Hilary Billing six months after their mother's accident, but after the age of sixteen they seem to have disappeared off the radar."

"What about Mr and Mrs Billing?" DC King said.

"Both dead. They were killed in a light aircraft accident in India in 2018."

"The twins would have been seventeen then," DC Moore calculated.

"Did the adoptive parents own a property?" Bridge said.

"Not according to the records," DI Smyth said.

"Sharon Billing claimed that she was in the vicinity of Zak Lambert's house because she lived with her parents close by," Bridge recalled. "She lied. They're both dead."

"Why are we sitting here discussing this?" Whitton said. "If Penelope Bright is involved it means Smith is in danger."

"We'll know more when we get word back from the uniforms," DI Smyth said. "Smith will be fine. We'll get some answers from Penelope Bright. She knows what this is all about, and she's going to tell us everything."

"I knew she was a part of this," DC Moore said. "I knew there was something dodgy about Penelope Bright."

* * *

Smith stood up and he didn't know why. Penelope Bright walked over to the kettle and switched it on. Behind her was a teenage boy in a wheelchair.
"Robert," she said. "This is Detective Sergeant Jason Smith."
Smith held out his hand to the boy. "Good to meet you."
Robert shook the hand. He had a strong grip.
"You're that one from the TV. The Australian."
"Unfortunately. How are you?"
"I'm good."
"I forgot what day it was," Penelope said. "The school finishes early on Wednesdays. That's what the phone call was about. My stubborn son thought he'd make his own way home, rather than wait for me."
"It's a hundred metres down the road, Mother."
Robert said this in the manner only a teenager can pull off.

Penelope made him some tea, and he informed her that he was going to his room to catch up on some social media.
"He seems like a good kid," Smith said.
"He is," Penelope said. "Despite all the odds."
"How severe is his paralysis?"
"His spine was damaged in the accident. He has paraparesis, which means he has partial paralysis in his legs. He was told he would never walk again, but he's determined that he will. He's undergoing physical therapy and it's extremely tiring, but he's adamant that he will walk again, and I believe him. His upper body is fully functional as are his bladder and bowels. He's able to get into bed himself, and he can go to the toilet with no problem. We have a modified shower so he's able to bathe himself, which he very rarely does. You know what teenage boys are like."

"I have three girls," Smith said. "You've done a great job with him."

"He's the strongest person I've ever met. He refuses to let what happened to him rule his life."

"He's an inspiration to us all," Smith said.

"Are you sure you won't have some coffee?" Penelope said. "The kettle's boiled anyway."

"Thank you."

"You mentioned some new information that you wanted to talk to me about," Penelope said.

She spooned some coffee into two cups and walked over to the fridge.

"I want to talk to you about Lucas and Sharon Billing," Smith said.

The effect of hearing their names was a physical one. Penelope stopped dead next to the fridge. She stayed frozen to the spot for a few seconds and then she took the milk out.

"Why are you asking me about them?"

"Your parents adopted them in 2012," Smith said. "Is that right?"

"I still don't know why they did that."

"I don't understand."

"I knew there was something wrong with them the moment I met them."

"What was wrong with them?" Smith said.

"It wasn't anything I could pinpoint, but there was something rotten in them – something evil. Sharon was the worst."

She made the coffee and put the cups on the table. Her hands were shaking, and she had to concentrate hard so as not to spill it.

"What have they done?" she said.

"We're looking into them regarding the recent murders in the city," Smith said.

"Why?"

"We've uncovered certain connections. I'm afraid I can't tell you any more than that. Did you not get on with the twins?"

"I'd already left home by the time Mum and Dad took them in. I was a lot older than them."

"So, you didn't really have much to do with them?"

"I'd see them when I came home from university, but I didn't stay long. I would always make an excuse, so I didn't have to be in the house with them. They had this way of making me feel uncomfortable. Like I said, I couldn't put my finger on it – it was just a feeling."

"I know exactly what you mean," Smith said. "Do you know the details of how they came to be up for adoption?"

"Vaguely. Something about an accident. The father was out of the picture, and the mother was unable to take care of them."

"You didn't know anything more than that?"

"I wasn't interested, to be honest. I tried to have as little as possible to do with them."

They were interrupted by the sound of the doorbell.

"Are you expecting anyone?" Smith asked.

"Not that I recall," Penelope said.

The doorbell sounded again, followed soon afterwards by a voice Smith knew well.

"Police. Please open up."

CHAPTER FIFTY EIGHT

"What is that smell?"
Sharon Billing put down her spoon and scrunched up her nose. The pistachio ice cream didn't taste the same as she remembered and she'd barely touched any.
"It's Mr Porter next door," her brother said. "It's worse when the wind blows in a certain direction."
"You should have got rid of him. Someone's going to find out what you did."
"You've barely touched your ice cream."
"I can't eat with that stench in my nose. I don't know how you can stand it."
"I won't be here much longer. I love you."
Sharon felt his hand on her thigh. She stood up when it crept upwards.
   "You haven't finished what you were told to do," she said.
"I can't. They've taken him away and I don't know where he is."
He stood up too and pulled her close. He moved in for a kiss, but she turned away.
"It really stinks in here," Sharon said.
"I want you. I need to feel your warmth."
"No. Why are we doing this?"
"For Mum."
"Why?" Sharon said, much louder this time.
"For Mum. For MUM!"
   The man the city of York had dubbed *The Spider* reached out and put his hands on his sister's neck. He tightened his grip and kept it up until Sharon's eyes bulged. He released her and brushed his fingers over her chest. Then he sat back down.
"I'm sorry."
"You're losing control," Sharon said.

"I keep having the dream. And the girl I kill is you."

"It's not real," Sharon said. "You need to finish this."

"I don't know where they took him."

"Then find out," Sharon said. "Someone knows where he is. Find someone. The Australian will know something – Smith. I know how to bring him here, and you're going to make him talk – kill him if he doesn't."

* * *

Smith was gathering his thoughts in the canteen with a strong cup of coffee. He was convinced that they now had the identity of *The Spider*, and he was also sure that he hadn't been working alone. DI Smyth was still of the opinion that Penelope Bright was involved somehow, and Smith was starting to smell something *off* about her too. Her only obvious role in this had been a Facebook page that somehow her adopted siblings had found out about, but Smith sensed that there was more to it than that.

He took a sip of coffee and thought about the *You're not Alone* page. It was common knowledge that he was no friend of coincidence, but the fact that the three people responsible for Corine Perry's paralysis had ties to that group proved that coincidences did happen. Smith tried to justify it by theorising that the kind of person who could seriously injure someone and leave the scene was the type of person a member of the support group might discuss.

Penelope Bright had been arrested, and she was waiting in one of the holding cells. Coincidentally, it was the same one that Zak Lambert had recently vacated. Penelope's son was staying with a friend. Smith had been conflicted about the arrest, but DI Smyth had insisted. Too many mistakes had been made already, and he wasn't going to take any chances with Penelope. There were too many things linking her to *The Spider* to ignore. Eventually, Smith had to admit that there was enough on Penelope Bright to justify the arrest. He insisted that he be the one to formally interview her and DI Smyth didn't argue. They were waiting for Penelope's lawyer to arrive.

Whitton came in and sat down next to Smith.

"We're getting close, aren't we?"

"I don't know what Penelope Bright's role in this is," Smith said. "But too many things lead back to her. Me and the DI will be interviewing her when her lawyer gets here."

"If she has nothing to hide," Whitton said. "Why insist on a lawyer?"

"Who knows? I need to tell you something."

"Can't it wait?"

"No," Smith said. "It can't wait. I might have done something stupid."

"I've heard that one before."

"This is serious, Erica. Robert Rogers's arrest was my doing."

"What have you done?"

"Before you get mad," Smith said. "Just hear me out. I bought a couple of ounces of weed from a mate of Gary's."

"That's why you were acting strange the other night."

"And that's why the car repair cost a bit more than it should," Smith said. "I gave the drugs to PC Bowler, and she promised to help me."

"You're an idiot."

"I'm aware of that. I phoned in an anonymous tip-off about a drug deal going down in the Green Man on the Tang Hall estate and PC Bowler and PC Griffin were sent out. I'd arranged to meet Robert Rogers there and he was searched."

"Let me guess," Whitton said. "PC Bowler planted the drugs during the search."

"It should have been simple," Smith said. "PC Griffin was witness to the bust, and two ounces was enough for the arrest. Robert has no evidence of our conversation – he'll probably get a suspended and a bit of a fine, but it means that his claim on Fran falls away. There is no way the adoption agency will consider the petition of a convicted druggie."

Whitton looked him in the eye. "What went wrong?"

"It should have been plain sailing," Smith said. "But I didn't consider PC Bowler. She was waiting by my car earlier and she threatened me. And it scared the shit out of me. Her whole personality changed, and I don't know what to do about it."

"She's got as much to lose as you if the truth comes out," Whitton pointed out.

"That's the disturbing bit," Smith said. "It's like she doesn't care. The woman is a bit of a psycho, and I had no idea."

"Leave it with me," Whitton said.

"What are you going to do?"

"Just leave it with me."

"I'm sorry," Smith said. "I was an idiot."

"You were. But your intentions were good. I don't condone what you did, but I'm sort of glad you did it. Family is everything to you, isn't it?"

"I didn't have one for a very long time," Smith said. "And now I've got one, I'll do anything to keep it that way. I'm going to see what's happening with Penelope Bright."

His phone started to ring. One glance at the screen told him that the investigation was about to explode. He answered the call and listened carefully.

"I have to go," he told Whitton when the call was over.

"Where are you going?" she said.

"With any luck," Smith said. "I'm going to squish a spider."

CHAPTER FIFTY NINE

Smith's thoughts were racing as he drove to the house in Bootham. The traffic was light, but he still took his time. He knew that he was probably going to end up right in the middle of the spider's web, but he didn't have any other options. The *Spider* investigation had consumed him, and it was time for it to stop.

He parked outside the terraced house and when he got out of the car, he was suddenly aware of a terrible stench. It was a reek he was familiar with, but he was unsure what it meant in the current context. Was the trap he was being lured into much worse than he originally thought?

He looked up and down the street. It was late afternoon and there were very few people around. The putrid funk crept inside his nostrils, and it made him feel slightly ill. He approached the house and knocked on the door. It was opened by a woman who Smith now knew was twenty-one years' old.

"Where is he?" Smith asked Sharon Billing.

"You've just missed him."

"It's over, Sharon," Smith said. "I know everything."

"I don't think you do. And it's over when I say it is. I want Zak Lambert and you're going to give him to me."

"I don't think so," Smith said.

A movement above him made him look up. A figure had emerged from the upstairs window, and it was making its way down the wall. Smith was too slow. Before he could react, *The Spider* was behind him, and Smith knew that the sensation in his lower back was caused by the tip of a knife.

"Come in," Sharon said, calmly. "I'll put the kettle on."

Smith didn't have much choice. The pressure of the blade in his back told him that this was an invitation he couldn't turn down. He went inside the house and soon afterwards the door was closed. Smith heard the sound of the key being turned in the lock.

"Where is Zak Lambert?" Sharon said.
"You said you were going to put the kettle on," Smith reminded her.
"Cut him," Sharon told her brother.
Smith winced when he felt the knife pierce his side. It was yanked out and Smith gasped.
"Fuck. What was that for?"
"You're going to tell us where Zak Lambert is," Sharon said.
"I don't know where he is," Smith said. "You've ruined my favourite T-Shirt."
"Cut him again."
"Wait," Smith said. "I'll tell you where Zak Lambert is."
"Don't lie to me. I will tell him to kill you slowly if you lie to me."
"Is she always this bossy?" Smith said to *The Spider*.
His question remained unanswered.
"Do you do everything she tells you?"

A noise close by caused all of them to look in the direction of the sound.
"There are some pissed off police officers out there," Smith said. "I'm not sure exactly how many there are, but my boss is a bit anal when it comes to backup. It's probably overkill. I mean – you're not really that good, are you? I think we even have a couple of snipers. The boss likes his snipers. As for me, I'm not a big fan – I hate guns. You don't have a gun, do you?"

There was a crash outside, shortly followed by a very clear expletive.
"Shit," Smith said. "Now they're really mad."
"Shut up," Sharon said. "I'll tell him to cut out your tongue if you don't shut up."
"You never did get your ice cream, did you?"
"Shut up."

"How did you know who they were?" Smith said. "There were no witness reports, and the incident was never investigated by the police. How did you know who caused your mother's accident?"

"Stop it," Sharon said. "Stop talking."

"You saw it, didn't you?" Smith said. "You saw her fall. That must have been terrible for an eleven-year-old."

"Ten," Sharon corrected. "I was ten."

"My mistake. Come on, tell your robot to put down the knife and we can talk. I can get my boss to call off his snipers."

"You don't know anything," Sharon said.

"So, my wife keeps telling me."

"You don't know where Zak Lambert is, do you?"

Smith was unprepared for *The Spider's* voice. He sounded like a scared child and it chilled Smith to the bone. Here was a cold-blooded killer, and he had the voice of a teenager who'd only recently reached puberty.

"I'm not important enough to be privy to that kind of information," Smith said. "Protected Persons is the remit of the National Crime Agency, and those bastards like to think of themselves as an extension of MI5. They take secrecy very seriously. For what it's worth, I wouldn't lose much sleep if you did take Zak Lambert out. I think he's a dickhead of the highest order. But I'm not allowed to think like that."

The wound in his side was throbbing now, and he could feel blood trickling down his lower back.

"Penelope has been arrested," he said. "It won't be long before she cracks. I had my doubts about her involvement, but some of the things she said, caused me to wonder. You took no pleasure in killing them, did you?"

"Shut up," Sharon said. "I will get him to kill you."

"I don't think he will. The people you made him kill were innocent. They played no part in what happened to your mother."

"It was necessary."

Smith sensed that *The Spider* had been made to believe this.

"Time's up," he said. "This is what's going to happen. Soon, an army of police officers are going to swarm in. Given your history, they'll come in hard, and contrary to popular belief, police officers are authorised to use as much force as necessary in situations like these. If you resist, you're going to get hurt."

The faint crackle of a police radio could be heard somewhere close by.

"Would you have any objections to me making a sharp exit?" Smith said. "The officers out there are hyped and seriously wound up, and I don't want to be here when they come in."

Sharon looked at him and then her eyes found her brother's.

"The roof," she screamed.

Smith watched them go. Their speed was astonishing. He heard their footsteps as they raced upstairs and then there was a scream. A few loud bangs followed and then the house fell silent. Smith put his hand to the wound on his back and winced. The hand was covered in blood, but he didn't think it was too serious. He was more annoyed about his Pink Floyd T-Shirt. He didn't think the shirts were still available. He left the room and made his way to the front door. He turned the key and opened it. He nodded to the four uniformed officers outside and took out his cigarettes.

CHAPTER SIXTY

"Of course, we considered the fact that you would try to escape through one of the upstairs windows," Smith said.
Sharon Billing looked different today. Smith looked across the table at her and for a brief moment, he could see the little girl who'd witnessed the accident that changed the twins' life forever.

When Sharon had phoned him claiming to have seen *The Spider* again, Smith was instantly awake. DI Smyth had broken all records, and it had taken less than twenty minutes to mobilise the biggest team of reinforcements in the history of York Police operations. No fewer than twenty-two officers were on the scene before Smith even arrived at the house in Bootham. Smith wondered if the boss was in line for some kind of commendation. The operation had been a huge success.

Lucas Billing hadn't spoken a word since his arrest, and Smith didn't think he was going to find his voice anytime soon. He'd withdrawn somewhere deep inside himself, and he would be evaluated by a specialist before any hard decisions were made. The man the city knew as *The Spider* had retreated to the darkest depths of his web, and he was refusing to come out.

Certain aspects of Penelope Bright's behaviour had sounded warning bells in Smith's head and when he looked more closely at her, his instincts told him that she'd played a big part in the plot to avenge the accident that resulted in Corine Perry's death. Penelope had crumbled more quickly than Smith expected. She was the one who was controlling the narrative. It was Penelope who'd seen the potential of the Facebook group when she realised that the three people who were responsible for the accident were connected to people on the support group. *You're not Alone* had since been shut down. Smith had questioned her about the death of George Baron and the subsequent maiming of his abusive father, and it turned out that they were both collateral damage. They were simply chosen to throw the police off the scent of the real motive. There had been an abundance of answers – many things had been cleared up, but there were still a few questions Smith needed to ask.

"How were you actually planning on getting away?" he asked.

"Through the bedroom window," Sharon said. "It's an easy climb to the roof. All the houses are connected, and we would have been at the end of the terrace and into the alleyway behind it before you knew what was happening."

"We've cleared up a lot of things," Smith said. "Penelope orchestrated the entire thing. Her son was the inspiration, wasn't he?"

They'd since learned that Penelope had lied about her son's accident. It was true that he'd been in a car crash, and he'd suffered damage to his spine, but that's where fact ended and fiction came into the equation. Robert sustained his injuries recently and he hadn't been in the wheelchair for six years like his mother claimed. And it hadn't been his father who'd caused the accident. Smith knew there was something fishy about that as soon as Penelope had mentioned it. The driver of the car Robert was in was a friend's mother. She was sober, and she was cleared of all blame.

Penelope's claim that she was terrified of the twins was too dramatic for Smith. The words she'd spoken felt too rehearsed and he knew she was lying. She wasn't scared of the twins – she was in total control of them. The photograph of her at the school sports day reinforced this. With her arms around Sharon and Lucas, Penelope was clearly a proud older sister. She didn't hate them – she didn't fear them; she was as close to them as any sister can be with adopted siblings.

"Robert was the catalyst, wasn't he?" Smith said. "His accident had similarities with your mother's. He was confined to a wheelchair. What can you tell me about that?"

"You seem to have all the answers," Sharon said. "Why don't you tell me."

"OK," Smith obliged. "I think Robert's partial paralysis brought back memories of your mother's accident. It can't be easy to deal with something like that. I think you confided in Penelope about what you'd seen that day on the beach, and you felt the need for retribution. Am I close?"

"They got away with it."

"Now we're getting somewhere. Talk to me. Tell me about that day. It was a sunny day in Bridlington. You, Lucas and your mum were enjoying a day on the beach. She went to buy ice cream, didn't she?"

Sharon nodded.

"For the benefit of the tape," DC King said. "Miss Billing is nodding her head."

"I wanted pistachio," Sharon said. "Lucas told me I was being a bitch."

"Why would he say that?" Smith said.

"Because the shop that sold the fancy ice cream was right at the end of the esplanade. Mum said she would get pistachio, and when she didn't come back after a while I went to find her."

"You left your brother by himself?" DC King said.

"I thought he would be alright. I got to the walkway, and I saw these drunk people. They were loud and rowdy. Mum didn't seem to notice them."

"Did your mother see you there?" Smith asked.

Another shake of the head. "No. She had her back to the beach. Then she fell. I mean, she was pushed. She fell back and all I could think of was she'd dropped the ice creams. I didn't know..."

"Take your time," DC King said.

"I didn't think she was too badly hurt. It wasn't a high fall, and I waited for her to get up, but she didn't."

"That must have been a terrible experience for you," Smith said. "What happened then? Did you go to her? Did you try to help your mother?"

"No," Sharon said. "I'd seen what had happened, and nobody was doing anything."

"Nobody came to help?" DC King said.

"Lots of people came to help," Sharon said. "I mean nobody stopped those three people from getting away. So, I followed them."

"You left your mother and followed the three students?" Smith said.

"I needed to know who they were."

"How did you find out who they were?" Smith said.

"One of them dropped his wallet. It was Zak Lambert. They were really drunk, and he didn't realise he'd dropped it. Inside was a student union card. That's how I knew who he was."

"What did you do with the wallet?" DC King said.

"I kept it," Sharon said. "And when I got back to York, I took it to the university."

"You were ten years old," DC King said. "That's a very responsible attitude."

"I didn't do it because it was the right thing to do," Sharon said. "I did it so I could get closer to Zak Lambert. The wallet was full of cash, and I didn't touch it. He didn't even thank me. I didn't expect a reward, but that man didn't even say thank you. Then we started to follow him."

"How did you manage that?" DC King said. "You were ten years old."

"Lucas and me were put into foster care. We didn't have anyone to look after us, so we were put with a family who didn't really care what we got up to. One day at the university campus I spotted all three of them together. Zak, Peter and Georgia. They were laughing like they'd done nothing wrong. It didn't take much asking around to find out who they were."

For once, Smith was lost for words. Sharon Billing's story was an extraordinary one.

"Who came up with the plan to maim them?" he asked.

"Penelope and me got talking one night. She knew that Lucas and me ended up with them because of an accident but she didn't know the details. I told her about the accident, and I told her how I'd found out who was responsible."

"When was this?" Smith said. "When did you tell Penelope all this?"

"A couple of months ago. She was still coming to grips with Robert's condition, and she said the people who ruined my mum's life should pay for what they did."

"So, you hatched the plan to kill the people closest to them and then sever their spines, like they'd severed your mother's."

"They deserved it."

"But the people you made your brother kill didn't," Smith said.

"It was necessary.

"How did you persuade your brother to go along with it?" DC King said.

Sharon laughed. "Lucas would jump in front of a bus if I told him to."

"Hmm," Smith said. "You manipulated your own brother into committing terrible crimes."

"Lucas would do anything for me."

"Why?" DC King said.

"Because I'm the only one who can comfort him. He needs me. When I left him alone on that beach it affected his whole life. He depends on me, and I can make him do anything I want. We've been sleeping together for six years. I own him."

Smith had heard enough. If there ever was a time to bring an interview to its conclusion, that time was now. He was feeling sick to the stomach. There was still a long way to go. Lucas Billing wasn't going to tell them anything, but his twin sister and Penelope Bright were. They still needed the details of the murders, and they still needed to know a lot more, but right now Smith had only one more question to ask.

"Why did Lucas kill Martin Porter? He was an old man who played no part in any of this."

"It was necessary," Sharon said. "He was a member of the *You're not Alone* group and he happened to live next door. Lucas assumed his identity. It was necessary. Will my brother go to jail?"

"That's not up to me," Smith said.

He stated the time for the record and got to his feet. He couldn't bear to be in the same room as Sharon Billing for one second longer.

CHAPTER SIXTY ONE

Smith stepped outside into the late afternoon sun and lit a cigarette. He savoured the hit of the nicotine and looked around the car park. His eyes stopped on the two women deep in conversation by the exit. It was Whitton and PC Angie Bowler. From what Smith could see, it was Whitton who was doing most of the talking and her body language told Smith that the conversation wasn't a friendly one. He watched as PC Bowler put up her hands and took a step backwards. He could see her lips move but he couldn't hear what she was saying. PC Bowler held up her hands again and walked back towards the station.

She reached Smith and stopped.
"I'm sorry."
"Good to hear it," he said.
"The planting of the drugs never happened," PC Bowler said. "I really am sorry."
"It's been a long, shitty day, Angie," Smith said. "And I'm about to go home."
"Can I ask you something, Sarge?"
"Make it quick."
"Do you sleep with one eye open at night?"
"Not that I'm aware of."
"I would. If I was married to DS Whitton, I would sleep with one eye open."
With that, she made her way inside the station.

Whitton came over.
"What did you say to her?" Smith asked.
"I just gave her a friendly warning," Whitton said. "I made her aware of some of the things I've done, and I explained what I was capable of doing, should the need arise."

"That clears that up then."

"Clears what up?" Whitton said.

"She asked me if I slept with one eye open at night."

Whitton laughed. "Sounds like I got the message across then. Zak Lambert is suing for the damage to his wine cellar."

"I thought he might," Smith said.

"Apparently, that wine you obliterated was worth close to fifty grand. Zak is suing the Home Office for the cost."

"He doesn't have a leg to stand on."

"I know he doesn't," Whitton said. "Webber has put it on record that the wine was broken during the break in. It's in the forensic report."

"Webber is a strange man. Remind me to thank him."

"I'll see you at home."

"See you at home," Smith said. "We're a proper power couple, aren't we?"

"Where did that come from?"

"I have no idea. I'll see you at home."

He finished his cigarette and got into his car. As he was putting the key in the ignition something caught his eye. A house spider had crawled onto the glove compartment door, and, with its eight eyes, it was observing him. Smith debated whether to squish it, but he didn't. He started the engine and disengaged the hand brake. He glanced at the spider. It was still watching him.

"I've never really liked spiders. Just so you know."

The spider still had its eyes on him as he put the car in gear and drove out of the car park.

When he parked the car outside his house, he realised that the spider was gone.

THE END

Printed in Dunstable, United Kingdom